LAST CHANCE

DEE MARVINE

Last Chance

A DOUBLE D WESTERN
DOUBLEDAY
New York   London   Toronto   Sydney   Auckland

A Double D Western
PUBLISHED BY DOUBLEDAY
a division of Bantam Doubleday Dell Publishing Group, Inc.
666 Fifth Avenue, New York, New York 10103

Double D Western, Doubleday
and the portrayal of the letters DD
are trademarks of Doubleday, a division of
Bantam Doubleday Dell Publishing Group, Inc.

Library of Congress Cataloging-in-Publication Data

Marvine, Dee.
Last chance/Dee Marvine.— 1st ed.
p. cm.
I. Title.
PS3563.A7433L37   1993
813'.54—dc20   92-561
CIP

ISBN 0-385-46794-X

Printed in the United States of America
February 1993
First Edition

To my family

LAST CHANCE

One

THE BUFFALO, thousands of shaggy, grunting animals, lumbered over the dry Dakota plains that flanked the Missouri, picking up speed as they struggled toward the muddy smell of water.

Squinting into the dawn light, Captain Garnet Tanner on the steamboat *Big Muddy* saw the rising dust cloud and ordered the boilers shut down. Such sights were to be savored. He rang the bell to signal those on board. Soon sleep-fogged passengers, pulling on shirts and buttoning suspenders, hurried to the forward deck to stare in awe as the buffalo spread out along the river's edge, snuffling and snorting their fill before moving into the current for the crossing.

In a cramped cabin on the upper deck, Mattie Hamil listened as the strange rumble rose above the familiar grinding of paddle gears and the slap of the river against the steamer's bow. She accustomed her eyes, in the early light from the small window, to the crude cubicle that had served as her cabin in the weeks since the *Big Muddy* left St. Louis. Despite her hasty decision to book passage, she'd been lucky to get a cabin on the upper deck away from the boiler noise.

The boat shuddered against the sudden tug of current as the engines were cut, and Mattie heard men shouting on the main deck below. Stepping into her petticoat and dress, she hurried out onto the promenade where acrid wood smoke, perpetually in the air, now mingled with powdery dust and a strong animal scent. Other passengers—three quartermaster soldiers bound for Fort Shaw, two brothers seeking Montana gold, and a whiskey peddler—stood at the forward rail. In the water toward shore, she saw swimming animals, their low primal sounds punctuating the scuffle and splash as their hulking forms plunged down the bank and into the river.

The captain, a weathered, muscular man, glanced at Mattie. "Buffalo!"

Buffalo. She had hoped to see buffalo.

"Don't worry, Miss Hamil. We're safe—unless one of them critters decides to come aboard." She smiled at his joshing.

The churning herd flowed into the current like poured molasses, while the lead animals, having reached the other side, spilled between two shallow bluffs and out onto the prairie beyond.

Mattie reveled in the spectacle she knew was rare now in 1875, and she wanted to remember every detail to record in her journal. Already she had made notes on deer, elk, coyotes, and wolves, as well as the straggly bands of Indians that appeared at the riverbank wood yards where the boat refueled. The voyage thus far had taken her through country more vast and splendid than she could have imagined, yet entirely untamed and unsettled—wild, like these buffalo. Was that why Cal had been drawn to it? Perhaps by the time she found him, she would understand why he'd given up a comfortable life for it. If she found him.

"Will you join me for breakfast, Miss Hamil?" The captain's kind gray eyes showed no condescension as he tipped his cap, a well-worn Union army issue. His tousled sandy hair, along with sandy brows and generous mustache, made him appear younger than his actual age, forty.

"Thank you, Captain Tanner. I'd like that." This was the first time he had asked her to his table. Everyone on board knew she was on her way to join her fiancé, and the glances of several of the men at the rail followed them as they moved along the deck past barrels, kegs, bundles, and crates spilling over from the hold.

"These buffalo could hold us up for a while," the captain commented, stepping aside to allow her to pass a stack of cordwood.

"Surely it won't be long."

"Probably just a few hours, but a sizable herd can take days to cross."

"Days? But I must get to Bismarck as soon as possible. Isn't there something you can do?"

"Nothing short of growing wings and flying over them." His humor crinkled the deep lines at the corners of his mouth. She laughed, too. It had been so long since she had found much of anything amusing.

"All right, Captain. Then I guess we have time for breakfast." They had reached her cabin. "I'll join you in a few minutes." Closing the door behind her, she stood for a moment, recalling his words. The buffalo crossing could take days. She had no time for delays. There were so many uncertainties. Marriage to Cal—if she could find him—

would be tenuous at best. Had it been a mistake to come? Had she underestimated the difficulties? The hardships?

She took a fresh shirtwaist from her trunk, retrieved the pitcher and bowl from under the bunk, and splashed cool water on her face. No, leaving St. Louis was not a mistake. Only shame and disgrace awaited her there. A twenty-six-year-old spinster schoolteacher had few choices.

Mattie buttoned the tiny wrist buttons of her shirtwaist, the kind her mother would have found appropriate. That dear, strong-minded woman had worked as a seamstress to support her through normal school only to suffer a fatal stroke shortly after Mattie's graduation. At least she had lived to applaud her daughter's valedictory speech—a tirade against the tyranny of appropriateness, the conventions by which all women are bound. Mattie smiled recalling the furor it had caused. Her mother's pride in her. Still, her mother would never have approved this impulsive trek into the wilderness.

Mattie quickly tamed wayward wisps of hair by tucking a tortoise-shell comb below the coiled blond braid. The old tyranny of appropriateness again. Making herself presentable despite the fact that she was stalled on a Missouri River packet, somewhere in Dakota territory, with buffalo on every side, choking prairie dust hanging in the summer heat, and nothing but rough-board walls separating her cubicle from the deck on one side, the dining cabin on the other. She preferred eating alone to the stilted conversation of the male passengers, all of whom regarded her as something of a curiosity. The only other woman aboard was Mrs. Schwartz, plump wife of a German homesteader bound for Bismarck. The Schwartzes slept in the open on the lower deck with their two small children and a coop of Leghorns, while their team of Belgians and a Guernsey milk cow enjoyed straw-filled stalls in the hold. "My wife, she don't talk no English," Schwartz had explained. Mattie hoped there would be English-speaking women in Bismarck.

Captain Tanner stood as she approached his table. "I'm afraid the oatmeal scorched. Cook was more interested in watching the crew set out after fresh meat."

She seated herself across from him. "Coffee will do. I'm not hungry."

"Hot for June. Gets to you after a while." He passed the tray of sourdough rusk. "Should be cooler when we get upriver—if these buffalo see fit to let us."

She sipped her coffee. Expressing more concern over the delay might make him inquisitive. "I've always found steamboats fascinating."

"You've ridden the packets before?"

"My father was often called to treat patients on boats that docked in St. Louis. I used to go with him."

"I thought I'd seen you somewhere." The captain leaned toward her cordially. "You're Dr. Hamil's daughter. That spunky girl who used to come along as his helper. I recall seeing you and your father a few times just after the war."

"Yes. That was me. Odd that you should remember." She didn't want to admit she couldn't recall the captain. But of course, she was young then and starry-eyed only about doctoring.

"You seemed a determined young lady," he said. "I would have thought you'd follow in your father's footsteps."

"He was killed by a runaway team when I was seventeen, and I'm afraid my dream of becoming a doctor died with him. The medical profession doesn't take kindly to females. Anyway, there was no money for study."

The captain nodded with understanding. "Well, I certainly never expected to see you traveling into the territories alone."

Mattie smiled. No one could be more surprised than she.

"I spend a good deal of time in the river settlements," he said, "since I lost my wife."

Mattie studied the lines on his rough face, lines she now realized expressed a certain sadness.

"Childbirth," he continued. "Lost them both seven years ago."

"In St. Louis?"

"She was with me on the boat, two hundred miles into Montana territory. The baby came early."

"You weren't able to get a doctor?"

He shook his head.

"How terrible."

"This old boat keeps me company now. The river towns."

They gazed in silence through the open window as the sunrise fringed the hovering dust cloud with gold and skimmed the backs of the swimming beasts.

"Your fiancé is meeting you in Bismarck?"

"Yes." Mattie tried to sound convincing. She *hoped* Cal would be in Bismarck. That's where his letter, posted in Omaha shortly after he left St. Louis, said he was headed.

"Maybe I know him," Tanner said.

"Probably not. He's new to St. Louis, and his trip a month ago was his first upriver. His name is Calvin Bodein."

The captain waited for her to continue.

"He's an outfitter," she explained. "Plans to set up a trading post for the Ottsbergs." Actually Cal had talked about establishing a saloon, a gambling hall, carrying a small line of Ottsberg goods to attract business, but she saw no reason to clarify this to the captain.

"He works for the Ottsbergs?"

"He did in St. Louis." Cal had spent only two weeks with the Ottsbergs after leaving the bank-clerk position arranged by his father with prominent financier Wallace Nesbit.

"Can't recall hearing about any Bodein shipping supplies upriver lately."

"The Ottsbergs will ship as soon as he's found a place."

The captain spooned his oatmeal. "Has quarters for you, does he?"

Mattie avoided his eyes. "A boardinghouse, I think, for a while." She wished he would stop asking questions she couldn't answer.

"Bertha Murphy's? She's about the best in Bismarck."

She turned her attention to the animals in the river. "Tell me, Captain, have you encountered this many before?"

"Only once, about three years ago. The big herds are mostly gone." He relaxed then, leaning back in his chair as if realizing he had been too nosy. The man had a fine quality about him. Mattie was glad he wanted to be friends. She felt less alone.

"You're lucky to have come now," he continued. "To see the real West, I mean, before it disappears. It won't last long. There's even talk of statehood for the territories. Folks are coming thick and fast. Good folks." He looked earnestly at her. "Like you and your fiancé."

Calvin Bodein stretched his lean arms across the table and drew in the scattered pile of coins and folding money. The tilt of his expensive hat and the gold of his University of Virginia signet ring, winking its blue-and-orange Cavaliers crest, identified a southern gentleman.

"Thank you, boys. It's been a pleasure." Amusement shone in his dark eyes as he stuffed his winnings into the pockets of his coat. The three mule skinners seated with him around a table in the riverfront Bismarck Hotel grumbled.

"If that don't beat all. Drawin' four deuces to beat my full house."

The stocky one stood angrily. "Bodein, your luck just ain't natural."

He glared at the silky-sideburned gambler, who responded to the insult with a wide grin that softened his patrician features.

"Don't know when the cards have been so good to me." Bodein untangled his long legs from his chair. "Gentlemen, I'm sure you'll agree it's best to quit when you're ahead."

"Now just a doggone minute." The angry skinner moved toward Bodein. "You ain't goin' nowhere till we get a chance to win back some of our money."

Bodein edged away with good humor. "I'll be glad to schedule a rematch, boys, but it's late. I need to hit the hay. How about tomorrow night?"

The freighter scowled. "We're headin' west at noon."

"In the morning then," Bodein said. "Say nine o'clock?"

The skinner looked at the other men, who nodded their agreement, then warned, "Bring that bankroll with you."

"You bet." Bodein again flashed the wide grin. "I never go anywhere without it." Turning, he walked toward the hotel stairs with the confident, casual stride that had carried him from confrontation many times before.

Upstairs in his room, he counted his winnings, adding to a fat roll of bills and a handful of gold coins secreted in a sock in the depths of the neatly packed valise that stood on the bedside chair. He'd soon have enough to build his hotel. Everything just the way he wanted it. Bodein House. High class. A downstairs emporium with saloon and gaming room, plus rooms upstairs for travelers. Girls, maybe. No, Mattie wouldn't like that. But he couldn't make his plans around a schoolteacher's values. From what he'd seen of the West, it didn't seem like much of a place for an educated woman anyway.

He stuffed the money into the sock and replaced it deep in the valise. Then, removing his coat and hanging it over the chair, he lay back on the bed. Maybe he should forget Mattie Hamil and make the most of what the frontier had to offer. Not that she had asked him to change. She knew what he was.

"There's opportunity right here in St. Louis," she had suggested. But he loathed even the thought of the tidy, small life of a bank clerk, just as he had hated the dull routine of an army corporal. After leaving the university, he had joined the Union army to escape the heavy hand of his father, whose loyalties were with the Confederates. But he had run away then, too. Away from the slaughter at Shiloh.

"Please don't leave me, Cal," Mattie had whispered that last night in

St. Louis. Her voice had a soft assurance to it. Enough to convince a man to stick around just for the sound of it. When he held her in his arms, her tender murmur told him he was a fool to think of leaving. Even temporarily. And when he loosened the honey-colored braid so that her hair fell across her breasts, her intelligent eyes showed not a flicker of coyness, only longing. He knew he could never be content with a lesser woman.

"You know I'll be back for you," he murmured, realizing for the first time that he couldn't bear to leave her without taking something of her with him. His lips searched the warmth of her neck.

She caught her breath. "I need you, Cal."

Ever conscious of her maidenhood, he had always maintained control when she responded too ardently. A gentleman always respected a lady. But this time he couldn't help himself. And why should he? He loved her. He was sure of it. And she loved him. He was sure of that, too. One day soon she would be his wife.

But come morning, he had to be on that riverboat. "A man's got to do what he's got to do, darlin'. Or he isn't a man."

Now he woke with a start and squinted at his pocket watch. Three-thirty. Sounds from the saloon had faded into the night. The Bismarck Hotel was stone quiet. He got up and, without lighting the lamp, put on his coat. Then, taking the valise, he crept down the darkened stair and out into the deserted street. At the stables not far from the hotel, he saddled the sorrel mare he had won in a wager the day before. A cowboy had challenged his marksmanship, forcing him to target six shots from the cowboy's pistol through a small knothole in the stable roof. Cal never carried a weapon—he hated guns since Shiloh—but the pistol practice his father made compulsory during his teen years finally had paid off. He hadn't realized the mare would come in handy so soon.

He felt a certain excitement in the change of plans. Bismarck wasn't much of a town. His fortune would be made farther upriver, Fort Benton maybe, or Last Chance Gulch. He chuckled to himself. Those mule skinners would be in a murderous mood when he didn't show up for the morning game. But they couldn't do much but speculate on his whereabouts before their wagons headed out. He'd make himself scarce till they were gone, then come back into town just in time to board the *Big Muddy*, due at the Bismarck wharf that very afternoon, and head on up the Missouri.

In the darkness he passed the shadowy barns and sheds that marked the edge of town, then headed east. As the first light spread across the prairie, he came upon a winding creek with a deep-cut bank that would screen a mounted man from view. Guiding the mare down into the gully, he rode a distance downstream before he unsaddled and spread the saddle blanket beside the creek. Using the valise for a pillow, Cal Bodein settled down to wait till the angry freighters had harnessed their teams and headed west.

Two

CANNON FIRE greeted the *Big Muddy* as it steamed into Bismarck. The welcoming volley was acknowledged by a single round from the ship's brightly polished brass cannon. On the riverbank, horses skittered at a sudden blast from the boat's whistle while clusters of people, waving and shouting, scurried among the buggies and wagons awaiting passengers and goods. Small boys scuffled to get closer as a rope was looped over a piling and the steam-powered winch tugged the packet against the wharf.

In the clamor of the docking, Mattie evaded Captain Tanner. Having arranged for her trunk to be taken ashore, she made her way along the row of riverfront business establishments toward the two-story Bismarck Hotel, its painted sign bright in the late afternoon sun.

Stepping into the hotel, she barely avoided collision with a lanky, shirt-sleeved youth mopping the dusty floor. The few scruffy bullwhackers leaning on the bar turned to look at her, as did a woman who sat at one of the tables adjusting the hairpins in her upswept hair. Mattie could see the hotel's business did not depend entirely on room rentals.

The young man with the mop glanced around as if to determine whether the others also saw the fair-haired woman in the blue silk traveling suit who had entered the hotel unescorted. Conversation ceased as the men fixed their attention on her.

She hesitated. "I'm looking for a room."

"Well . . . uh . . . this is an old hotel, miss, and well, our rooms . . . our rooms are . . . ," the young man stammered.

"What Willy means, sweetie, is that you might be more cozy over at Bertha Murphy's boardinghouse." The woman got up from the table, her limp green satin dress drooping on her slim body. As she came closer, Mattie saw that she was a young girl in her late teens. Her voice was high-pitched and unpleasantly loud. "That is, if you'll be stayin' awhile," the girl added, a skeptical look on her pale, pinched face.

After the long river trip, Mattie welcomed the sound of a feminine voice, however shrill. "I'm not sure just how long," she said, smiling. "Captain Tanner also recommended Mrs. Murphy's boardinghouse. Is it nearby?" As the girl continued to scrutinize her, Mattie added, "I'm here to join my fiancé."

The girl raised an eyebrow at the word "fiancé." "You can take her over to Bertha's, can't you, Willy?"

"You betcha. Got the buckboard all hitched just in case the *Big Muddy* brought business." Willy stuffed the mop in the pail and banished it behind the bar before adding sheepishly, "I'm s'posed to charge a dollar."

Mattie frowned. "That much? Well then, maybe you can tell me if my fiancé has been in here. Calvin Bodein."

Willy's eyes widened in surprise. "Bodein? The gambler? Why, yes. I mean, no. I mean, yes, he was here. But no, he ain't now. Ain't that right, Cindy?" He blinked at the girl, whose narrow face screwed into a disdainful expression.

Mattie's hope soared. "He was here? When?"

"Well, let me think. It's hard to say." Willy seemed to have difficulty concentrating.

"You mean he's gone?"

"Let's see, today's riverboat day. I think he came in on the last one. Stayed right here. Room four." He pointed up the open staircase.

"He was here all right." Cindy's voice held a candid quality despite its deficiencies. "Last night he cleaned out a bunch of mule skinners in a poker game."

Willy's memory revived. "Yeah, they sat right there at that table." As he pointed, everyone, including the men at the bar and the aproned bartender, turned to look at the empty table.

"Then he must still be in Bismarck." Mattie's excitement heightened. She had come so far with no guarantees.

"Not likely," Cindy chirped. "Them skinners said he lit out early this morning on that horse he'd left over at the stable."

"Did they say where he went?" Mattie searched the face of this frail girl who seemed to be so well informed.

Cindy shrugged her shoulders. "How would they know? They was fit to be tied when he didn't show up for their game this morning. I reckon if they was headed west, he probably went east."

Willy frowned. "Ain't nothin' east. I say he went upriver."

Mattie looked toward the bar hoping one of the men would comment, but the bartender quickly busied himself polishing glasses and aligning them on the shelf. The men hunched under their grubby hats.

"Didn't he know you was coming?" Cindy studied her own stubby fingernails.

"Well . . . there was . . . a mixup." Mattie decided to challenge the unscrutables at the bar and walked toward them. "Excuse me, gentlemen. I wonder if any of you have seen Cal Bodein."

They turned blank faces. The bartender came from behind the bar. "Lady, you musta come clear from St. Louie judging by them fancy duds."

Mattie glanced down at her stylish high-laced shoes barely visible beneath her bustled skirt. She blushed at the patronizing tone.

"A man like Bodein, I reckon he's long gone," one gaunt and grimy whacker volunteered.

"After cheatin' them freighters," another drawled, "I'd hightail it outta here, too." The others chortled agreement, then looked at Mattie for her reaction.

Mattie spoke confidently. "Cal's not a cheat."

"A fair man gives losers a chance to win back," the bartender said.

"And don't sneak away in the middle of the night with his tail between his legs." The whacker pushed back his hat with his thumb and peered at Mattie. "You look like a real nice lady. You sure you want to hook up with the likes of him?"

Mattie glared. "If he left suddenly, he must have had good reason." She looked around for more promising assistance. There was no one except Willy and Cindy, who watched with vacant expressions. Mattie turned back to the men. "Please. Do you have any idea where he might have gone?" There was a long silence before the bartender spoke.

"A gambler sticks to the river," he offered. "If you're set on catchin' up with him, I'd get right back on that boat and head upstream." The others nodded.

Her spirits sinking, Mattie murmured a thank-you and started for the door. Willy hurried along beside her to earn his fare.

One of the men called after her, "You're welcome right here if you change your mind."

"Wait up," Cindy said. "I'll help you get your stuff."

Outside, Mattie scanned the crowd milling about the wharf and dispersing in both directions along the waterfront. If Cal left early this morning on horseback as they said, where would he go? Surely he wouldn't ride very far across the prairies alone. Not Cal.

Cindy, too, studied the activities of the men involved with the ship's cargo. "If he's leaving on the *Big Muddy*, you could find out over there at the mercantile where they sell the tickets." She indicated a broad-fronted building almost at the river's edge.

"I'll go over to the stable and see if he brought his horse back," Willy said, sprinting off. He was capable of independent thought after all. Mattie followed Cindy into the mercantile, piled to the open rafters with goods of all kinds and smelling of new harness and tar soap. There they saw a placard announcing the *Big Muddy*'s departure for Fort Benton the next morning at sunup.

Mattie approached the stocky clerk. "Has a Mr. Bodein purchased a ticket on the *Big Muddy?*" She spelled out Bodein so there would be no mistake.

The clerk flipped a page in a leather log book and ran his finger down a column of names. "No Bodein listed."

"If he should come in here, will you tell him Mattie Hamil is waiting for him at Mrs. Murphy's boardinghouse."

He picked up a stubby pencil and a scrap of paper. "How's that again?"

"Mattie. Miss Matilda Hamil." He scratched out the note and stuck it in a crevice on the top of the cash register.

"Matilda Hamil." Cindy rolled the name across her tongue, tasting its sound as if it were a delicacy. "Is that your real name?"

"Yes." Mattie wasn't certain how friendly she should get with Cindy, whose pale young face shone with eagerness to help. "But you may call me Mattie."

The girl looked pleased. "Cindy here. Cynthia Dougherty."

As they emerged into the street, the low rays of the sun splashed the decks of the *Big Muddy* with yellow light, while in the cool violet shadow on the riverbank, a few rough freight handlers loaded their huge wagons. Shielding her eyes with her hand, Mattie saw her trunk standing near the coop of chickens and other goods on the wharf near the boat. Beyond, Captain Tanner directed the Schwartzes in unloading their Belgian team. The big horses pranced from the boat like trained circus ponies, sunlight gilding their flaxen manes and tails in the same way it fringed the captain's sandy mustache and the wavy hair below his cap.

Mattie regretted that she hadn't said good-bye to the captain. He had been kind to her. But it was his job to be concerned with all traffic on the Missouri, this umbilical of the Northwest. Helping that lifeline nurture the river towns was his livelihood. Mattie wondered at the disorderly tangle of frame structures huddled on the waterfront, the endless prairie stretching behind them. Who were these people who had severed connection with all but the river? Were they now to be her people?

A bony bay horse hitched to a buckboard careened into the street from behind the mercantile, Willy at the lines. He pulled the horse up beside the women. "Bodein ain't been to the stable today," he announced. "He took his horse and skedaddled."

"Well, I'm staying here till I'm sure he's not coming back." Mattie started toward the baggage on the wharf. "You can help me take my trunk to Mrs. Murphy's." Captain Tanner stood with his back turned as she approached.

"I didn't get a chance to say good-bye," she began.

He whirled around. "Miss Hamil. I was afraid I'd missed you. Did you find your fiancé?"

Mattie tried to sound lighthearted. "Cal didn't meet the boat. I . . . I don't know just why."

"He's here though," Cindy hastened to assure the captain. "He was at the hotel last night so he's around someplace."

The Schwartz couple approached with their horses, and Captain Tanner touched Mattie's arm to move her out of the way, calling to Schwartz, "You'll find the wagoner down that way." Schwartz, gripping the bridles, led the champing team with the strong, powerful hands of a seasoned farmer. Plump Mrs. Schwartz and the shy children hurried along behind.

Captain Tanner turned to Cindy. "You say Bodein was at the hotel last night?"

"There was a card game. He won money from some freighters and they weren't too jolly about it."

Willy added, "He rode out of here 'fore daylight."

The captain looked earnestly at Mattie. "I have a few more things to attend to, then I'll make some inquiries."

"I'd appreciate that, Captain. I'll be at Mrs. Murphy's."

While Willy hoisted Mattie's trunk into the buckboard, Mattie thanked Cindy for her help and held out her hand to the sallow girl. Surely this young girl has a home somewhere besides that hotel, Mattie thought. "Do you live with your folks?" she asked.

"Got no folks here." Almost defiantly, Cindy turned and started toward the hotel. "I take care of myself."

"But . . . how do you come to be in Bismarck?"

Cindy called back over her shoulder, "Captain Tanner brought me."

Willy extended his hand to pull the startled Mattie up onto the buckboard seat beside him. "Yeah, she came with Tanner all right," he said. "He set her up at the boardinghouse, but that didn't last. Bertha didn't take to her." He gave Mattie a look that implied she should understand the whole story from his brief account.

"And about the fare," he said. "It ain't a dollar. It's fifty cents . . . but for you . . . well, I reckon I can get you over to Bertha's for a quarter."

Three

BERTHA MURPHY, a faded calico apron covering her ample front, answered Mattie's knock at the planked door of the boardinghouse, a rough board-and-batten structure fronted with a broad porch and two eye-like dormers peering from the low roof. Bertha's rosy face blossomed with Mattie's inquiry and brief explanation.

"Willy, bring that trunk on in." She held the door open wide in a welcoming gesture and led Mattie into the central hall. "You come all that way by yourself to join your man?" A doorway to the left revealed a neat low-ceilinged parlor, and down the hall past several closed doors a dining room, its table set for the evening meal. "I'd say that's real brave."

"The boat trip was pleasant enough." Mattie hoped she wouldn't have to go into the whole story of Cal's absence. "I may be going on in the morning."

"Well, I have this nice front room I save for special guests." Bertha opened the door across from the parlor to the musty smell of old wallpaper, then scurried about opening the windows, adjusting the shades, and fluffing the starched lace curtains. "Lots of air comes through here these hot nights." She patted the towels on the washstand and picked up the pitcher. "I'll fill this so you can freshen up. Supper be ready soon."

"You're very kind," Mattie said.

"Not a' tall." Bertha shooed Willy out the door.

"I'll come for your trunk in the morning," he said, as Bertha closed the door behind them.

Mattie barely had time to take off her jacket and skirt and hang them in the chifforobe before Bertha tapped on the door and handed her the pitcher of water. Mattie latched the door then, removed her shoes, and stretched out on the feather bed in her camisole and petticoat. Bertha was right about the ventilation. The curtains had begun to stir slightly, the day's heat diminished, and the homey room provided a feeling of security, however temporary.

She awoke to another soft rapping at her door. The room was dark, and Mattie realized she had slept for some time. Bertha's voice called softly, "Miss Hamil, you have a visitor in the parlor."

Cal. He's come. She jumped up, felt for the matches on the bureau, and lit the lamp. Pouring water into the washbowl, she tried to splash away her fatigue before putting on the blue silk and hurrying to the parlor. There she found Captain Tanner talking with Bertha. She could not conceal her disappointment.

"Miss Hamil." He stood to greet her. "I'm sorry to call so late, but I wanted to let you know I haven't found a trace of Bodein."

Mattie sank onto the horsehair sofa.

"You're wore out," Bertha said, sympathetically. "But I saved you a supper plate. Have you eaten, Gar?" She seemed to know Captain Tanner well.

"No, guess I haven't."

"I'll fix you a plate then, too." Bertha bustled toward the kitchen.

Captain Tanner turned to Mattie, his light hair contrasting with his tanned face in the lamplight. "No one saw him leave the hotel. The stablemaster said he must have taken his sorrel horse before dawn."

"But he may come back," Mattie said.

"My guess is he's still around somewhere. Probably keeping out of sight till the *Big Muddy*'s ready to leave in the morning, or he may ride upstream and come aboard at one of the wood yards or Fort Clark."

"I'll be at the wharf in the morning, too, in case he comes."

For a moment his gaze held hers. "I'd like to help you in any way I can." It was Mattie who looked away as Bertha returned to the parlor.

"I set up supper for the two of you," she announced. "Help yourself if you want more. I got the kitchen to tend to."

"It's been a while since I've had one of Bertha's suppers." The captain gestured for Mattie to lead the way to the dining room, where one end of the big table was set for two. Steaming bowls of Irish stew, fresh-baked bread, and spiced apple sauce produced tantalizing aromas. For the first time in weeks, Mattie felt ravenous. The captain held her chair for her.

"Bertha's cooking always reminds me of when I was a kid at home in Massachusetts," he mused, seating himself and reaching for the bread plate.

"You're from the East?"

"Grew up on the Maryland waterfront. My dad had a fishing boat. It was his idea that I go to the Naval Academy at Annapolis."

"Then you were in the military?"

"Served with the Union fleet under Farragut. The battle of New Orleans. Just seemed natural to stay on the water when the war ended. But lately I've come to feel my home is out here in the West. These river towns are wide open. Lots of opportunity." He smiled at her as he savored the hot stew. "They need schoolteachers."

"I don't plan to teach again." She hoped he couldn't guess she'd soon be barred from ever teaching again. "I'm afraid I've lost patience with narrow-minded school boards."

"I'll bet you gave them something to think about." He raised his water glass in a mock toast.

"Yes, I'm afraid I did."

"A trip into the wild and woolly West will give you a fresh look at things for sure."

She chuckled, surprised at how comfortable he made her feel. "I've never shied away from adventure—or at least the contemplation of it."

Tanner grinned. "I'm the same way. I guess you might expect that from an old river rat like me. Not knowing what's around the corner has always been exciting to me." His strong features took on a serious look. "But more and more, I'm thinking about getting back on land where I can build something solid." They sat in easy silence as he poured coffee and she offered cream and sugar. She sensed something truly fine in this captain. Surely such a man had nothing to do with young Cindy's situation.

"Captain Tanner." She decided to come right out with it. "Cindy said *you* brought her to Bismarck."

"That I did. I found her in Sioux City where some mule skinner had dumped her. She was so young and pitiful. She'd had a wretched time, and I thought if I brought her here she could start fresh. Work for Bertha maybe."

Mattie felt relieved. His relationship with Cindy seemed honorable after all. "Why didn't it work out? Working for Bertha, I mean. The girl seems to have some appealing qualities."

"She's smart. Bertha wanted to help but couldn't accept . . . shall we say . . . her unconventional ways. Finally threw her out. Or at any rate Cindy moved over to the hotel." He grinned. "Cindy won't take much guff."

"I noticed," Mattie said. "That voice of hers is fair warning."

He laughed. "I'm hoping some eager young settler will see her good side one of these days." He glanced at his pocket watch. "It's getting late." He pushed away from the table. "Thanks for sharing your supper. I don't know when I've enjoyed an evening more."

"It was my pleasure, Captain."

As they paused at her door in the front hall, his hand rested lightly on her arm. "If Bodein shows up on the *Big Muddy*, we won't pull anchor without you aboard, too."

"Thank you, Captain Tanner."

"Good night, Miss Hamil."

Inside her room, Mattie listened to his footsteps cross the porch and fade in the dusty street. The prospect of continuing aboard the *Big Muddy* somehow seemed more appealing now. Yet she wanted to do what was appropriate. She could wait for Cal in this rowdy river town; she could go upriver in the company of Captain Tanner; or, if Cal showed up, follow along wherever he was headed. As if whatever she decided could possibly be appropriate.

Comfortable in her cool nightdress, she blew out the light, raised the shades, and stood looking out at the vacant street. A thin moon hung over the low buildings that spread up from the river—a pale silver crescent as precarious and delicately balanced in darkness as her future seemed to be. Feeling suddenly bone-weary, she climbed between the worn muslin sheets. A night breeze wafted through the lace curtains. But sleep did not come at once. The look in Garnet Tanner's eyes lingered. How silly, she thought. I should know better than to let the captain have such an effect on me. Obviously he enjoys looking after women in distress. Strays. Like Cindy and me.

A scraping sound came from the side of the house. Mattie bolted upright from a sound sleep. Moonlight outlined the dark form of a man at the window.

"Mattie?" A loud whisper filled the room. The voice set her heart pounding. "Mattie, it's me, Cal." Swatting at the lace curtains, he dropped a valise over the sill and climbed inside.

"Cal!" She leapt from the bed into his waiting arms.

"Cindy told me you were here." He drew her close. His kisses were sweet, loving, and gentle.

Tears of joy spilled down her cheeks. "Oh, Cal. I was afraid I wouldn't find you." Then, ashamed of her emotion, she pulled away to light the lamp. Cal Bodein was as she remembered—the dark silky hair and sideburns, the bright dark eyes, the wide grin.

"Glad to see me?" His lighthearted manner was also the same, his laugh still contagious. In answer, she went to him and kissed him again, grateful now that the worst of her journey was over.

"But what are you doing here?" he said with genuine surprise. "You came all this way alone? I told you I couldn't make plans till I got my place set up."

"I wanted to be with you."

"And I want to be with you, too, darlin'. I've missed you." Again he enfolded her in his arms. "But I've got to get on upriver in the morning."

"I know. I'm all packed and ready." She gestured to her open trunk bulging with all manner of goods. "Where are we headed, Fort Benton?"

"Whoa, now. I didn't mean . . . I mean, I'm not that selfish. The frontier is no place for you, Mattie."

"Of course it is. There are other women here." At least she knew of three, Cindy, Bertha, and Mrs. Schwartz.

He wrinkled his handsome nose. "But I don't much like this place."

"Cal, what happened in that poker game last night? Why have you been hiding?"

"Just avoiding some sore losers. I saw no reason to attend a rematch so I took a jaunt out east of town." He nuzzled her cheek. "It's good business, darlin', to quit when you're ahead."

She relaxed in his embrace, resting her head on his chest, hardly daring to think ahead. "Everything will be fine as long as we can be together," she murmured.

"That's my girl. A few more months and I'll be set up in my own place. Then I can feel right about asking you to marry me."

Mattie swallowed her pride. "Cal, I want to be your wife now."

"I know, darlin'. But I've got to travel light for just a little while longer." He held her at arm's length, his hands on her shoulders. "When I got back to the hotel tonight, I struck up a conversation with two prospectors headed for the Montana gold fields. Those greenhorns don't seem to realize the gold rush is over. There's lots more like them still swarming into Last Chance Gulch. I can make a fortune off them." His dark eyes narrowed with excitement. "Maybe you met those two. The Fike brothers? They must have come in with you on the *Big Muddy*."

Mattie nodded. But as she studied his charming, mobile features, she saw a side of Cal she didn't know. Surely he didn't expect her to go back. She managed a smile, pleading. "I can travel light. I'm very portable."

"Portable or not, it's just not seemly for a woman of your refinement out here. It's not only dirty and uncomfortable, it's downright danger-ous. Be reasonable, darlin'." Cal's voice, commanding and coaxing at the same time, still held its mesmerizing quality.

"Cal, I'm not going back to St. Louis. I can't go back."

"Now if you don't look like a willful little girl with those pretty blue eyes snapping." He kissed her forehead. "All right, if you insist, you can wait for me right here in Bismarck. There's a school. Maybe you can teach." He began to unbutton her nightdress.

"You're not leaving without me, Cal. If you get on that boat, I'm going with you." She stepped back, hands on hips, her firm tone leav-ing no doubt as to her seriousness.

Cal stared at her, surprised at her outburst. "Mattie, you're not being sensible." He took her hands in his, and they sat down together on the bed.

"I mean it, Cal. I love you, and I'm going with you."

He shook his head, amused. "All right, darlin', if your mind is made up. But I warn you, it could be rough. A woman on the frontier."

She threw her arms around him. "Oh, Cal. Things will go well for us. I can feel it." She clung to him. And when he pressed her back onto the pillows, she gave herself to him eagerly, longing to share the love she felt for the new life she already carried.

Four

MATTIE HAD LONGED for the moment when Cal would again hold her in his arms, but now that he lay beside her, the expected contentment, the peaceful sleep did not come. She ached to tell him about her pregnancy, but she could never accept his marrying her out of any sense of duty. He must initiate that responsibility himself. In return, she would be a good wife, she was sure of that. She would help him in his business ventures, become indispensable, make him proud to have her beside him. Mattie stared into the darkness of the low-ceilinged room. She would also help him to love the child they had conceived that last night in St. Louis. Perhaps he would help *her* understand why she had risked everything on a man with his restless spirit.

She could have married Jim Plumet or Matthew Carney. They had both adored her, and she'd felt a special affection for both. But choosing between them hadn't been the problem. That special spark just wasn't there. When she met Calvin Bodein at a New Year's Eve party given by her friend Clarissa Nesbit, she knew someone extraordinary had come into her life. At first suspicious of his polished manner and good looks, she was soon attracted by his sensitivity, and, yes, intrigued by his daring. Cal took to her, too. As they danced the evening through, he confessed that, though he had thus far wasted most of his thirty-two years, he had no intention of sitting day after day behind a teller's window simply to help old man Nesbit get richer. He talked of going west. But by midnight, when he welcomed in the new year by touching his lips to hers, she felt certain she could convince him that St. Louis offered many opportunities for a man of his promise.

It was Cal who did the convincing. Despite the romantic weeks that followed, he remained determined to go up the Missouri to look over the settlements along the river for a place where he could build their future. "I've arranged for a line of credit with the Ottsbergs to whole-sale goods to me when I get located," he told her one evening, his dark eyes keen with anticipation of the adventure to come.

"Then you're set on going?"

"I am, darlin'. I know our future lies out there somewhere."

"Then I'll go with you."

"What?" He had looked at her incredulously.

"If our future is out there somewhere, then that's where we both should be."

His surprise changed to the familiar grin. "Oh, no, darlin'. Not yet." The grin broadened to a chuckle. "A woman like you in that raw country? Why, I couldn't let you leave your life here to endure such a needless ordeal." He pulled her close and touched his lips to her forehead. "No, no, no. I want to know you're safe and comfortable, waiting for me right here in St. Louis till I've got things ready for you."

"But I want to be with you, Cal. I could be a help to you. And to others, too. I know that doctors are few in the territories. I'm trained in medicine. It would be fulfilling for me."

"Fulfilling? Mattie, you've no idea what it's like. I've done some traveling. I've had to put up with poor food. Poor lodging. Cold. Rough vagabonds. Even desperate outlaws. It may be even worse on the frontier. Think of the hardships. Hostile Indians maybe."

"Hardships don't worry me. I'm strong. It would be a challenge." She knew her enthusiasm perhaps overshadowed her judgment. "The worst hardship will be having to wait here alone, wondering where you are. Worrying about you."

"Hush, now." His tone softened. "As much as I want you with me, I could never forgive myself if you came to any harm." He gently kissed her lips. "No, darlin', you have to wait for me here. I'll come back for you soon as I can. I promise you that."

"Cal, stay with me." She had told herself she wouldn't beg. She knew that if he didn't love her enough to build a future with her here in St. Louis, or to take her with him; if he could simply walk away from what they meant to each other, then she would have to let him go.

But how could she? Just a glimpse of his long, easy stride set her heart pounding, and the depth of feeling in his eyes seemed to tell her as clearly as his touch how much he loved her, too. Here was the only man who had stirred her imagination, excited her spirit, aroused her passion. And he was leaving her. She must hold him. Keep him with her. If only for a moment more.

When he loosened her hair and pulled her to him, neither resisted the tender force that bound them.

After he'd gone, when she discovered she was carrying his child, she knew she had to find him. Her comfortable life in St. Louis had suddenly jumbled into uncertainty. The tyranny of appropriateness allowed no deviations. She would be discharged from her teaching job when she could no longer conceal her condition. Marrying to escape the scandal would still bar her from teaching; married women were not allowed to teach. And marrying simply for support would mean she must spend her life with Jim Plumet or Mat Carney, a dismal prospect. Even worse, women faced with disgrace and poverty were often reduced to the very worst that could happen to a woman. Mattie had alluded to such tragedies in her fiery valedictory address. Ironic that she would now face such ruin herself. Her choice was clear. She booked passage on the next steamer upriver.

Now, here on the Dakota frontier, she lay beside a man who seemed almost a stranger. It had been little more than two months, yet Cal was somehow different. Or perhaps it was she who was different. As dawn filtered through the shades, she rose and began to dress.

Cal awoke with a start. "Oh, Mattie, it's you." He sighed and his look of alarm changed to one of relief. "I dreamed those freighters had me hogtied." He leaned back on his elbows admiring Mattie as she dressed, then bounded from the bed and wrapped his arms around her camisoled waist. "Are you always this wide awake in the morning?"

She smiled and kissed him lightly before slipping from his grasp to step into her blue silk. "I am on my wedding day." She felt lighthearted, actually happy, for the first time in weeks.

"Wedding day?" The wide grin spread across his lean, handsome face. "You mean you're fixing to find a preacher right here in Bismarck?"

"No time for that." She worked at buttoning her tiny sleeve buttons. "Maybe Captain Tanner can perform the ceremony."

Cal shrugged. "Never thought of that." He poured water into the bowl and soaped his face, then squinted at her through the suds. "I can see I got myself one spunky little gal." He splashed, toweled, and turned to her looking like a fresh-scrubbed little boy. "Darlin'," he said, "you may just turn out to be my ace in the hole."

Bertha prattled happily as she scurried about the big dining table, serving Mattie and Cal along with three scruffy boarders. Cal's unexpected appearance at breakfast, after obviously having shared Mattie's room, had ruffled her sense of propriety, but her indignation faded with his announcement that he and Mattie were to be married that very day. "How romantic now," the older woman clucked as she stacked steaming flapjacks on their plates. "Her coming all this way to find you." She gazed affectionately at the pair. "And getting married today. Well, that calls for some of my special strawberry preserves." She poured their coffee into china cups, the only two she had, and was proposing a wedding toast when Willy arrived with the buckboard. Willy seemed pleased to see Cal.

"Gosh, Mr. Bodein. I guess you came back."

"Guess I did," Cal said, to the amusement of Bertha and the boarders.

Willy beamed at Mattie. "Will you be needin' me to take your trunk then, Miss Mattie?"

"Yes. Thank you. We'll both be leaving on the *Big Muddy.*"

"They're getting married." Bertha beamed happily and the boarders nodded approval. "But wait just a minute before you go," she said. "I have something for you." And she darted toward the kitchen door.

Cal tossed a fifty-cent piece to Willy. "Fetch my sorrel mare from the stable and see that she gets aboard, will you, Willy?"

"Yes, *sir*, Mr. Bodein." Willy pocketed the coin.

Outside, the intense morning sun tipped the horizon, heralding another hot day. Cal helped load the trunk and valise into the buckboard, then boosted Mattie onto the seat next to Willy and swung up beside her. Bertha came hurrying from the back of the house clutching in her rough hand a small bouquet of purple and yellow pansies.

"Here, my dear. These are for you. A girl can't get married without flowers."

"Thank you, Mrs. Murphy." Mattie took the blossoms and sniffed their faint fragrance. "Thank you for everything."

"Not a'tall." The ample woman closed her eyes for a moment, savoring the sentiment of the occasion as Willy snapped the lines and the bony bay in the traces plodded off toward the riverfront.

At the wharf, the hulking *Big Muddy* tugged gently at the tie lines as passengers hurried back and forth over the gangplank attending to last-minute preparations and freighters stowed final cargo. Alighting from the buckboard, Cal waved at the Fike brothers who stood on deck watching. Mattie scanned the crowd for Captain Tanner, recalling his sturdy silhouette against yesterday's late afternoon sun. Was that only yesterday? she thought. It seems like a lifetime ago. Willy shoved the trunk onto the wharf among other baggage to be taken aboard.

Cal, his valise in hand, led Mattie toward the mercantile to book passage. As they rounded the corner, Captain Tanner came out the door, nearly colliding with Mattie.

"There you are." He scanned her face. "I was looking for you. We're about ready to shove off." His eyes darted to Cal's wide grin, then to the pansies Mattie held.

Mattie caught her breath. "Captain Tanner, I'd like you to meet Cal Bodein. He came back after all," she said. "We're going to Montana."

Cal held out his hand. "Thanks for looking after Mattie on her trip upriver."

The captain looked sternly at Cal before extending his hand.

"We're getting married," Mattie hurried to explain. "And we'd like you to perform the ceremony on board the *Big Muddy.*"

An uncomfortable look came over Garnet Tanner's face. "Well, I couldn't do that. I mean . . . that is, I'm afraid I don't have that authority." Mattie hadn't seen the captain at a loss for words and his fluster surprised her.

"That's all right, Captain," Cal said. "We'll find a preacher when we get to Fort Benton."

"But how long will that be?" Mattie asked.

"With good luck, about six weeks," Tanner said.

"Six weeks?"

"There's a chance you could run into a missionary or a priest at one of the stops," the captain said. "But don't count on it." He sounded almost gruff. "I'll see you on board." With a brief nod, he started off toward the wharf.

Cal grinned. "I think the captain's a little sweet on you himself."

Mattie felt her cheeks flush and she pushed on into the mercantile. Cal followed and approached the stocky clerk. "I'd like to book passage to Fort Benton for Mr. and Mrs. Calvin Bodein."

The clerk glanced up. "Bodein? Wait a minute." He took the slip of paper from atop the cash register. "I have a message for you. From a

Miss Hamil." He peered at Mattie from over his glasses. "Says she's at Bertha Murphy's boardinghouse."

Cal turned his most disarming smile on the clerk. "Miss Hamil is now Mrs. Bodein," he said. "Do you have appropriate accommodations available?" Mattie started to protest but Cal's wink stopped her.

The clerk returned Cal's smile. "There's a cabin on the promenade deck away from the smoke. Cabin five." He copied the spelling of Cal's name from the slip of paper into a log book. "It's good to have you young couples coming west," he said. "Plan to settle in Fort Benton?"

"Don't know for sure, yet." Cal paid for the two passages with twenty-dollar gold pieces.

The clerk counted out his change. "Well, good luck to you both."

On board, Cal guided Mattie along the main deck to where the Fike brothers stood at the rail. The older one was small, slightly built, and wore an awkward brace on his right leg. He tipped his worn derby politely as he recognized Mattie.

Cal maneuvered her forward. "Mattie, I believe you've met Boot Fike."

"Booker," he said. "My name is Booker Fike. They call me Boot." Mattie nodded as she turned from his narrowed stare to the younger brother, a strapping fellow with heavy lips and dull, close-set eyes.

"And his brother Alf. Or Alfred, am I right? Boys, Miss Hamil."

"So you're the fella she came to meet." Boot Fike gave out a low cackle as he noted the tiny bouquet of pansies in her hand. "I thought you said last night you were traveling light." His grin produced an uneven row of teeth.

"This is the future Mrs. Bodein." Cal put his arm around Mattie's shoulders. "She's our business partner."

"Wait a minute." Boot's dark eyes narrowed. "You didn't say anything last night about a four-way split."

Cal grinned. "Last night I didn't know she would be coming along. But our deal remains the same—a three-way split. One share for each of the two of you and one for Mattie and me."

Boot again narrowed his eyes at Mattie, who tried to conceal her surprise at Cal's statement. She couldn't let on that he had told her nothing. He had said only that a fortune could be made from "green-horns" flocking to the already worked-out mines.

Cal explained casually. "We'll be outfitting the Fikes for their prospecting venture—at reduced cost," he emphasized. "In return, we claim a third of any mine they bring in."

"I still think you're hoggin' the best of the deal," Boot grumbled. "A third of everything just for discounting our grubstake."

"You said yourself you didn't have enough to get started," Cal countered. "This will set you up in good shape and get you through the winter. I'd say that's a fair deal."

Alf grinned his satisfaction. Boot was less convinced. "Maybe so. Seems like I feel more trusting, Bodein, now that your missus is with you." He gave another cackle. "Knew you was a fine lady when we seen you on the boat, Miss Hamil."

Mattie managed a weak smile.

"I'll buy you boys a drink," Cal said, "as soon as we're settled into our cabin. Maybe we can get up a friendly poker game this evening." He guided Mattie along the deck.

"You didn't tell me you were in business with them," she said when they were out of earshot.

"I'm not." Cal grinned. "I don't expect them to find any gold."

"Then what was that all about?"

"I'm outfitting them through Ottsberg's for a small profit."

"But you said at reduced cost."

"At a discount from my usual quadruple markup, darlin'. They don't know prices. I'll sell for what money they've got and we'll have a stake in what they dig up, if anything. There's no gamble. I can't lose. If I can work enough of these deals . . . well, who knows?"

Mattie hesitated, frowning.

"What's the matter, darlin'? You look as if there's something illegal about it. Quite the contrary. Everything is strictly legitimate. I have our future to think about now." He smooched her cheek, looking so appealing she had to smile. So this is the man I'm going to marry, she thought. At least life won't be dull. And it certainly won't be bound by appropriateness.

As they turned to wave to Willy leading Cal's sorrel mare toward the hold, a commotion rose from mid-deck. The sound of rapid, heavy steps and a loud voice shouting, "If the sonofabitch is here, I'll kill him!"

Mattie and Cal exchanged puzzled glances just as a burly man pushed through the crowd and came running toward them. Huge and unkempt with a full growth of black whiskers, he carried a bullwhip. "There he is!" The man pointed the long whip directly at Cal.

"I better vamoose," Cal muttered. He slipped his valise into Mattie's hand and darted away. Before she could respond, he had disappeared around the forward deck. The black-bearded man rushed past her and around the corner in close pursuit.

She heard a loud crack as the whip was unleashed. Then a splash in the river below. A passenger shouted, "Someone's overboard."

At once, continuing heavy steps traced the burly man's race for the gangplank. "The sonofabitch is getting away. Stop him!"

Mattie rushed with other bystanders around the forward deck to the far rail. She saw Cal in the river flailing his arms toward the opposite shore as he was swept downstream in the swift current. The swirl of the muddy water dizzied her. She steadied herself at the rail, still clutching the wilting pansies, and stared after the churning figure in the water, dipping and bobbing, now visible, now lost to view.

The morning sun beat down on the river, engulfing the hissing steamboat in an intense white heat. Under the wide dome of sky and the enormity of her predicament, Mattie crumpled against the rail. Her fist opened and the pansies dropped to the river. They spread momentarily on the surface, then sank into the murky water.

Five

"MISS HAMIL, what's happened?" Captain Tanner ran to help when he saw Mattie gripping the rail. "Who's overboard? Bodein?"

With the deck reeling beneath her, she pointed downriver at the figure struggling in the current. The captain grasped her arm to steady her as they watched Cal being swept into the branches of a fallen cottonwood jutting onto the river.

"Can you send a rowboat after him?"

"I'm not sure he wants to be rescued right now." The captain indicated the burly bearded man raging along the shore. "Bodein may be safer where he is."

Mattie moaned. How could Cal be safer hiding in a tree, drenched, maybe hurt, and on the wrong side of the river? How would he get back to the boat? She bent her head to steady her dizziness.

"Let me help you to your quarters." The captain took the valise and led her toward the forward cabins.

"I'm sorry. I felt faint for a moment."

"Your fiancé seems to have a talent for trouble."

"I don't understand any of this." She walked now on her own, embarrassed at having displayed such weakness. "But I must get off this boat and go back to Mrs. Murphy's. Cal will find me there."

"You look tuckered out," he said. "Sit for a minute." Her cabin was stifling and cramped but, as the clerk had promised, contained a double bunk beneath the narrower one above. The captain put the valise on the floor next to her trunk and opened the small window.

"Captain Tanner, you've been more than kind but this needn't concern you. Cal and I plan to be married and go on to Montana territory." She sat down on the bunk. "It's just that those men seem to have some angry feelings over Cal's winning at cards, and . . ."

"I'd say that bearded fella had murder in his eyes."

"Cal's a clever poker player. I can see how some losers could hold a grudge, but not to this extent."

"They might if they've been cheated." He raised an eyebrow.

She looked at him squarely. "Cal's not like that. He's impulsive, but he's not a cheat." She wished the captain would stop looking at her with such intensity. "What happened to that man with the whip?"

"He went ashore muttering something about getting up a posse."

"A posse?"

"Probably find a couple of men who'll ride with him, that's about it."

"But where can Cal go? Would they hurt him?" She jumped to her feet, alarmed by the thought.

"I doubt it will come to that."

"But we've got to help him." She searched the captain's face for a solution.

"Not much we can do. If I were you I'd stay right here on the *Big Muddy.*"

"I can't do that. I have to wait for Cal."

"What if he doesn't make it back here? He knows we're heading for Fort Benton. He'll catch up with you there. I'd hate to leave you here alone . . . if he doesn't come back, I mean."

If he doesn't come back. Mattie refused to accept that bleak possibility. "But he left his bag." She gestured toward the scuffed valise.

"I'm sure Bodein can take care of himself. For all we know, he could show up anywhere along the way. He's not going to be keen on venturing back into Bismarck. Stay aboard. I'll see that you get to Fort Benton safe and sound."

"Maybe it *would* be easier—for Cal, I mean—if I stay on the *Big Muddy*," Mattie said, almost convinced. "But he has both our passages."

"I can arrange to have yours credited."

Mattie nodded her decision. "All right. I guess that is best."

"Good." The captain clasped her hands. "Now you rest, and I'll see what I can find out about this whole thing before we shove off."

"Thank you for your concern, Captain Tanner."

"If you feel up to it, come up on the forward deck when you hear the whistle." He stepped out on the promenade, then turned to her before closing the door. "No matter how many times you head upriver, there's always a certain excitement in every departure, new adventure in the air."

When he was gone, Mattie stretched out on the wide lower bunk. Her head ached. What if Cal didn't follow? What would she do when her savings were gone? When the baby was showing? Maybe Cal was right. The frontier was no place for a woman. For any woman. Certainly not for a woman alone . . . and expecting. She rolled onto her side, trying to ease the nausea.

A muffled sneeze came from directly beneath. Mattie sprang to her feet, nearly tripping over the valise in her haste, while from beneath the bunk a mop of mousy hair and a small, pinched face emerged.

"Cindy!"

"Didn't mean to scare you." Cindy, her usual high-volume voice hushed to a hoarse whisper, wriggled from under the bunk till the faded green dress emerged, followed by thin ankles and worn shoes. "I didn't want you to find me till we was up the river a ways, but dust got in my nose." She stood up and brushed at her limp garments. "You won't tell on me, will you?"

"Cindy, what are you doing here? Are you running away?"

"No. I'm startin' a new life." She looked out the window, up and down the deck, before slumping possessively onto the bunk. "I don't like Bismarck. I figure if Captain Tanner brought me here, he can take me away."

"But you can't hide all the way to Fort Benton."

"The captain won't find me for a while, and when he does he won't kick me off. I know he won't."

"But how did you find my cabin?" Mattie didn't know whether to be angry or amused at this resourceful girl.

"I was on the wharf when that mule skinner started raisin' a ruckus. I saw your man go into the water, so I decided kind of sudden like to come aboard. Willy said you'd be in number five." The girl's expression changed from triumph to desperation. She grabbed Mattie's hand. "Please don't tell on me. I can work for you." Her pale green eyes pleaded. "I'll be a big help, honest I will."

"But don't you have someone who'll wonder about you?"

"Nope. My pa left when I was little. He was no 'count. Always hittin' on me. And my ma . . . well, she died." She bowed her head as if ashamed. "Left me on my own 'fore I got my monthlies."

Mattie patted the girl's arm. "All right. I won't give you away. But how will you manage?"

Cindy jumped up and whirled around the room. "I can stay right here with you . . . seein' as how your man ain't here." Again she flopped onto the bunk as if testing for comfort, then indicated the water pitcher, bowl, and chamber pot beneath. "There's everything I need. And I won't eat much."

The *Big Muddy*'s whistle gave a long, deafening blast. The boat was leaving without Cal. "I'm going on deck," Mattie said, remembering the captain's invitation. Then at Cindy's apprehensive look, "Don't worry, I won't tell anyone."

Joining Captain Tanner on the forward deck, she anxiously scanned the river as the boat swung out into the current, its huge paddle wheel churning the yellowed water. No sign of Cal. Another blast from the whistle and final shouts of farewell. A breeze wafted the smell of the river on the morning air, and she looked back at the fallen tree where Cal had pulled himself from the water. The incident seemed as unreal as Cal himself. But the smoke-belching riverboat now heading up the Missouri for Montana territory was, regrettably, all too real.

Mattie smiled wistfully at the irony of it and began to relax in the gentle undulating motion as the *Big Muddy* fought the current, moving slowly but steadily now between the cottonwoods and willow groves on either bank. Nothing is ever as bad as it seems, she thought. It's fear and dread that torture. She would simply wait for Cal in Fort Benton, the end of the line. He was sure to find her there. She took a deep breath. Captain Tanner was right about the sense of newness. "It's pleasant out here on the river," she said.

"I thought you'd like it," the captain concurred. "Heading away from the settlements into open country. It's almost like nobody's ever made the trip before."

I wonder if anyone has, she thought. Anyone like me. For my reasons.

In response to a final blast from the whistle, Captain Tanner waved to a round, rosy-nosed man up in the pilot house, but his attention remained fixed on Mattie. "Hodgewarden is a fine pilot," he said. "You're in good hands with him at the wheel."

"I'm sure of that. I'm just worried about Cal."

"If Bodein has the sense I think he has, he'll make himself scarce. I left word for him with Willy that you're on board."

"And that I'll be waiting in Fort Benton?"

"Yes, that, too," he said. "Now if you'll excuse me, I have chores. Join me at supper tonight and we can talk further."

A sudden image of Cindy pacing about the cabin prompted her response. "I'm sorry, Captain, but I'd prefer to take my meals in my cabin if I may."

"All right, then." The polite manner in which he tipped his cap did not conceal his disappointment. "Maybe another time." She watched as he hurried along the deck and up the narrow stairway that led to the pilot house, issuing orders to crewmen along the way.

At noon, Cindy remained concealed in their small quarters while Mattie went into the adjoining dining cabin and brought back her meal on a tin tray. "Look, there's plenty for the two of us." Mattie divided the fried potatoes and sausage into two parts and handed the girl a fork. They sat, the tray between them on the bunk, and Cindy quickly downed her portion. Mattie's stomach turned at the sight of the heavy food. "You may have mine," she said, indicating the uneaten sausage. The girl helped herself, then finished off the stewed tomatoes. Mattie drank the tepid coffee.

"You know, Mattie, this is going to work out just perfect." Cindy licked grease from her fingers. "As soon as they find me on board, we can have fun together, walking on deck, going ashore at the different stops. I'll teach you everything I know about this part of the country."

"That will be nice, but right now I'd like to rest awhile. I have a few books with me. You may read them if you like. To help pass the time." Opening her trunk, she rummaged among the things she'd brought.

Cindy peered over Mattie's shoulder at the carefully folded clothing and fabrics, lace-trimmed underthings, linen towels, stockings, books, mysterious small boxes and bottles, paper-wrapped parcels.

"Gee," she whispered. "No tellin' what all you got in there."

Mattie took out Emerson's *Essays,* Whitman's *Leaves of Grass,* and Darwin's *Origin of Species.* Then, noticing the girl's puzzled look, she added Harriet Beecher Stowe's *Uncle Tom's Cabin* to the stack.

"Oh, I don't guess I'll have much time to read." The wispy girl sashayed around the trunk as if the tiny room offered limitless possibilities.

"Of course you will," Mattie said. "What else do we have to do?" She picked up *Uncle Tom's Cabin.* "Here, take this."

Cindy took it gingerly, rubbing her hand over the embossed cover, then looking with interest at the illustration inside. "Oh, the little girl's on an icy river."

Mattie understood at once that the girl could not read. "Perhaps we could read it together," she said, sinking back wearily onto the bunk. "Come here, we'll start right now."

Cindy's pale eyes shone in their hollow setting as she climbed onto the bunk beside Mattie. The poor girl is hardly more than a child, Mattie thought. Maybe I can teach her. I have to do something. Propping the pillows so that each of them could comfortably see the pages, Mattie began the story of Little Eva's travail.

Six

CALVIN BODEIN'S LEAP into the Missouri River surprised him as much as it did those watching from the *Big Muddy.* The river ran deep on the far side of the steamer, and he felt himself sinking rapidly. Down. Down. Though a strong swimmer, he hadn't reckoned with the weight of his clothing, and his boots touched the soft bottom before he could reverse his plunge. Flailing his arms and kicking wildly, he propelled himself to the surface, spitting and gasping. Quickly taking his bearings, he struck out for the opposite shore, an easy swim under normal conditions. He didn't want to slip out of his coat and boots unless he had to. He could simply let the current carry him along, while he gradually worked toward the other shore. There was no real danger . . . if that galoot with the whip didn't start shooting.

But he underestimated the power of the river. Struggling to keep his head above water, his arms grew leaden. He considered shedding coat and boots. Then, where the current swirled into a bend in the riverbank a short distance ahead, he saw a large fallen cottonwood, some of its leafy branches still arching high over the water, some trailing in the current. If he came near enough, he could grab onto it.

He pulled hard for the fallen tree. But just as he reached for a projecting branch, the undertow created by the rushing water slammed him against the cottonwood trunk, a startling, hard blow, and he felt himself being sucked under. His face and hands scraped painfully against twigs and bark. His knee took a sharp crack. One leg twisted in the tangle of submerged branches. How could this be happening? He knew about currents around fallen trees. "Widow-makers" they were called. Terror rose in his throat. His lungs screamed for air. For once, his bluff was called. He thrashed about crazily, powerless against the pounding. All further bets were off. In the black water, he thought he saw his valise floating away.

Then he felt a strong tug at the back of his collar and his body being lifted from the roiling river and onto the half-submerged cottonwood trunk. Daylight returned as air surged into his lungs. He gagged and river water spasmed from his throat. Trembling, he gripped the log, grateful that the leafy arbor of branches screened him from view of the *Big Muddy*.

A sharp pounding on his back brought him to full consciousness. He blinked at the shaggy, white-haired, and bewhiskered old man hunched over him. "Only a dag-nabbed fool would try to get out of a river in a whirlpool." The stranger seemed amused as he grasped Cal's arm. "You best get your bones on dry land."

Cal coughed, spitting the murky taste from his mouth as he crawled among the branches to the safety of the riverbank, where he sprawled exhausted for a few minutes, arms and legs limp, and treated his lungs to glorious air.

"I guess I owe you," he said, sitting up and brushing at the muddy water that ran in rivulets from his hair. He could see that the old geezer, who moseyed about reclaiming a crumpled hat and a string of fresh-caught catfish, was not one of the men out to get him.

The man's wayward eyebrows knitted in merriment. "Looks like you had to leave that paddle boat kind of sudden."

Cal peered from the screen of branches. Nearly a quarter of a mile upriver the paddle wheeler stood ready to depart. He could barely make out a spot of color that could be Mattie in her blue dress among the passengers on deck. Poor Mattie. What a rude way to take his leave. He would make it up to her when they got back together. But how would he accomplish that? On the wharf, a noisy group of men milled around the whip-toting mule skinner, who stood waving his arms and pointing across the river toward the very spot where Cal was hidden. Would he get his cronies and come across in pursuit? Cal thought it best not to wait to find out.

The old man took hold of Cal's dripping shirt sleeve. His squinting right eye glinted with steely brightness, but the left was milky. Blind. "Better come with me if you're set on gettin' out of here with your skin." Dangling the fish over his greasy buckskin shirt, which probably accounted at least in part for his rank odor, he led the way toward a nearby willow grove.

Cal scrambled after him. "I'm much obliged, mister."

"Call me Doc."

"I'm Cal."

"Well, Cal, I figure a gent like yourself has good reason to be runnin'. Had to skedaddle once myself."

"That so?" Cal kept his reaction slow and casual, but Doc didn't explain. In the shade of the grove stood a scrawny mule, its ribs out-lined under a scruffy brown hide. "This is Buttercup," Doc said, taking the mule's halter rope in his free hand. "But don't get any ideas about hightailin' it out of here with her. She's too old to ride. I just keep her for companionship." He led the mule off through the underbrush.

Cal followed him, taking one last glance at the steamboat. His valise would be safe with Mattie. He slapped his coat pockets. A deck of soggy cards. His pocket watch with water under the crystal, no longer ticking. His wallet containing a few dollars. And the soaked steamer tickets.

Mattie would expect him to follow. In a way he was glad she'd come to find him. He liked the idea of having her with him, but marriage he hadn't planned on. It would cramp his style now while he was trying to accumulate a bankroll big enough to finance his hotel. He had to travel fast and free, and he couldn't ask that of her. No, Mattie could join him after he was set up. She would understand.

Deeper into the grove, Doc stopped only long enough for Cal to empty water from his boots and wring out his socks, then was off again. When dense undergrowth hindered their progress, the old man emerged from the trees onto a dusty wagon trail, and they skirted the river groves, Cal's wet coat and trousers steaming in the hot sun.

For a time, Cal listened intently for sounds of pursuit but, hearing none, soon began to feel a certain exhilaration in his tenuous safety. The singing of birds in the willows, insects chirping in the roadside grasses, and the occasional hollow splash of a fish near shore provided pleasant summer music as they moved at a comfortable pace. When the sun began to beat down on his face and neck, he regretted having lost his hat in the river.

Several times Doc tramped to the river's edge to check another of his fish lines. "You figure on eatin' tonight?" He dangled a fish toward Cal.

"Obviously I hadn't planned that far ahead."

"You can grub with me if you've a mind to. Got a place yonder." The old man pointed across a shallow swamp to a sandbar overgrown with willows. "Come on. They ain't gonna find you."

Cal hesitated. "What makes you so sure?"

"Quicksand," he said with a wink of his good eye. "Best defense I know of."

Cal followed in appreciative silence as his agile guide threaded across the swamp, hopping through weeds onto sandy fingers of solid footing among mossy, stagnant pools, and leaping across trickles of clear water from a network of creeks flowing to the main channel. Reaching the sandbar, the old man led the way through the dense underbrush for some distance before announcing, "Here she is, home sweet home."

Cal looked past Buttercup's bony hind quarters into the small clearing where he focused on a hut constructed of driftwood and brush, almost indistinguishable from the tangle of fallen trees and assorted vegetation. In front of the deerhide door was a blackened fire pit, where a rusty grate propped on rocks supported an iron kettle. Nearby a stream of clear water cut through the sandbar.

Doc slipped off Buttercup's halter, hung it on a twig projecting from the hut, and began to clean the fish in the stream while the mule foraged among the weeds. Shuffling to and from the hut, he soon had a fire going, a dollop of grease in the kettle, and fish frying. He heated an opened can of beans and made coffee in a battered pot. "Not fancy," he said, "but tasty."

Cal sat down on the log beside the fire pit and took the deck of cards from his pocket, peeling them from the pack, one by one, and spreading them on the log to dry out. His only deck. All but ruined. As dusk came on, squadrons of mosquitoes zeroed in on him. Swatting at first strategically, then wildly, he tried to concentrate on salvaging the sodden cards.

Doc scooped beans and charred catfish onto a tin plate and held it out to Cal. "I get a hankerin' for company sometimes," he said. "I didn't spring full-grown in this swamp, you know."

"How long you lived out here?" Cal asked between bites.

"Awhile."

"Where you from?"

"Upriver."

Cal spit a tiny catfish bone into the fire. "I was headed for Last Chance Gulch," he said, "till some itchy bullwhacker claimed I cheated him at poker and slowed me up some."

Doc's fork remained suspended in midair as he squinted skeptically at Cal.

"He was mistaken. I beat him square," Cal said. "Got a talent for cards."

The old man's good eye gleamed as he resumed shoveling beans into his mouth. "Got a talent for cards, eh? Well now, ain't that somethin'. Think you could see your way clear to a little game?"

Cal frowned. He wouldn't want to skin this old man. Still, he glanced at Buttercup grazing near the hut.

"Oh, not with me," Doc said. "I never gamble. This would be a match with some . . . acquaintances of mine."

"Acquaintances?"

Doc put down his plate and leaned forward. "I'm runnin', too. You maybe guessed that."

"That how you lost your eye?"

"Yup. Got this little souvenir for doin' a good deed." He glanced at Cal, then continued. "The varmints who poked me in the eye deserve a comeuppance. Now if you was to get 'em into a game—take 'em for all they got—it would do my old gizzard good."

"I'd like to help you, Doc. But . . . well, my stake is on the *Big Muddy*."

"You got a stake, huh?" He savored the information for a moment.

"Access to some cash could get us both out of trouble. It's lack of a stake that's kept me bogged down here, that's kept me from gettin' on down the river respectable like."

"I have to overtake the *Big Muddy* for another reason," Cal said. "My woman's on that boat, too."

"Your woman?" Doc's good eye snapped to attention. "Well now, ain't that somethin'."

"So, I'll be moving on," Cal continued, "first thing in the morning."

Doc thought for a moment, absently wiping his fingers on his shirt. "Tell you what. Maybe we can help one another. You need a guide to catch up to that steamer, and I need some gettin' even with the pole-cats that wronged me."

He knows this country, Cal reasoned. There are probably shortcuts that would save time in catching up with the *Big Muddy*. Maybe his offer isn't such a bad bargain. "Just where are these . . . polecats?" he asked.

Doc slapped his hat against his knee. "That's the dag-nabbed beauty of it." He began shuffling his boots in a kind of seated jig. "Last Chance Gulch! Helena they call it now. That's where they are."

"Let me get this straight," Cal said. "You want me to clean out some fellas there in return for help in overtaking the *Big Muddy.*"

"There's considerable to clean out." Doc leaned closer, squinting pointedly. "Them skunks are powerful men in Helena. The territorial government's there now, you know." Then, as another thought intervened, "Course I wouldn't want you to *lose.*"

"I seldom lose, Doc."

"This is one time you'll *have* to win. Fair or foul." Doc's milky eye seemed to gaze into the future. "Have we got ourselves a deal?" He held out his gnarled hand.

"But I thought you said Buttercup was too old to ride."

"Buttercup?" Doc's chuckle rose to a gleeful shriek. "I got horses. Two good horses. That's just the dag-nabbed beauty of it."

Two horses. Cal felt a rush of excitement. Maybe the plan wasn't hopeless. I'll get out of this scrape first, he thought, then see whether I can help the old codger. "All right, Doc," he said. "It's a deal." He shook the old man's outstretched hand.

But he declined the offer of Doc's lumpy ticking after an introduction to the odoriferous interior of the hut. Instead, he bedded down outside, huddling under his coat to ward off the mosquitoes that, coupled with the fiery sunburn on his face and neck, produced sufficient discomfort for him to dream he had died and gone to hell.

At the first morning light, Doc was up rekindling the fire and frying the rest of his catch, offered this time without beans, but with enough strong, hot coffee to revive his aching guest. While Cal sat in misery, sipping a third cup and patting his waffled deck of cards back into their box, Doc tied a parfleche filled with supplies to Buttercup's sagging back, reserving two worn bridles, which he carried off into the underbrush. A short time later, he returned leading two horses, a small black gelding and a lanky strawberry-roan mare.

"Take your pick," he said. "The black's feisty. The roan's balky."

Cal sighed, suddenly weary of the whole plan, but indicated he'd ride the mare.

"Bareback's better'n walkin'." Doc swung aboard the black horse and started off, leading the pack mule. Cal locked his long legs around the roan, but the mare's prominent backbone served as painful reminder that he was accustomed to a more genteel way of life.

"Don't let her get the upper hand," Doc called back, "or you'll be in for it." With Cal prodding the reluctant roan to bring up the rear, the procession moved out of the willows, retracing the precarious route off the sandbar and across the swamp.

"The boat'll be stoppin' to wood up," Doc said after a while. "But with a day's start on us, ain't much chance overtakin' her till she lays over. May take us a day or two."

"That long?" Under his breath Cal cursed the luck that had placed him in such a circumstance. "What if we don't catch her?"

"Well, steamers can't climb the great falls, so Fort Benton's the end of the line."

"How far is that?"

"'Bout thirteen hundred river miles, I reckon."

Cal shuddered at the thought of such an extended association with Doc and the bony roan. Before I'll ride that far, I'll catch a boat somewhere along the line, he thought, again patting his pocket for reassurance that the steamer tickets were intact. He wasn't entirely dependent on the old man.

Doc looked back over the champing black's rump, squinting his good eye in a way now all too familiar to Cal. "If we miss the boat, Benton's where you'll find your woman." He cackled merrily. "If she don't run off with someone else first."

Seven

DURING THE *Big Muddy's* first layover at the village grown up around old Fort Clark, Mattie went ashore to stroll along the riverbank, determined to overcome her queasy feeling away from the constant motion of the steamer. Getting reacquainted with solid ground, she made her way up a small knoll and sat overlooking the river, where the big boat, luminous in the evening light, bobbed gently at the water's edge. She regretted leaving Cindy alone in their stuffy cabin but it was best if the plucky stowaway stayed out of sight, at least for the time being. Mattie noted the scene in her journal as she watched crew and passengers moving between the ship and the village. Among them were three women. Since Mattie had thus far remained in her cabin, she had had no chance to talk with them. As soon as this Cindy business settled out, she promised herself, she wanted nothing more than to get acquainted and enjoy their company.

She felt satisfaction in helping Cindy learn to read. Having something to occupy them would surely make the journey pass more quickly. Immediately, the girl had shown considerable skill in sounding out the words in *Uncle Tom's Cabin*, parts of which moved her to tears and made her reluctant to stop when Mattie admitted her need for some time on shore.

"I don't know why the boat makes you sick," Cindy had commented. "It don't bother me none."

Mattie knew all about morning sickness from her work with her father's patients. She'd heard all the complaints and had stood by at several births. Her experience had given her the confidence to undertake this journey. But listening to symptoms and watching deliveries had not prepared her for her own pregnancy. She had assumed many women carried on unnecessarily about minor discomforts, but now she understood she had done them an injustice. A brief morning sickness she expected, but why did she feel so weak and weary all day? What if something wasn't right? Perhaps the ladies on board . . . But no, she couldn't reveal her condition. If only I could see a doctor, she thought. He could reassure me. Oh, why didn't I learn more about these things when I had the chance?

She scanned the silver river winding into the distance, the prairies on either side lavender in the twilight. Such beauty alone made her heart ache. But now with all the uncertainty . . . Where was Cal? Was he safe? She mulled over every detail of his disappearance among the fallen cottonwood branches. Where had he gone from there? Was he trying to find her? Could he overtake the *Big Muddy?*

"Mattie, you up here?" The shrill voice startled her. She turned to glimpse Cindy coming up the hill, her stringy hair undone and flowing about her shoulders. Grinning as she approached, she looked like a little girl—except for the faded satin dress. "I came to find you. You might get lost by yourself."

"What if someone sees you?" Mattie teased, glad for the company.

"Nobody noticed." Cindy flopped down on the grass, happily clasping her knees with her thin arms. "Anyway, it's too hot in that little room."

Mattie breathed deeply of the evening fragrance. "It's lovely up here."

"Yeah. Real peaceful." Then almost as if a moment's tranquillity was as much as she could bear, Cindy bounded to her feet. "Mattie, I got an idea. With me learnin' to read now and all, I'm intendin' to make something out of myself." Her pale eyes shone as she hurried on. "I thought if your man don't show up—not that he won't, but if he don't —you and me might start us a business."

Mattie smiled. She couldn't help liking this girl who had seen so much, yet remained so childlike.

Cindy continued. "You're real pretty and educated, Mattie, but I know about business. I figure we could hook up together. I'm talkin' about if Cal—your man, I mean—if he don't come back."

Mattie saw no reason to dampen her enthusiasm. "That's something to think about, Cindy, but right now we better attend to the business of getting you back on that boat without Captain Tanner seeing you."

Darkness had settled in by the time they reached the waterfront. Crew members, having finished the wooding, prepared for the next morning's departure, while passengers lingered on shore enjoying the cooler air and solid footing. When the captain appeared at the head of the gangplank, Mattie pulled Cindy into the shadows behind a woodpile, saying, "I'll distract him so you can slip aboard." She strolled toward the boat. "Lovely evening, Captain Tanner," she called.

"That it is." He stood waiting for her. "I was about to come looking for you. I made some inquiries in the village. No sign of Bodein. I'm sorry, but if he doesn't show up by morning, we'll have to move on."

"I know." She strolled along the deck, the captain beside her.

"I'll keep my eyes open," he said. "If I can help in any way, you've only to ask." As they rounded the pilot house, Mattie glimpsed a furtive figure in a limp green dress hurrying along the rail toward her cabin.

"We have three nice ladies aboard," the captain continued. "All headed for Helena. I'm sure they'd like to meet you. One is the wife of Pastor Parkington, who's setting up a new church in Helena. The other two, Mrs. Steinbaum and her daughter, are on their way there to join Mr. Steinbaum. We're carrying goods for his store."

"Yes, I want to meet them. And I will soon. It's just that . . . well, I'm still feeling a bit under the weather." Should she reveal so much to Captain Tanner?

He showed genuine concern. "Sometimes these old tubs can rile your insides. After what you've been through, I'm not surprised you feel a little shaky." While they lingered in front of her door, she felt a special warmth in Tanner's attention—she needed someone concerned about her welfare just now—and was reluctant to cut short the pleasant moment. Then she heard a muffled voice from inside the cabin. It was Cindy reading in her most dramatic Little Eva voice.

"Thank you, Captain," Mattie said abruptly. "Good night."

He hesitated, then touched his cap. "Good night."

She opened the door and eased herself inside, putting a finger to her lips to silence her clever pupil until the sound of the captain's footsteps faded down the deck. Cindy reclined in tattered knee-length drawers on the upper bunk, her book extended toward the wall lamp. Without the ugly dress, she looked much like any schoolgirl doing her lessons.

It's only a matter of time till the captain finds out about Cindy, Mattie thought. I can't let him send her back. She opened her trunk and, rummaging near the bottom, pulled out a length of yellow calico.

"Cindy, come down from there. Let's see how you would look in yellow." Cindy reverently ran her fingers over the smooth fabric.

"Can you sew?" Mattie asked.

"Nobody never showed me," Cindy replied with disappointment, as if her admission would deprive her of the new garment.

"Well, I'm going to teach you now." Mattie, returning the girl's broad smile, saw even more possibilities. "And we're going to wash and fix your hair." She extracted her sewing materials from the trunk, along with a bar of castile soap and a bottle of vinegar. "Our smart little reader is also going to be pretty."

Cindy brightened. "I get it." She clasped her hands with eagerness. "Then when the captain finds me, it won't be me he finds."

To make more work space, Mattie stowed Cal's valise out of the way under the bunk and shoved the trunk closer to the light to use as a tabletop. They giggled as they smoothed out the calico on the trunk, and Mattie cut the cloth using one of her own dresses as a pattern. They worked through the night, climbing into their bunks toward dawn and scarcely noticing the blare of the whistle announcing the *Big Muddy*'s departure.

Two days later, with Cindy's willing but inept assistance, Mattie had transformed the assorted pieces into a dress—the style becoming to Cindy's spare figure, the color flattering to her now shiny clean and attractively arranged hair. Surveying her handiwork and Cindy's glowing face, Mattie announced, "Tonight we'll be dining with the other passengers."

That evening when the dining cabin filled with hungry passengers and Captain Tanner had seated himself at his usual table, Mattie entered the room dressed in her best summer dress of apricot voile. The captain sprang to his feet. Half hidden behind Mattie was a young woman in yellow calico, a stranger. He tried to recall just who the newcomer might be and where she might have come aboard. Something in her animated demeanor seemed familiar. But it was Mattie in her apricot dress, her honey-hued hair piled high, who held his attention. All heads turned, and Mattie seated herself quickly as the captain held her chair. It was then that he recognized her companion.

"Cindy! Where did you come from?"

"The stork brought me," Cindy quipped, sliding onto the chair opposite Mattie.

"She wants to start over," Mattie whispered when the attention of the other diners returned to their plates and normal conversation resumed.

"You ain't sendin' me back, are you, Captain Tanner?" Cindy's pleading look changed to one of pride. "I got plans."

The captain raised an eyebrow at Mattie. "I see now why you had those meals sent to your cabin."

"And Mattie's teachin' me to read."

"She's eager to learn," Mattie said. "And I don't mind sharing my cabin."

"Looks like you two have me over a barrel." He held out the platter of fried chicken to Cindy. "Let's just say having such fine ladies aboard gives the old tub a touch of class. If you're willing to share your quarters, Miss Hamil, I have no objection to providing an extra plate at the table. On one condition . . ." His pause brought a worried look to Cindy's scrubbed face. "That both of you dine at my table each evening."

"It would be our pleasure, Captain." Mattie intended to joke about having to share her food with the voracious Cindy, but before she could say more, a tall man in a cleric's collar approached the table abruptly. Nervously, he ran his hand over his graying hair, smoothing it back from a center part that divided his long, clean-shaven face into two unmatched halves.

"Captain Tanner, may I have a word with you?" When he spoke his nose wrinkled in a way that reminded Mattie of a cat.

"How are you, Reverend?" The captain stood and gestured toward Mattie. "Reverend Parkington, may I introduce Miss . . ."

"Captain, please." The reverend sputtered, glaring at Cindy. "I feel it my duty to protest this . . . this woman's presence when there are ladies dining." The clergyman clipped his words through clenched teeth.

"What?" Tanner frowned.

"I will not have my wife subjected to such an indignity. I also feel it my duty to speak for dear Mrs. Steinbaum and her lovely daughter. We saw this woman—inadvertently, of course—at the Bismarck Hotel."

"Now just a minute . . ."

Parkington continued, "I had thought that paying for first-class passage on the *Big Muddy,* one of the *best* steamers on the river, would assure the company of *decent* people."

"If you'll just calm down, Reverend." Tanner placed a venomous emphasis on the word "Reverend." "I'd like to introduce Miss Mattie Hamil, en route to join her fiancé in Fort Benton, and her traveling companion, Miss Cynthia Dougherty."

Cindy smiled her most charming smile and absently touched her upswept hair. Once again all eyes turned toward them.

The reverend pulled Tanner aside. "Perhaps you're not aware, Captain," his hissing whisper could be heard throughout the dining cabin, "that this . . . this person," he pointed a long finger at Cindy, ". . .

worked at the saloon in Bismarck. She's a . . . well, she's no traveling companion."

Cindy raised her chin haughtily. "I am, too. I'm on the boat, ain't I?"

Tanner's face flushed with anger. "Look, Reverend, this is not the time or place. You're upset over nothing. Now let's finish our meal. We can discuss this later."

"You expect us to dine," the reverend sniffed, cat-like, "with . . . with *her* at the captain's table? I tell you, I won't have my wife and the Steinbaum ladies insulted this way." His lips pressed into a thin line as he nodded across the room at a prim, mousy woman dressed in gray seated with the two other women; the older, a heavyset matron with a jolly face despite sharp, swarthy features; her pretty black-haired daughter, angular but graceful in a rose velvet traveling suit.

The captain spoke in a confidential tone. "Reverend Parkington, let's have a little Christian charity. Miss Dougherty isn't . . . well, she's changed." Tanner grinned to lighten the situation. "You can tell that by just looking at her. I don't know how you even recognized her."

The reverend snorted his disdain.

Tanner continued. "I think in this case we'll just let bygones be bygones. Isn't that your domain, Reverend? Forgiveness. Now surely Miss Dougherty has as much right to be here as anybody else."

"She has no right to embarrass innocent women, Captain. No telling what is going on here. Now I must insist that she be put ashore . . . at the first settlement, of course . . . or I'm going to report you to your superiors for harboring women of questionable reputation on this ship."

Captain Tanner reddened with rage. "Sir, I assure you that no one will be put ashore."

Parkington drew himself to full height with a long intake of breath. Then he turned on his heel and walked back to his table, his narrow shoulders hunched stiff around his collar.

He took his wife's arm. "Come, my dear," he said in a deliberate voice. Mrs. Parkington rose to her feet and marched from the dining cabin beside her husband.

Eight

CAL FAILED TO SHARE Doc's good humor as the two mounted travelers leading the old pack mule, Buttercup, kept a steady pace along the river, sometimes cutting off across grassy plains on shortcuts Doc knew about. Mosquitoes and underbrush made it uncomfortable to ride among the trees along the riverbank, and Cal knotted his handkerchief around his head to provide some protection from the blistering sun. He ached in every bone and muscle as he gripped the mare's mane and eased from side to side in a futile attempt to find a comfortable position. Folding his coat and stuffing it with grass to simulate a saddle provided little relief. He longed to give up the chase, but now he had no choice. The only way out was to continue on, overtake the *Big Muddy*, or any steamer that came along, and proceed to Fort Benton, where Mattie—and with luck, his valise—would be waiting. He resolutely downed the beans and hardtack the old man produced from Buttercup's pack that night when they camped for a few hours' sleep.

Rising in the pre-dawn dark, stove up but determined, Cal insisted they push on. The whereabouts of his valise now loomed foremost in his mind. Did Mattie still have it? Chances are the money was safe. But if it fell into other hands, it would be gone for sure. Doc claimed all he needed was a stake, but could he be trusted? Queer old goat. Yet he seemed harmless enough. Might even be good company under different circumstances.

"Rain comin'," Doc said, sniffing the air, as they headed out. Dawn light revealed a bank of towering thunderheads to the southwest. "A gully washer would slow that steamer some."

"Could bog us down, too," Cal said. "Let's make tracks while we can. I intend to part company with this razorback as soon as humanly possible." When he dug his heels into the roan's sides, she jerked forward in such a tooth-jarring trot that he soon settled her into her usual plodding gait, the mare now and then heaving a sigh of protest, or flattening her ears and tossing back a disdainful glance at her rider.

The rain began about mid-morning, a pleasant shower at first that Cal thought a welcome relief from the hot sun. But soon the heavy, dark clouds dumped a torrent on the travelers.

"Slight precipitation," Doc called back, his voice almost lost as rain poured from his hat brim.

"A damn cloudburst," Cal muttered, wondering if he should shift the padded coat from beneath him and put it on over his drenched shirt.

The rain turned to hail. "Take cover," Doc shouted as chunks of ice the size of pullet eggs bounced in the grass. He swung down and huddled beneath his horse. Cal dived under the roan, shielding his head with the padded coat. The roan stood stoically against the pelting hailstones, but Doc's black panicked and whirled and the old man, clutching one rein, tried to take shelter beneath the docile Buttercup.

Cal laughed at the old man's tussle. "Good thing you have that hat, Doc, or your brains would be lumpy about now." He gave the roan an affectionate pat as the hail gave way to a steady rain, and he ducked from beneath her belly.

"Takes more'n a little storm to do me in." Doc, too, remounted, and they continued on for some time in silence, heads bowed against the driving rain.

At the peak of the downpour, Doc pulled up short, signaling a stop as they emerged from a willow grove. Before them lay an Indian camp—a few pinto ponies picketed near three bedraggled tipis, smoke wisping from top flaps open to the rain. Several scrawny dogs barked threateningly.

"Small hunting party," Doc said in an undertone. "From the look of those dogs, I'd say it's been lean pickin's."

"Let's get out of here." Cal tugged the reins to turn the roan as voices rose from the lodges.

"Stay put. I doubt they'll be threatened by a couple of rained-on roosters."

"I'm not waiting around to find out."

"Too late now."

A gaunt young man wearing only a skin breechclout and carrying a rifle came on the run from the nearest tipi. Several men, women, and children, poorly dressed in dirty skins and tattered bits of white man's garb, followed. The men viewed the visitors through an assortment of rifle sights.

"Mornin'." Doc waved his hand in a friendly gesture. "We're wet." He flicked his hand at his soggy buckskins.

An older man wrapped in a frayed trade blanket, wisps of graying hair framing his leathered face, stepped forward. His eyes narrowed to dark slits as he scrutinized Doc, then Cal, and finally their horses, then gestured for them to follow.

Doc dismounted, looping his reins over a dripping willow branch, and when Cal did the same, the rifles were lowered. Before one of the tipis, the old man, who seemed to be the leader, motioned away all but three, who invited Cal and Doc inside by nudging them with the gun butts.

The smoky interior was crowded with family members. An old woman in a greasy buckskin dress bent over a kettle set on coals in the center fire pit. Three younger women and two near-naked children, their dark eyes wide, huddled against the left wall among a tidy stack of bundles. Animal skins spread around the fire pit provided seating, and the chief settled himself onto a woven-rawhide backrest opposite the door, motioning the visitors onto a buffalo robe spread to the right of the fire. The three braves squatted behind them.

Cal nudged Doc. "What now?"

"Don't get antsy," Doc said, focusing his attention on the old woman dipping a stew-like mixture from the kettle into a tin bowl. "They may just be inviting us to supper." The woman gave the bowl to the chief, who took a hunk of meat with his fingers, blowing on it before putting it into his mouth and passing the bowl to Doc. Doc helped himself and indicated Cal should do the same. "Rabbit," he said, licking his fingers.

Two young women began tugging at the visitors' clothing, while the old squaw assembled a drying rack of willow sticks beside the fire.

"They're offerin' to dry our clothes," Doc said, raising his arms to help the woman remove his shirt. Cal hesitated but, deciding Doc was right, peeled off his coat, shirt, and trousers. One of the young women passed them to the older woman to spread on the rack, then pointed to his underwear. Doc, who stood in a disreputable-looking union suit, winked at Cal and stripped down to his skin, which was white as a trout belly. The children giggled. Cal stepped out of his drawers and socks and handed them over. The two visitors then reseated themselves cross-legged on the buffalo robe and proceeded with second and third dips into the hot stew.

"Reminds me of the time I lost my shirt in a New Orleans poker game," Cal joked.

"Can sure make you cautious about spilling," Doc replied.

The meal was eaten with little conversation among their hosts, but Cal sensed no hostility, and by the time his stomach was comfortably full, his nervousness had subsided. So had the rain. He stood up and reached for his clothes, saying, "Well, we best be getting along." The young braves rose to block the door.

"Can't eat and run," Doc said. "Wouldn't be polite. Got to show we appreciate their hospitality. Got something we could give 'em?"

Cal reached for his coat on the drying rack and came up with the deck of cards from one of the pockets. He held it up to imply the cards were the reason he had stood up in the first place. Seating himself again, he took the deck from its box. Some color had faded from its river dunking, a few peeled areas distorted the numbers, and some of the edges were ruffled, but Cal shuffled with a deftness that intrigued his audience. Motioning the three young braves to gather around the buffalo robe, he dealt a card face up for each. They edged closer, observing Cal's distribution of the brightly marked rectangles.

"The idea," Cal said as though they understood him, "is to . . . ," he hurriedly invented a game he could convey without words, ". . . to get as many cards with the same markings as possible." He spread the deck, pointing to show that it consisted of diamonds, hearts, clubs, and spades, then shuffled and dealt a second card to each of the players. The first player, whose original card was a club, received a heart. Cal frowned and shook his head. The second, whose first card was a diamond, also received a heart. Again Cal shook his head. The third brave picked up his card, a club, and held it on his outstretched palm to receive another. This time Cal made sure a club appeared, accompanied by smiles and enthusiasm to show that cards of the same suit constituted a winning hand. He held up five fingers to indicate a player must have five of a suit to win. The chief moved his backrest closer and tapped his finger on a spot in front of him indicating he, too, wished to receive cards.

"Better have a reward for the winner," Doc muttered.

"All I have is my watch, and it doesn't run."

"That'll do just dandy," Doc said. "I got a couple of fishhooks. Might be a good idea to see that each one wins a hand."

"Right you are, Doc." Cal leaned toward the drying rack to retrieve his watch from his pants pocket, then displayed it to indicate it would be given to the winner. He dealt a third round of cards, giving three to the chief to catch him up with the others. By the fourth round, the men were whooping with delight as each card turned up on the buffalo robe. Cal prolonged the game to increase the suspense.

"Flush!" he shouted when one of the braves at last held five of the same suit. "And here, my good fellow, is your prize." He handed the watch to the young Indian and showed him how to make the hands go around by twisting the stem. The brave grinned and demonstrated the delicate operation for the others.

Doc tossed two fishhooks onto the robe. "These are for the winners of the next two hands," he said. The players seemed equally keen on winning the fishhooks, and Cal made sure that each went to a different brave.

"We need another prize for the chief," Doc reminded. "What else you got?"

Cal slapped his naked sides as if to check his absent pockets. "Nothing. Don't you have another fishhook?"

"Yes, but we may need it," Doc said. "How about that ring you're wearing?"

Cal rubbed the blue-and-orange crest on the Virginia Cavaliers ring he'd worn since he departed the university. "Do I have a choice?" he muttered, slipping the ring from his finger.

The ring stimulated even keener interest in the card game, and each brave in turn received cards that could have led to his winning, but in the end it was the chief who turned up with five hearts to win the ring. He smiled broadly as he put it on the middle finger of his right hand, then stood, at ease now with arms folded across his chest, while Cal and Doc slipped into their still-damp clothes. Doc gave a friendly wave as they backed slowly toward the tipi entrance. The chief nodded and the braves made no move to stop them.

Patches of blue dotted the southern sky promising sunshine as Cal and Doc rode from the camp, yapping dogs worrying their horses. They turned to wave one last thanks for the hospitality of the hunting party, who called out to them in friendly farewell. The chief stood tall, holding up the middle finger of his right hand in a Cavalier salute.

After slogging over the muddy plain without another stop, Cal and Doc rode into the sparse village at Fort Clark late that afternoon and made their way directly to the low, log trading post.

"Doggone, you just missed 'er," the grubby proprietor announced. "The *Big Muddy* left first thing this mornin'."

Cal's whole body sagged. The steamer was almost twelve hours ahead of them. Twelve hours. He felt too exhausted to sit that lanky mare another minute. The horses needed rest, too. "When's the next one due?"

"No more'n a week. Could be somethin' sooner. The river's full of boats this time of year."

Cal mustered a dispirited groan. All that way for nothing. Yet waiting in this godforsaken place, while the *Big Muddy* moved farther out of reach, was even less acceptable.

"Get yourself a hat," Doc advised. "You'll feel like a new man."

The proprietor sprang to the back wall where three black sombreros hung on pegs. "Yes, sir, best selection this side of Mandan." He took one and brushed at the dust on its brim. "How's this?"

Cal pointed at the one with the widest brim and paid for it from the few dollars in his wallet.

"The way I look at it," Doc summed up as they walked outside into the clear air, "we can wait here for that next boat, or ride on. River'll be runnin' high and swift with the storm runoff. May slow that steamer some. She'll soon stop to wood up in any case, maybe lay over again."

Cal pictured Mattie's lovely face, framed by the soft blond braid. Then he pictured his valise with the money nesting in its depths. Mattie, the dear girl, he knew would wait for him. But the valise and its contents might not be so faithful. "Let's ride on," he said, pulling himself once again onto the roan's back. "And when we catch up with that boat, I'm going to shoot this horse."

Nine

STANDING AT THE DECK RAIL watching the rush of the water, Cindy breathed deeply, savoring the fresh storm-washed air. "The rain's made the river muddier," she called through the open cabin door to Mattie, who lay on her bunk looking out at the bright, clearing sky.

At that moment, the boat shuddered against the muffled rumble of an explosion. Cindy lurched against the rail. Mattie jumped up and ran out on deck. "What was that?"

Sounds of clanging pipes and hissing steam brought Captain Tanner on the run, shouting at crew members, who followed him along the deck toward the hold. Passengers hurried from their cabins, coughing from the black smoke that hung in the air. From below came the clamor of animals milling in distress and horses whinnying. The captain reappeared on the lower deck. "It's a boiler break," he shouted above the racket. "Blew a hole in the hull just at the water line."

"Are we on fire?" Reverend Parkington gasped. "Are we sinking?"

Captain Tanner shook his head. "No. But we've taken on some water. We'll have to tie up for repairs."

Abigail Steinbaum caught her breath. "Father's goods will be ruined."

"You men lend a hand," Tanner ordered. "Keep the rest of that cargo dry."

The larger Fike brother pushed toward the steps, followed by the smaller one dragging his braced leg. Reverend Parkington looked distressed. "I'll just go and change my suit," he said.

Mattie started after the Fikes. "Come on, girls. We can help, too."

Abigail nudged Cindy. "Yes, let's. If I know men, they'll save the tobacco before the dry goods." They followed Mattie to the lower deck, where they peered into the dim hold at crates and barrels bobbing about in clay-colored water. Wading crewmen tugged at cargo stowed at one end near the stalls where Cal's sorrel and two mules skittered in the rising flood. The girls quickly removed their shoes and stockings and stowed them on deck.

A crate of squawking geese, floating half submerged, bumped against the ramp. Mattie stood aside to let the hulking Alfred Fike lead one of the mules out on deck, then gathered up her skirt and petticoat in one hand and plunged knee-deep into the water to reach a handle of the crate. Abigail, too, hiked up her skirt and waded in to take the handle on the other side. Cindy lifted her yellow dress above her knees and waded after a wooden box marked baking powder.

Again the boat shuddered, bucking the current while the pilot, Hodgewarden, edged it toward a barren stretch of grassy shore. It settled with one last heave as crewmen secured lines at either end to cottonwoods on shore. Hodgewarden immediately came down from the pilot house to pitch in with the others carrying crates out on deck. But hardly had he begun when a nail keg toppled from a disarrayed stack and struck him on the head. Abigail gave a frightened cry as he crumpled into the muck.

Mattie sprang to his side, holding his face above the water. Blood flowed from an ugly gash behind his ear. "Help me get him on deck," she commanded the crew. "And bring soap and boiled teakettle water from the galley to clean this wound. Cindy, get the rubbing alcohol from my trunk. And bring the sewing basket." Cindy sprinted toward the upper cabins.

While members of the crew carried the heavy Hodgewarden out on deck, Mattie knelt beside the injured man applying pressure to the bleeding with the edge of her petticoat. "I'll take care of him," she said, and the men hurried back to their tasks in the hold while she cleansed, then closed the raw edges of the gaping cut with carefully laced stitches of silk thread.

Captain Tanner appeared carrying a hand pump and knelt beside them. "Silt baked onto the boiler," he reported. "Kept the iron from cooling and a spot melted through."

Hodgewarden moaned, returning to consciousness.

"A nail keg conked you," the captain explained. "Miss Hamil is fixing you up."

Dazed but trying to comprehend, Hodgewarden stared after the men toting cargo to and from the hold.

"I'll need a sheet to cut for bandage," Mattie told the captain.

Abigail smiled at him. "Let me get it for you."

The captain directed Abigail to the supply room on the promenade where she found a stack of muslin sheets and hurried back with one to the little group crouched over the sprawled, round-bellied pilot.

"That should fix you up," Mattie said, tying the final strip of cloth around the pilot's head. "Now you need to rest a few hours."

Fully aware now, Hodgewarden struggled to get up. "I gotta get back in there and help the men." He grinned. "Don't want any of that good whiskey to get damaged." But too shaken even to sit, he slumped back on the rough decking.

"You take it easy," Captain Tanner ordered.

"I don't need no coddlin'," the pilot said gruffly. "Leave me lay here out of the way till I get my sea legs back." He gripped Mattie's hand. "A swig of whiskey wouldn't hurt me, would it, Doc?"

"I guess not," she said, "if it will keep you quiet."

Tanner grinned at Hodgewarden. "Just keep in mind you're our pilot, not a stevedore. We'll need you when we get this tub patched up." Then as an afterthought, "Miss Steinbaum, would you find a pillow for him? I want to get this pump started."

Abigail's face lit up. Captain Tanner had spoken her name. "Of course I will." Her eyes still fixed on him, she hurried up the steps toward the supply room.

As Mattie gathered her things and stood up, she reeled with a sudden dizziness. For a moment she thought the boat was swirling in the current. But it was her head that was swimming. She slumped against the wall.

Captain Tanner saw her and, handing the pump to a crewman, ran to her. "Are you all right?"

"Just felt a little faint."

"This is all too much for you. Let me help you back to your cabin."

"You mustn't bother with me at a time like this," she murmured. "Your men need you." But he had pulled her arm around his neck and was half-carrying her up the steps and along the promenade to her cabin, where he gently eased her onto the bunk.

"I'm all right. Really I am."

"I'll have someone look in on you," he called as he hurried out the door.

Mattie's head spun, whether from dizziness or from the captain's touch she couldn't be sure, and she barely had strength to remove her soiled petticoat and wash the river water from her feet and legs.

A short while later, a light rap sounded at the door. "Miss Hamil, are you there? It's Mrs. Steinbaum. And Mrs. Parkington."

"Yes, come in." Mattie raised her head as the two women entered. Mrs. Steinbaum carried a tray of tea and toast. "Forgive me for not getting up. I'm afraid I'm a little under the weather."

Mrs. Parkington, standing near the door, glanced suspiciously about the tiny room. She looked the same as she had in the dining room the night before, the prim gray suit with black collar and cuffs, her mousy hair parted in the middle and pulled tight into a bun. "At least you're not down there in the filth grubbing around with deckhands like . . . like that little harlot." She sucked in her breath. "Heaven knows why we have to put up with her kind." Her comment came in an unpleasant whine. "Now the captain says we can't possibly continue on till the boiler is fixed."

Mrs. Steinbaum sat down on the edge of Mattie's bunk. "I'm Sophie," she said. "Captain Tanner says you're ailing." Her short, ample body was wrapped in a lacy, crocheted shawl, and her pudgy face, framed in tendrils of salt-and-pepper hair straying from the knot at the back of her head, had a kindly look about it. "It's everywhere, the summer complaint." Mattie acknowledged her diagnosis.

"We're on our way to Montana, my daughter and me. If you think this boat is a misery, you didn't ride that railroad train from Chicago to Bismarck." Sophie chatted as she folded Mattie's soiled clothing and emptied the washbowl. "Already my husband Lionel has a store—with a nice flat above—waiting for us in Helena. That boiler leak we didn't ask for." She gave a pointed glance at Mrs. Parkington. "My Abigail, also, is down underneath helping Captain Tanner." She assisted Mattie with her nightgown and eased her under the sheet.

"You're very kind," Mattie murmured.

"To Fort Benton you're headed?" Sophie seemed eager to talk.

"My fiancé will join me there, then we'll go on to Helena." On impulse, Mattie added, "I'm a teacher."

"How nice, dear." Sophie's plump cheeks crinkled upward, nearly hiding her bird-like eyes. "Schoolteachers we need. Abigail took normal training, too." She plumped the edges of Mattie's pillow as she talked, her chubby fingers adorned with a wide gold wedding band worn smooth. "Who would have thought when Abby was a little girl in Chicago, that someday we'd be off across the wilderness. Lionel is like that. Opportunity he sees. I told him, how will Abby find a nice husband in the wilderness—she's twenty-two now, already—and he told me Helena's just the place. The men outnumber women, he says. Yes, I told him, but what kind of men . . . ?" She remembered the tea tray and poured a steaming cup for Mattie. "Here, my dear, try some."

Mrs. Parkington interrupted. "Oh, I do hope the good Lord will fix that leak so we can get off this awful boat."

"Him and who else?" Sophie quipped as she plumped Mattie's pillow.

Mattie raised her head to sip the warm liquid. "Do they know how long it will take?"

Sophie frowned. "Don't ask."

"And now we'll probably all get this sickness." The grim set of Mrs. Parkington's thin lips eloquently expressed her distaste for sickroom visits.

"Maybe you have more important things, missus," Sophie suggested curtly.

"Very well. Yes, I'll see if I can help with . . . with the Lord's work." Mrs. Parkington left hurriedly.

"That one gives me a regular pain." Sophie chuckled. "Can you imagine her lugging crates." Then, assuming a confidential tone, "To save sinners, she told me, she and the reverend came west." Sophie raised her eyebrows, her dark eyes bright as a blackbird's.

When Mattie woke, still feeling shaky, Sophie Steinbaum was gone, and Cindy, stripped to her drawers and camisole, stood in the wash-bowl placed on the floor, scrubbing vigorously at her feet. "We saved the wallpaper, the hats and shoes, and the ladies' underwear," she announced when she saw that Mattie was awake. "One barrel of flour is ruined and we're having to dry out some of the yard goods. Got it draped along the railing." She bubbled with eagerness as she brushed at the mud spatters on her dress. "It was mostly tinned tomatoes and stuff like that on the bottom, and they can be washed off." She sat on the trunk to dry her feet, her cheeks still flushed with excitement.

Through the open door Mattie saw that the sky was nearly dark. A pale star hovered over the gentle hills sloping up from the river's edge. She felt as far from reality as the dim star from this wilderness place. She had never before been in such a predicament. She remembered her mother once saying physical strength had nothing to do with moral courage. Did that apply to Mattie now? What did moral courage mean? Had she forfeited her right to claim moral anything?

"Would you like me to read to you?" Cindy asked cheerfully. "Abigail gave me a history book. Did you know that our President is Ulysses S. Grant? I don't know what the S stands for." She settled herself on the trunk and opened the book but sat quietly for a moment. "No, I guess you don't feel like listening," she said. Then Mattie heard only the flutter of pages as Cindy searched for pictures.

Late that night, Garnet Tanner's back ached with fatigue as he but-toned his clean shirt. The hot bath had eased his overworked muscles, but his concern for Mattie Hamil remained. Her handling of Hodge-warden's injury this afternoon was remarkable, he mused. Still, she's pale and seems ill. He stretched out on his bunk and tried to sleep. A husky voice outside his cabin startled him. "Captain, you in there?"

Reluctantly, Tanner got up and went to the door, where a crewman waited near the rail. "Yes, what is it?"

"We have visitors. Two saddle tramps. They hollered from shore. Said they had business with you. I put down the plank for them. An old geezer and a younger fella. They're in your office."

One of the visitors, a tall, dark-haired man wearing a wide-brimmed black sombrero, stood when the captain entered. His once dapper clothing now hung limp and grimy, but even though Tanner had seen him only briefly in Bismarck, there was no mistaking the tall, aristocratic manner.

"Captain." Calvin Bodein extended his hand.

The captain did not offer his. "About time you showed up, Bodein."

Cal gestured toward Doc. "May I present Doc, my friend and guide. We've ridden a hard piece to overtake the *Big Muddy*."

Doc tipped his battered hat. "We got horses to bring aboard before we start upriver."

Tanner scowled at the old man's weathered face, the wild white hair, and scraggly beard. "It may be a while. Our boiler is down and we've a leak to patch. And, Bodein, Miss Hamil isn't well."

"Mattie?"

Doc blinked his bright eye. "What's wrong?"

"Where is she?" Cal asked.

Tanner hesitated. "Look, it's after midnight . . ."

But Cal spoke sharply. "Captain, she's going to be my wife." He produced the ticket packet. "It wasn't my fault I had a temporary change in travel plans."

Tanner knew he had no right to prevent Bodein's seeing Mattie. Anyway, knowing he's here should make her feel better. "All right, I'll take you to her. But you'll have to bunk with the crew." He took his lantern from the peg.

Cal flashed his boyish grin. "Don't these cabins sleep two?"

"Cindy's staying with her," Tanner snapped.

"Cindy? The one from Bismarck? What's she doing with Mattie?"

"It's a long story." Tanner paused outside Mattie's door and rapped softly.

Inside the dark cabin, Cindy climbed from the top bunk and opened the door, her finger to her lips. "Shhh. She's sleeping."

But Mattie woke with a start and sat upright.

"Mattie, it's Cal. I'm here." He pushed into the room. The captain held the lantern while Cindy lighted the wall lamp. Cal stood as if stricken himself when he saw Mattie's ashen face. She did indeed look ill. "Oh, darlin' girl. What's wrong?"

But Doc stepped forward and pulled Cal back from the bunk. "Don't touch her. You're mangier'n a dead coyote." Doc tossed his hat into the corner, went to the washbowl, and began to soap his hands.

"Not here." Tanner tugged at Doc's sleeve. "You can clean up with the crew."

"You old coot," Cal snapped. "Can't you see Mattie's sick?"

"That's exactly what I see." Doc squinted through his good eye. "Now get out of the light so's I can help her."

"How are you going to help?" Tanner said. "Mattie needs a doctor."

"You're lookin' at one." Quickly drying his hands, he reached for Mattie's wrist to take her pulse.

Cal scowled. "Are you saying you're a *real* doc?"

"I ain't imaginary." Doc gently placed his hand on Mattie's forehead and pulled back her eyelid with his thumb. "Just checking you over, miss. I'm a doctor." Turning to the others, he snapped, "The rest of you better wait someplace else. Bring the horses aboard, Cal, and get my medical kit from the parfleche in Buttercup's pack. And, Captain, you better leave that lantern. My old eye ain't as good as it used to be."

Ten

MATTIE BLINKED in the dim light at the shadowy figure bending over her, an old man with straggling white hair, a leathered face, and one milky eye. He seemed disheveled and dirty. Not at all like a doctor, but the battered medical case and the motley instruments he had deftly soaped and rinsed in the pot of hot water showed longtime wear. He worked in silence, gently and methodically.

She searched his face. "Doctor, I'm . . . in the family way."

"I see that." Doc raised one bushy brow and grinned. "Near three months along, I'd say."

Mattie nodded. "I've been dizzy. And I feel so ill. I'm afraid something's not right."

"This trip ain't exactly your typical confinement. Your body's tryin' to warn you. My guess is that you got poor blood. Some fresh buffalo liver should do the trick. And milk. Lots of milk."

"I've been craving dandelion greens."

He chuckled. "Got to listen to cravings." He pulled the sheet up around her. "Everything seems normal. Those dizzy spells are tellin' you to go easy." He fixed her gaze with his good eye. "I take it Cal don't know."

"No, not yet. I'd rather he didn't. You won't tell him, will you?"

"Not my place to tell him."

"I don't want him to know till after we're married."

"And if that don't come to pass?"

"I've always managed by myself," she said. "I'm a teacher."

Doc rinsed and dried his hands. "Not much welcome out this way for an unmarried woman with a child." Then he added soberly, "Or anywhere else for that matter."

"But Cal wants to marry me." She lay back on the pillow, feeling less panic now with the doctor there, someone to confide in. "I know he does."

"Reckon so." Doc carelessly tossed his equipment into the case. "Now you rest. We'll get started on that buffalo liver in the morning."

"Thank you, Doctor . . . uh . . ."

"Austin," Doc said, looking a bit surprised himself at the sound of it after all this time. Then with a wink of his good eye, "Elsworth Austin."

Cal, Captain Tanner, and Cindy stood on deck not far from Mattie's door watching the moon's reflection on the rain-swollen river and lulled by the warm night air, the hum of insects, the peaceful lap of the water against the boat.

Cal repeated, "I can't get over him being a real doc."

"Can he be trusted?"

"Nobody but a real doctor looks under eyelids," Cindy said.

Mattie's door opened. Doc stepped out and walked toward them, giving Cal a long, meaningful look.

The captain frowned. "So what's the matter with her?"

Doc leaned his elbows on the railing, gazing thoughtfully across the moonlit water, before turning to Cal. "I don't know why she's having a tough time of it."

"That settles it," Cal snapped. "You're a damn fake."

Doc shook his head. "No, just not a magician."

Tanner stepped forward. "She's not in any danger . . . ?"

"No, no. Nothin' like that." Doc tilted his grizzled head toward the far end of the deck, suggesting a private conference with the captain. Tanner strode impatiently beside him, leaving Cal and Cindy staring after them. When they had moved out of earshot, the squint-eyed doctor turned to face the captain.

"I told Mattie I wouldn't tell Cal, but since you're in charge here, I think you need to know what's goin' on." He glanced around to be sure they were alone. "Mattie's close to a miscarriage. She don't want Cal to know. Don't want to get hitched just 'cause of her condition. You know how women are."

Tanner stared at the wizened face. "A miscarriage. She's . . . ?"

"Gonna have a baby." Doc finished his sentence. "She's pregnant."

"But she can't be. Not Mattie. She's . . . I'm . . . She's a doctor's daughter."

"Whatever. But she's about three months along."

"Is it Bodein's?" Tanner spat the words.

"Don't think there's any doubt there, with her coming all this way to find him."

Tanner muttered between clenched teeth, "I could kill the bastard."

"Makin' Mattie a widow before she's even married wouldn't help, now would it?"

The captain's face twisted. "I'd never have thought it of her. Why would she do such a thing? And with that good-for-nothing fancy pants?" He hit the rail with his fist.

"Nothin' so unusual about it," Doc said.

Tanner turned toward the old man. "Will she be all right?"

"She needs rest, good food, and maybe a little hand-holding with Cal."

Tanner glowered.

"A strong tonic might help," Doc continued, "but I doubt there's any between here and Fort Benton. Best we can do is feed her good and see that she rests."

Tanner nodded. Retracing their steps, they found Cindy alone on the deck.

"Where's Bodein?" Tanner asked.

"He went to be with Mattie." Cindy sighed, gazing dreamily at the diamond-like sparkle of moonlight across the rippling water. "It's like a real romance."

The captain snorted and turned toward his office.

Cal carefully latched the door behind him as he entered Mattie's cramped cabin and tiptoed toward the bunk, the lamp flickering his shadow onto the ceiling. Mattie seemed to be sleeping peacefully. Could the old man actually have helped her in some way?

"It's Cal, darlin'. How're you feeling?"

Mattie opened her eyes. "Cal." He looked leaner and his handsome nose was peeling from sunburn. "I'm better," she reached her hand toward his, "now that you and Dr. Austin are here."

"Dr. Austin?" He realized he'd never heard Doc's name.

"I'm sorry to worry you, Cal. I'll be up and about in a day or two. It's just . . . well, you know . . . female complaint."

"Oh." Cal took her hand and kissed it. "You had me worried for a minute."

She smiled to reassure him. "I guess the trip was a little too much, the heat and all. But never mind that. You're here now. That's what matters."

He stroked her hair and she closed her eyes. Everything would be all right now. Cal was with her. And the doctor. How silly to have been so apprehensive.

"Mattie," Cal murmured. "My valise. Do you have it?"

She gestured under the bunk and he found the scuffed leather bag.

"The captain assigned me a bunk with the crew," he said. "I'll take this with me." To reassure himself, he undid the clasp and dug beneath the clean shirts. A smile came over his face as his hand closed around the rolled sock. The weight of the coins and the fat crinkle of bills were unmistakable through the fine wool. He closed the bag with a smart snap of the clasp, a particularly pleasant sound. "Thanks, darlin', for taking care of this for me." He kissed her forehead lightly and moved toward the door. "Happy dreams."

Sunlight streamed in through the door as Cindy, her hair neatly combed into two puffs over her ears, entered carrying a tray. "Doc's special order." She sounded unusually cheerful as she placed a steaming plate of fried liver, buttered carrots, and boiled dandelion greens on Mattie's lap. "I went ashore for the dandelions myself."

Mattie stretched, smiling. "Is it morning already?"

"It's afternoon. You've had a good long sleep."

Mattie ate ravenously, feeling stronger almost at once.

"I knew he was a real doc right away," Cindy said. "Bodein and the captain weren't sure."

"I'm so glad they caught up with us." Should she tell Cindy about the baby? No, not yet. She might let it slip. "Will you let Cal know I'm up and feeling better already?"

"Bodein? He's gone."

"Gone!" Mattie's fork dropped to the tray.

"Yep. Rode off this morning with the Fike brothers."

"He what?"

Cindy shrugged. "You were sleeping. I guess he didn't want to bother you."

"Bother me?" Mattie pushed the tray aside, her voice rising. "Bother me?"

"I don't blame you, Mattie." Cindy put a comforting arm around her. "But don't fret yourself. He ain't worth it."

Mattie glared at the girl. "You don't understand. He's going to be . . . ," then suppressing the impulse to reveal her pregnancy, ". . . my husband."

Cindy wrinkled her nose. "I'd sooner marry a wild goose." On impulse, she tucked her hands under her armpits, flapped her elbows, and began to make honking noises.

"A wild goose would be easier to keep track of," Mattie snapped. But she had to smile at Cindy's audacious display. "I think I better get well real quick. Here, let me finish that liver." She attacked the few morsels left on the tray.

Doc and Captain Tanner, appearing in the sunlit open door, had witnessed Cindy's goose imitation. "What's this, migrating season?" Doc, having bathed and borrowed a clean shirt and trousers from Tanner, presented a more civilized appearance. He carried his medical bag.

"Miss Hamil," Tanner began awkwardly, "Bodein went on ahead." He hurried to add, "Dr. Austin thought it would be a good idea to get some medicine for you."

"When I told Cal you needed a tonic," Doc explained, "he volunteered to send it downriver from Fort Benton."

They're trying to spare my feelings, Mattie thought. She searched Doc's face for a clue as to whether Cal knew about her condition. Doc understood and responded with a slight shake of his head. She didn't know whether to be relieved that Cal didn't know about the baby or disappointed because the truth might have kept him with her.

Either way, he was gone again. She should have told him. He would have stayed with her then. Married her. That would have been the appropriate thing to do. Still, she now knew that an uncertain future loomed ahead even if she did marry Cal.

Captain Tanner stood back. He offered no fond, lingering look as he had yesterday. No extension of his hand toward her. Instead, his eyes avoided hers, his mouth a grim line of resignation. It was obvious. He knew about her indiscretion. She had counted on his friendship, and now he was abandoning her.

Despair rose in Mattie's throat. Was Cindy right? Should she sooner marry a wild goose than Calvin Bodein? Cal loved her, but the problem seemed to be he didn't need her. At least not at the moment.

Doc prodded Cindy and the captain from the room and closed the door.

"Now, Mattie, how you really feelin'?" He drew the trunk close to the bed and sat down.

"I'm scared, Dr. Austin. Not for my health. I'm better. But why would Cal go off again like that?"

"Beats me." Doc lifted her wrist to take her pulse. "Some men just can't stay put. Course if we'd told him about your urgent need for his presence, it might have made a difference." He stopped talking while he counted her heartbeats. "But I doubt it." Then, squinting at her through his good eye, "You sure you want to hook up with him?"

Mattie considered Doc's words. Even *he* thought Cal a poor risk. "What choice do I have?"

Doc looked at her for a moment as if trying to decide whether to say what was on his mind. "You don't *have* to become a mother just yet, you know."

What was he saying? Had she heard him correctly? His solemn look left no doubt as to his meaning.

"It's not too late to . . . to interrupt your condition."

"Dr. Austin!" Mattie gasped. "Surely you aren't suggesting . . ."

"Ain't suggestin' nothin'. I'm just tellin' you there's more'n one way to skin a cat."

Mattie straightened. "Why, I wouldn't even consider such a thing." Angry tears sprang to her eyes. "This baby is part of me. I love it already. I'd die for it."

"All right. All right." He patted her hand. "If you're set on goin' it alone, I'll do what I can to get you through it in good shape."

Mattie stared speechless as he stood to go. He turned as he reached the door, his white eyebrows knitted into a wild tangle over his questioning glance. "Just between you and me?"

Mattie nodded. But the encounter left her shaken.

Eleven

THE MAIN STREET of Fort Benton in mid-August bustled with the kind of activity Calvin Bodein had missed since he left St. Louis. He strolled along the boardwalk that edged the dusty riverfront thoroughfare, feeling renewed after the purchase of a new suit of clothing from Power's mercantile, a bath, and a comfortable night at the Overland Hotel. The hotel, a squat frame structure, occupied a narrow lot between the Wells Fargo office and the Diamond R Transportation Company, where twenty oxen stood in their yokes before a covered freight wagon, tails switching at flies as they chewed their cuds. A few saddled horses waited at hitching posts.

Near the small adobe courthouse, Cal nodded cordially to two well-barbered men alighting from an expensive buggy pulled by a fine harness horse, their eastern polish a refreshing respite, he thought, from the motley bullwhackers and miners palavering in front of the saloons. Perhaps these gentlemen, too, could be engaged in a friendly poker game.

Cal and the Fike brothers had arrived in Fort Benton on a freight barge they had overtaken near Fort Bufford. After sleeping on deck with their horses, suffering mosquitoes, heat, and drenching rain, Cal vowed that once he got to a town where he could cultivate the kind of life he was born to, he would never again undertake a journey of any kind. It pleased him to see the prim, starched housewives with energetic children going in and out of Baker's general store. It was clear that Fort Benton offered opportunity.

Still, Last Chance Gulch—or Helena as they called it now—seemed a more attractive prospect for a permanent home. Despite its isolation, a prospering community continued to thrive there after the gold played out. With hotels, banks, a daily newspaper, and growing industries, the town had just been named capital of the territory, and it was rumored that a railroad would soon connect it to the rest of the country. Yes, with Mattie bent on getting married, the new capital seemed the more likely place to settle.

He made his way toward a physician's shingle hanging in front of a newly built adobe-and-log pharmacy. Dr. Will E. Turner, a pleasant general practitioner, surgeon, and partner in the store, listened sympathetically to Cal's explanation of Mattie's condition. "Female complaint, eh? Well, this should put the roses back in her cheeks." He held two large bottles of the tonic requested on the note signed by Dr. Elsworth Austin.

"Austin? That name rings a bell," Dr. Turner said, scratching his graying goatee. "Seems like I heard about a fella by that name got himself in trouble over at Last Chance Gulch a while back." He looked questioningly at Cal.

Cal shrugged. Maybe this was a chance to find out why Doc had hidden out on that hellish sandbar. "What kind of trouble?"

"Don't rightly remember. Probably not even the same fella." Dr. Turner wrapped each of the tonic bottles in layers of brown paper from the large roll on the counter, then packed them in a small wooden box.

"I'm much obliged," Cal said, disappointed that Dr. Turner's poor memory failed to provide a clue to Doc's mysterious past. "And I'd appreciate it if you'd see Miss Hamil when she arrives on the *Big Muddy.*"

"Glad to do what I can," Dr. Turner promised.

On the way to the steamship office, Cal mulled over the new bit of information. It seemed clear that Doc was in trouble with Helena authorities. Were these the men he wanted Cal to trounce in a poker game? Seemed an odd sort of revenge. And wouldn't the old coot be picked up if he went anywhere near the place? In any case, Doc certainly was not fit to be looking after Mattie. Or to be accompanying her to Helena.

Cal obtained the steamship clerk's promise that the package would be sent downriver the following afternoon on the steamer *Rosebud* and transferred to the *Big Muddy* when they met. The *Big Muddy*, Cal learned, was repaired and under way, due in Fort Benton in ten days.

Ten days. Cal's cash reserve showed a small increase from last night's game at the Exchange Saloon and dance hall. The Exchange, a rough establishment where gamblers kept their pistols on the table to discourage cheats, harbored an assortment of Frenchmen, Métis, and others whose thirst for whiskey equaled their passion for gambling. Cal had witnessed a quarrel between two belligerent miners that ended when someone fired a shot into the ceiling.

Amid this distraction, and aided by a testimonial from the Fike brothers, he had signed two more prospectors to outfitting contracts. As soon as he found a place, he would send an order to the Ottsbergs for enough supplies and equipment to establish a modest business. If the river held high, the shipment could arrive in little more than two months, a bit late for this season but in plenty of time to stock prospectors in the spring. He had made arrangements with the Diamond R freighters to haul the goods to the Gulch. But ten days seemed too long to delay. The sooner he got there and found a place to house his business, the better. He could have much of the order sold by the time it arrived.

Cal, spirits crisp as his new straw skimmer, continued along the walk toward the Exchange Saloon. Best to mingle with the miners in the morning before they got roaring drunk. He stepped around a sprawled, snoring Frenchman, whose scraped knuckles and bruised cheek recalled the melee Cal had witnessed there the night before. The man slept undisturbed as Cal went through the swinging doors. Despite the lingering stale smell of whiskey and tobacco, the near-empty saloon appeared freshly swept and tables and chairs had been placed in order. Three cowboys sat talking at one of the tables. Boot and Alfred Fike stood leaning against the bar while a balding, garter-sleeved bartender refilled their glasses.

"Hey, Bodein!" Boot turned, shifting the brace on his leg and narrowing his eyes at Cal's dapper new suit of clothes. "Figured you wouldn't show up this early." He cackled at his implication that Cal would be hung over. "Don't look like you're sufferin' much." The burly Alfred grimaced with the burn of hastily swallowed whiskey.

"Morning, boys." Cal joined them at the bar and ordered whiskey, placing a small stack of silver dollars on the counter. The gesture usually eased the way into a poker game. "I've been tending to business. Getting up an order for our supplies. With luck, the shipment will be here in two months."

"Wanted to talk to you about that," Boot said. "Those other two prospectors lit outta here early this morning. They're aimin' to get to diggin' 'fore the weather goes bad. And me and Alfie here, well . . ."

"We're fixin' to do the same." Alfie flushed his remaining whiskey through his teeth.

"We think alike," Cal said. "There's a freight wagon over at the Diamond R now getting ready to leave. We can ride along with it down through Sun River Crossing. Might be nice to have company along the way . . . in case we meet up with unfriendly tribes." Cal wanted keener men than the Fikes with him if they should be forced to defend themselves.

"You mean Indians?" Alfie poised his empty glass in the air.

"Not too likely, but I ran across a bunch outside of Bismarck." Cal glanced at his naked ring finger. "Anyway, the Mullen Road goes by way of Fort Shaw." He regretted Doc hadn't come with him. Despite his outlaw status, or perhaps because of it, Doc knew his way around this country. Maybe it was a good thing after all that he was looking after Mattie.

"Can't just start across a prairie half-cocked." Boot nudged his brother. "This ain't Detroit, you know."

"It's only a hundred and fifty miles," Cal said. "A few days' ride. Let's grab some grub and hit the trail." He picked up his change and, glancing at the three men seated at the table, regretted there wasn't time for a game of five-card stud.

Another warm August day waned as the *Big Muddy* steamed upriver. On either side, the Montana plains rolled out a stark and constant landscape of amber grasses, mottled in the last low rays of sunlight by rocky outcroppings. The Missouri had become surprisingly blue beyond its confluence with the muddy Yellowstone, and Mattie, energetic again even before taking the tonic delivered by the *Rosebud,* strolled on deck with Cindy and Abigail while the paddle wheel churned away the daylight hours. The steamer's wake trailed off behind them in deep, foamy furrows that broke into rippling waves before settling into the quiet flow.

"Let's go up on top where it's cooler," Mattie said, gathering her calico skirt about her for the climb up the steps. "I prefer to see where I'm going, not where I've been."

"Mattie, we've gone up there more times than I can count." Abigail's merry manner showed how much she enjoyed the company of her two new friends. "I think I know more about steamboats than I care to." She liked the prairie air and sunshine, too, and, despite her mother's admonitions, refused to carry her parasol on deck. Now, a rosy tan complemented her expressive dark eyes and shining hair, which she wore in a high puff. She had put aside the rose velvet traveling suit for comfortable cotton shirtwaists and a navy twill skirt.

"Could be Captain Tanner's up there." Cindy's teasing carried even above the noise of the wheel. Her narrow face had lost its pallor during their on-deck sunning, and her pale eyes were emphasized by the green-and-white-checked gingham dress with ruffled sleeves and a saucy flounce she'd sewn from another length of Mattie's fabric.

Mattie raised an eyebrow in mock haughtiness. "Don't be silly. It's that pilot, Mr. Hogwharton or whatever his name is, that I find attractive." The three giggled happily.

On the top deck, Cindy ran to the front railing. "You're right, Mattie, there's a breeze up here." She plopped down, scooting between the balusters, letting her legs hang over the edge. "Come on, you two."

Mattie and Abigail exchanged glances, still laughing as they positioned themselves on either side of Cindy, their feet dangling amid their petticoats, their faces caressed by the rising evening breeze.

They sat for a long moment gazing at the golden panorama of sun-tipped hillocks and purple-shadowed plains stretching away on either side of the river. Mattie spoke. "It's really rather magnificent, isn't it?"

"Like another world," Abigail murmured. "I can feel my old life trailing off downriver. Up ahead somewhere," she gestured at the expansive landscape before them, "is a whole new existence waiting for us. Something we can't even imagine."

"Yeah, what's gone don't matter," Cindy said.

Mattie took a deep breath of resolve. This strange and wild country was her country now. She would thrive here—with or without Calvin Bodein.

"Watch out! There's a sandbar!" Cindy looked back at the pilot house, where the ruddy-nosed pilot, having already spotted the expanse of sand looming just beneath the surface of the water, spun the ship's wheel forcefully. The river's shifting bottom presented an ongoing challenge for even the *Big Muddy*'s shallow draft. Despite the pilot's effort, and his recitation of a complete repertory of seagoing oaths, the boat glided onto the submerged sandbank and shuddered to a stop that nearly pitched the three young women off their upper-deck perch.

Captain Tanner appeared below directing the men. "Set the legs," he shouted as steam hissed through the capstans. The pole-like "grasshopper legs" at either side of the forward deck could be lowered onto the sandbar where they would serve as stilts or braces so that blasts of steam into the capstans would bounce the boat, allowing the current to wash sand from underneath.

"Give it everything you got!" Tanner ordered. But the steamer's bottom sucked stubbornly into the sandy bar. "Again!"

All three women admired the captain's easy authority, his strength and sureness. Yet three times, with the capstans under a full head of steam, the boat only mired deeper into the sand as the grasshopper legs failed to bounce it free.

"We better try the chain!" Tanner and the men positioned themselves, some on the starboard side and some on the port, to drag a heavy chain back and forth in a sawing motion beneath the boat. When they had pulled the chain the length of the boat, the captain ordered the paddle wheel reversed to backwash the loosened sand. With a reluctant groan, the boat heaved off the sandbar into the current, rocking gently once again against the steady force of the river.

Acknowledging success by waving to the pilot, the captain noticed for the first time the three young women seated precariously at the upper rail. He touched his cap in a brief salute, then hurried below.

"The captain seems to be avoiding us," Abigail said, wistfully.

Cindy glanced sharply at Mattie. "It ain't *us*, Abby. It's Mattie he don't want to see. I reckon if a certain party don't meet us in Fort Benton, the captain'll be hangin' around plenty."

Mattie scrambled to her feet. "Of course Cal will meet us in Fort Benton."

But Cal was not at the riverfront when the *Big Muddy* steamed up to the Fort Benton levee. Mattie, standing on the lower deck in her blue silk suit and straw bonnet, waited in vain for a glimpse of his lanky build among those on shore. "We'll see you at the hotel," Abigail, toting her share of the Steinbaums' hand luggage across the gangplank, called to her. The Reverend and Mrs. Parkington glared at Cindy as they passed, a reminder that they intended to report the captain's lack of discretion in allowing her aboard. Cindy swished the flounce of her dress at them, holding her head high as she took Mattie's arm and led the way off the boat toward the baggage being placed on shore.

Mattie, scanning the milling crowd, waved absently to Doc Austin, who led his black saddlehorse and aging pack mule toward a saloon hitching post. Cindy complained about the heat, her chatter increasing Mattie's apprehension that Cal would not be there to meet her, that he had met with another unfortunate circumstance, that perhaps he would never come for her. Her eyes and throat burned as dust swirled around them, stirred by the wind from the parched hills hovering along the river. There seemed to be little to Fort Benton except the one avenue of meager establishments now absorbing the steamer's passengers—squat, scruffy buildings, barely more than shanties. She looked back toward the *Big Muddy,* the comfortable haven captained by Garnet Tanner, who had avoided even telling her good-bye.

Cindy seemed to sense her thoughts. "It ain't what you expected?"

A goateed man wearing small, round spectacles approached them, his white shirt sleeves rolled neatly in the heat. "Which of you is Miss Hamil?" He looked from one to the other.

"I am." Mattie held her breath. Perhaps he had word from Cal.

"I'm Dr. Turner. I promised your fiancé I'd see that you found lodging."

Mattie eagerly searched his face. "Is he here?"

"He went on to Last Chance Gulch more'n a week ago."

Mattie sank onto her trunk.

"He told me you hadn't been feeling well. Did you get the tonics?"

She nodded wearily.

"She's better now," Cindy said.

"Yes. I . . . I'm fine."

"Just the same, come on over to my office there." He pointed toward the little adobe-and-log pharmacy down the riverfront street. "I'll check you over before you go on. There's a stage leaving for Helena in the morning. Mr. Bodein paid your fare."

Cindy frowned. "Just hers?"

"Don't worry, I can pay for you," Mattie assured her. Then to the doctor, "This is my friend Cindy Dougherty." Cindy grinned, pleased to be properly introduced.

Dr. Turner nodded. "Maybe you'd like to take a room at the Overland for tonight. I'm afraid that's about the best we have to offer."

Mattie handed Cindy a bill from her handbag. "Could you get us a room and have my trunk taken there while I talk with Dr. Turner?"

"I'll check on the stage, too." Cindy scanned the area for a likely helper and before Mattie and Dr. Turner reached the drugstore had recruited a cattleman with a buckboard to deliver the trunk to the hotel. Mattie smiled, saying to the doctor, "Cindy's very resourceful."

"Is she meeting her fiancé, too?"

"She's working for me," Mattie improvised.

Dr. Turner led the way through the small, medicinal-smelling phar-

macy into his office, which Mattie noted was equipped with an examination table and a glass-front cupboard containing equipment and
medicines, along with a framed diploma from a Philadelphia medical
school. The doctor indicated one of the chairs. "How long have you
been feeling poorly?"

"Doctor, I'm going to have a baby."

"Well now, that explains some of the problem."

"Mr. Bodein and I are getting married as soon as possible."

"I see. Then we best have a look at you." The doctor accompanied
his examination with practical advice for a comfortable confinement.
"You're doing just fine," he said when he had finished. "There's a doctor
in Last Chance, a Dr. Ward. Get in touch with him when you get there.
He'll take good care of you."

"I'm grateful to you," she said.

"Glad I could help." He indicated his fee had been paid by Cal and
led the way back out through the pharmacy before adding, "Oh, one
word of caution. I understand Dr. Elsworth Austin was on the boat
with you. Watch out for that one, Miss Hamil. He's a bad apple.
Wanted by authorities."

"Wanted? Whatever for?"

"Happened a while back, but I recently made some inquiries to
refresh my memory on what the furor was all about."

"Furor?"

"Yes. Seems he killed a young woman."

Twelve

DISTURBED by Dr. Turner's warning against Elsworth Austin, Mattie
hurried from the Fort Benton pharmacy directly into the path of Captain Tanner.

"Mattie, I've been looking for you."

"And I wanted to see you." She was pleased that he had dispensed
with calling her Miss Hamil, yet unsettled by the effect he had on her.

"To tell you good-bye. I've had a message from Cal. He's waiting for me in Helena. I'll be going on tomorrow."

"Mattie, I must talk to you." He led her to the side of the pharmacy out of the way of passersby. "Mattie, I . . . I know about the baby."

She pulled herself up to her full height.

"I'm worried about you," he continued. "I can't let you go chasing around the frontier hoping Bodein will hold still long enough to marry you."

"But I must. This has all been a series of unfortunate incidents beyond Cal's control. Everything will be all right when I get to the Gulch."

"I've thought about it, Mattie. I can't let you go like this. When Doc Austin told me what you'd gotten yourself into . . . well, I didn't know what to think. It's all so hard to talk about."

"You needn't think anything, Captain. It doesn't concern you."

"I thought when you realized what a fly-by-night Bodein is, you might come to care for me. But since you haven't . . . Well . . . I feel you're letting yourself down. That somehow you're letting *us* down."

Mattie gasped. "Letting *us* down?"

"I know it's not rational, but dammit, Mattie, these things are never rational. I'm just being honest. I owe you that."

"You owe me nothing!"

"I didn't mean it that way. What I'm trying to say is . . . Mattie, stay with me. I want to take care of you. Can't you see how much you mean to me?" He gripped her shoulders, his eyes commanding hers.

Mattie stood stricken. She longed to fall into his arms. To say, "Yes! Yes, Garnet Tanner, I'll stay with you." This dreadful journey would be over then. One word from her could put an end to her shame.

"Captain, you must understand. I can't."

"But, Mattie, I'm sure in time . . ."

"It wouldn't be fair to you . . . or to anyone else. It's not just my own feelings I have to consider now."

"You mean you do have feelings for me?" He clasped her hand.

"No, I don't mean that at all."

"Please, Mattie, is there anything I can say? Anything I can do?"

"No. I'm sorry." The words seemed to come from someone else. She saw the dull syllables strike his dear face.

He released her then. "I think you're making a terrible mistake."

Abigail Steinbaum appeared from the Wells Fargo office and hurried toward them. "Mattie, the stage leaves at six in the morning." She came up to them, her dark, intelligent eyes taking in the flush of emotion binding Mattie and the captain.

"Mama insists that the two of you join us for supper tonight. A farewell party. Bon voyage and all that." She took the captain's arm, moving along with them, her contagious smile lighting her face. "Unless, of course, we can talk Captain Tanner into coming to Helena with us."

"I'm sorry to have to refuse such a charming invitation," Tanner said. "But I . . . I've much to do this evening. I wish the very best to you both." He tipped his hat, turned, and strode away without looking back.

Abigail's bright smile faded abruptly. "If only he were in love with *me.*" She looked away to hide welling tears.

"Oh, my dear Abby." Mattie touched her friend's hand. "I didn't realize."

Doc Austin, who had seen them passing by the saloon where he had downed a glass of port, hurried up behind them. "Afternoon, ladies." Mattie startled at Doc's greeting, as much from her awareness of his reputed crime as with his slightly tipsy appearance.

"I'm ridin' on," he said. "I prefer travelin' alone." Then, tipping his scruffy hat, "I'll let Cal know you're comin'." And he shuffled off.

"He's a weird old duck." Abigail dabbed at her eyes with a handkerchief.

"Yes, he is." Mattie did not relate Dr. Turner's warning.

Six horses pulled the bulky Gilmer & Salisbury Stage Lines coach as it rolled out of Fort Benton just after dawn the following morning, the weathered green lettering on the door nearly obscured by swirling dust. The coach swayed sharply as the heavyset driver gripped his handful of lines and persuaded the skittish team to assume a steady pace.

Mattie, wedged between Cindy and Abigail in the forward seat opposite Sophie Steinbaum and the Parkingtons, looked from the window back toward the riverfront. A whistle blast from the *Big Muddy* announcing the steamer's impending departure now seemed a mournful lament rather than a cheerful leave-taking as the boat eased into the current that would carry it to St. Louis. St. Louis, Mattie mused sadly. So far away.

Sophie craned her plump neck for a last glimpse of the boat. "That nice Captain Tanner. I wonder if we'll ever see him again."

"Hummph." Mrs. Parkington's voice was even more brittle than her expression. *"Never* will be too soon." She avoided looking at them.

Cindy, shining and eager in her yellow calico, said firmly, "I have a feeling we will." But her remark did little to ease the melancholy of each of the two young women beside her, and soon, in the breaking rays of sunlight, the sound of the *Big Muddy*'s whistle faded into the crunch and jolt of the coach wheels.

Jonah Parkington, the lone male in the coach, appeared embarrassed to be so closely confined with the three unmarried young women. "Perhaps you will see the captain again when you go back down the river, Miss Dougherty." His comment changed his wife's icy stare to one of outrage. She kicked his ankle.

"I ain't goin' back," Cindy said. "I mean," she glanced at Mattie, "I'm *not* goin' back."

Parkington seemed to be softening to Cindy's ingenuous appeal. He took a small leather-bound prayer book from his pocket. "Perhaps a reading, ladies," he suggested, "to pass the time away?"

"Let me read it to you," Cindy volunteered, bending across to peer at the printed verses.

"But that wasn't what I . . . ," Parkington stammered. "I mean, I thought . . ."

"Please let me try." Cindy took the book from his limp grasp. "Let's see now." She flipped through the pages. "Here's one." She squinted at the first word. "All . . . all . . . What's this word?" She shoved the book toward Parkington, marking the place with her finger.

"Almighty." He looked down his narrow nose at her small tapered nails. "Almighty God."

"Yes, Almighty God," Cindy began. "Lead me through the . . . the dark shadows to . . . to the . . ." Again she leaned toward the reverend, sharing the prayer book.

"Everlasting light," he prompted, staring at the glowing face of the girl in yellow.

Cindy, suddenly aware of his gaze, drew back. "Maybe this *is* too hard for me," she said quietly.

"No, no," Parkington assured her. "Keep trying. I'll help you with the difficult words." He twitched as his wife's pointed shoe again came in contact with his ankle.

The Mullen Road, connecting Fort Benton with the Montana mining camps and beyond to Walla Walla and the Oregon country, proved to be quite unlike any Mattie had experienced before. There had been no rain for weeks and, along with the increasing heat, the stage passengers endured an ever-present dust that irritated their eyes and gave their clothing, the coach, and everything in sight a chalky appearance. The rough wagon trail wound westward over miles of open country, flanked by scattered scrub pines and low-growing junipers, with occasional brief stretches hacked through forests of fir and tamarack at the higher elevations. Fort Shaw and the other stations along the way, spaced a day's drive in between, provided poor accommodations and poorer food. Mattie sought some degree of comfort in the coach by folding her shawl behind the small of her back, but by the third day, the bouncing and jarring made her fear for the child she carried. Must be a healthy one, she thought, to hang on through all of this. Again she braced herself while the horses struggled up a rocky rise and skidded down the other side.

"Why I ever came to this Godless country, I'll never know," Portia Parkington muttered. "Mrs. Steinbaum, how can you endure this insufferable jolting?"

"Don't ask," Sophie replied.

Portia's ceaseless complaining provoked no response from her husband, who seemed absorbed in his prayer book, but whose narrow-set eyes darted now and then in Cindy's direction.

At last they headed south through the Prickly Pear Valley on the final leg of their journey. The peaceful valley, buffalo grass browning under the blue late summer sky, provided a panoramic vista. To the west loomed the Rocky Mountains and, Parkington explained, somewhere up on the highest ridges lay the Great Divide, the continental watershed that determined whether rain and snowfall flowed west to the Pacific or sent its precious moisture inland down the Missouri and its tributaries.

"What are tributaries?" Cindy's pale eyes fixed on the cleric with such interest that he was forced to look away while he answered, "A tributary is a smaller stream or river that feeds into a bigger one." He braced for the expected kick on the ankle but Portia Parkington ignored the geology lesson, and he continued. "I can show you a map when I unpack the books in my trunk." That's when his wife gouged her heel into his instep.

Abigail nudged Mattie, suppressing a giggle that would seriously offend the Parkingtons, and Mattie responded with a knowing glance. How glad she was to have such a friend as Abigail, smart, cultured, and delightful to be with. And Sophie. So motherly and good. She felt less alone in their company. But how long could the friendship last? Would they, too, forsake her if it turned out that she must face her confinement alone, unmarried?

Pretending absorption in the scenic views from the coach windows, Mattie once again grew tense and uncertain. Would Cal be waiting for her? Would she have to tell him about the baby and force him to marry her?

It was late afternoon when a shout from the driver announced their approach to the gulch. The weary passengers strained toward the coach windows, while the horses trotted with renewed energy along Benton Road. They followed a side hill above the town from which Mattie and the others could look across a labyrinth of streets lined with rows of small frame houses. Last Chance Gulch appeared to be a rutted trail that zigzagged along a sluggish stream at the bottom of the gully.

As the stage proceeded, Mattie saw an occasional two-story brick or stone residence standing out among the more modest dwellings. At the point where a rough bridge spanned the stream, a string of business establishments testified to the prosperity of the community. A city hall and fire department, topped with a fine bell tower, were housed in two handsome new brick structures standing side by side. Streets teemed with a lively commerce of buggies and buckboards, mule-drawn freight wagons, and riders on saddlehorses, and Mattie observed with delight the many women and small children moving purposefully along the boardwalks.

"There it is!" Abigail shrieked. "There's Papa's mercantile!" She pointed down the slope to a whitewashed, two-story storefront near the bridge. Above the entrance hung a wide painted sign, Steinbaum & Company.

Sophie smiled. "It's a regular store." Then she shrugged. "A little small."

"It'll be big someday," Abigail said merrily.

Mattie scanned the streets for some sign of Cal's enterprise, but she knew it was too soon to expect him to have set up anything to compare with the Steinbaum store. She noticed other painted signs identifying Fred White's Dance Hall and the Helena Theater.

"And there's the newspaper Papa spoke of," Abigail pointed out. *"The Helena Herald."* She turned to embrace Mattie. "Oh, Mattie, we're here. And it's a fine place."

The stage pulled up in front of a stone house, final station on the

Benton line. A carriage hitched to a bay horse stood at the hitching post. Beyond it was a shiny new buggy pulled by a sleek black. On the stone steps a stocky man with an untrimmed graying beard, wearing a dark suit and homburg, peered anxiously toward the coach. As Reverend Parkington opened the door and stepped down, the bearded man hurried forward.

"It's Papa!" Abigail scrambled from the coach and flung her arms around him. "Oh, Papa, we're here! We're here!" He hugged her, then turned to help Sophie. "Hello, my dear." He lifted her to the ground and kissed her affectionately.

"Lionel, you could at least wear your best." She sniffed back happy tears as she adjusted his twisted tie. "Every day your wife and daughter don't arrive."

At that moment, a tall man in a rakish straw skimmer stepped from the shiny buggy. Mattie's heart skipped a beat. She could not mistake Cal's patrician features and graceful stride. Nor the familiar wide grin that brightened his face when he caught sight of her alighting from the coach.

"Mattie!" He took her in his arms, his dark eyes searching her face lovingly. She clung to him. He had come for her. He did love her. And she loved him more than she had thought possible after her long ordeal. His kiss was tender and lingering and Mattie longed to remain in his arms forever, but he eased away. "Come, darlin'. I've got a room for us at the hotel."

Suddenly conscious of her traveling companions silently observing the reunion, Mattie resisted his attempt to guide her toward the buggy. "Wait, Cal, please. You must say hello to my friends."

"I want you to meet my father," Abigail said. Lionel Steinbaum acknowledged the introduction by removing the homburg from his balding head, its untrimmed fringe of graying hair as unruly as his patriarchal beard.

"And this is Cal," Mattie said, feeling genuine pride. "Calvin Bodein." How truly handsome he looked in his summer haberdashery, shiny dark sideburns curling beneath the skimmer. His long, graceful fingers tapered to manicured nails, something she hadn't seen on a man since she left St. Louis. "Cal, Abigail Steinbaum and her parents." Cal extended his hand to Lionel, then to Jonah Parkington as Mattie introduced the clergyman and his wife.

Cindy, assessing Cal from his dapper hat to his expensive, well-made boots, extended her hand, too, announcing, "We met."

"Well, hello," Cal said, warmly. "I want to thank you for looking after Mattie."

"They've all been wonderful." Mattie clasped his arm for reassurance that he was indeed there, that he wouldn't disappear again at any moment.

"Then you must all come to the wedding," Cal said with an expansive gesture. "I've got everything arranged."

Mattie caught her breath. Wedding, he said. He *was* committed to her, to their life together. Her long journey had not been in vain after all.

He put his arm about her shoulders. "We'll be married tomorrow. If that's all right with you, darlin'."

Mattie flung her arms around his neck, resisting the impulse to smother him with kisses. "Oh, yes. As soon as possible," she murmured.

"We'll have the ceremony at noon at the International Hotel," Cal announced to the others, "followed by a fine reception for my beautiful Mattie." He held her at arm's length, grinning for a moment at her disheveled and dusty appearance, then started for the luggage unloaded by the stage driver. "Now which of these is yours?"

Sophie clasped Mattie's hand. "With us you should stay tonight," she said, her birdlike eyes twinkling. "The blushing bride he shouldn't see on the wedding day before the ceremony."

"There's a room extra," Lionel said.

"Oh, Mattie, do," Abigail chimed in. "Cindy will stay, too."

"I am available to perform the ceremony," Parkington offered.

Cal looked sheepishly at Mattie. "Guess I thought of everything but a preacher. Sure, Reverend, we can use your services. High noon at the hotel. And you and your missus must stay for the party afterward." Then, grinning at Mattie, "I'm inviting everyone I know."

She embraced Cal once more, her arms around his waist, her head resting on his snowy shirtfront. How could she bear separation from him one more night?

Sensing her reticence, he whispered, "I want to do everything up just right for you, darlin'." Still holding her, he said to the Steinbaums, "All of you must be worn out. Mattie and I will have some supper at the hotel, then I'll deliver her to your place."

"I'm not a bit tired," Cindy said.

Abigail gave Mattie a quick hug. "Mama and Cindy and I will get everything ready for you. Oh, Mattie, it'll be a beautiful wedding."

Thirteen

MATTIE SETTLED HERSELF on the soft leather seat of the shiny new buggy, and Cal picked up the lines and urged the black horse down a dusty road sloping toward Last Chance Gulch.

"And now for a proper welcome." He looped the lines over the lacquered dash and drew her to him. His ardor banished the last of her doubt and she eagerly returned his kiss.

A soft whistle interrupted. A tall, freckled youth on a swaybacked pony was riding along beside, ogling them with a gleeful expression.

"Hey, Mr. Bodein," he called. "Is this the one?"

"This is the one, P.J." Cal grinned. "Mattie, this is Patrick Joseph Calahan. One of my best pals."

P.J. whipped off his straw hat, revealing a cowlick of reddish hair.

"But nosy," Cal teased.

"Gosh, Mr. Bodein, I just wanted to say hello to your lady."

Mattie smiled. "Hello, P.J." Young Calahan was a most appealing welcomer. But, suddenly bashful, the youth clapped his hat on his head and reined his pony in the opposite direction.

Cal laughed heartily. "Mattie, this is the place for us. Good town. Good people. My supplies won't be here for a month but I've already sold about half and ordered more. I've rented a storefront to warehouse the stuff, and . . . and this is the best part. As payment for goods, I've negotiated with three different prospectors for a share of anything they bring in. It's silver they're digging for now." His expression softened. "We could be rich, darlin' girl."

She smoothed her fingers over the fine leather upholstery. "This buggy must have cost a fortune."

"Oh, the whole rig is rented." He gestured toward the handsome horse and buggy, indicating they were inconsequential. "To prosper in my business, you have to look as if you're already in the chips." He nuzzled her neck. "But we'll soon have our own."

"I only want you, Cal. You . . . and our life together." Was this the time to tell him? She would have to tell him before the wedding. He had shown he loved her and wanted to marry her. Now he must know the truth. "Cal, I . . ."

"Here we are." He pulled up sharply on the lines. "The *Hôtel International.*" He gave the French pronunciation as he stepped from the buggy and swept off his hat in a mock salute toward the two-story frame building. In the warm twilight, several men in work clothes lounged on benches along the covered porch, backlighted by the flickering ceiling lamps in the central lobby. Through the wide windows Mattie could see an open stairway flanked by the hotel parlor to the left and a dining room to the right. Two women in stylish plumed hats were seated among the diners. Cal grinned. "Just like St. Louis."

"It's wonderful, but . . . ," and Mattie brushed back the lank wisps straying from the bun high on her head.

"You can freshen up in my room," Cal said. "We'll be living here till we find a better place."

As they entered the lobby, a thin, middle-aged woman, her long nose and sleek, center-parted black hair further narrowing her, assumed a proprietary position at the desk. "Evening, Charlotte," Cal said. "I want you to meet my intended. Mattie Hamil, Charlotte Gaines."

Mattie smiled. "I'm happy to meet you."

"Miss Hamil would like to refresh herself before supper," Cal said. The woman managed a curt nod. When they were up the stairs out of earshot, Mattie murmured, "Not especially friendly, is she?"

"Oh, Charlotte's all right. All kinds of people here, and everybody's standoffish till they get to know you."

His spacious room was furnished with a four-poster bed, a chiffonier and washstand, a large armoire, two matching armchairs, and a small heating stove, pushed back into the corner for the summer. Once inside, Cal kissed her again, pressing his body against hers. "We could have supper sent up."

"Maybe it's best if we dine downstairs," Mattie said. "That woman at the desk . . ."

He grinned. "All right, my girl, tonight you will be formally introduced to society. And tomorrow, we'll be married all nice and proper."

"I can't believe I'm actually here." She caught a glimpse of herself in the mirror above the washstand and winced at her disheveled, fatigued reflection. This was not the time to tell him.

"Bodein valet service at your command," he said. "Give me your things. I'll get the dust out of them while you wash up." And he danced about the room, shaking and brushing her skirt and shirtwaist, even dropping to his knees at her feet to buff up a shine on her shoes. By the time she was washed, dressed, and combed, she felt revived and thoroughly amused by the many-faceted man she was to marry.

When they descended the stairs, Charlotte Gaines' thin black eyebrows raised ever so slightly as she forced a smile for Cal.

"Remember, you're invited to the wedding tomorrow, Charlotte," he said as they moved on toward the dining room. "High noon, right here in the parlor."

Cal nodded to several of the men in the dining room and selected a corner table covered in blue oilcloth. The two women in plumed hats and their escorts gazed in open curiosity at Mattie.

"You'll like it here," Cal said. "The country's ripe for any kind of enterprise. We'll have us a dozen businesses." His easy smile delighted her as much as his vision of their future. "We'll build us a fine house. Have us a fine family."

She sobered. Was this the right time? Would her confession ruin the beautiful reunion? The wedding? Perhaps the whole marriage? There would never be a right time to tell him.

"Cal, I . . . we . . ."

His smile relaxed into a quizzical look as he realized she was trying to tell him something, but just then a ruddy, plump woman in a crisp apron came to take their order.

"Evenin', Gertie." Cal turned on his usual charm. "How's my girl tonight?"

Gertie blushed. "Lordy, Mr. Bodein, how you do carry on." She turned up the flame on the small kerosene lamp at their table and glanced shyly at Mattie. "Tonight we have beef stew."

"How about beef stew?" Cal asked Mattie. "Gert, this is Mattie. We're getting married tomorrow."

"Well now, ain't that nice." Her round face glowed in the lamplight. "Pleased to meet you, missus."

"We'll have coffee and some of your special raisin pie later." Cal watched Gertie amble toward the kitchen before returning his attention to Mattie. "Now what's so serious as to put a frown on that beautiful face of yours?"

"Cal, the family you mentioned . . . What I mean is, we . . . well, we already have a good start on that."

"I know, darlin'. You and I will be the beginnings of one of the finest families in the West. When the money starts rolling in, we'll build us a big brick house, maybe stone, with plenty of room for babies and nursemaids. Got to have nursemaids. Can't have you overworking yourself and ruining these pretty hands." He lifted her hand to kiss her fingertips.

"No, Cal, we're not waiting till the money starts rolling in." She took a barely perceptible breath. "We're starting our family now."

"All right." He grinned happily. "We'll get to work on it first thing after the wedding. But what's your hurry?"

"Cal, can't you understand?" She lowered her voice to a bare whisper. "Our baby is on the way."

Suddenly she had his sober attention.

"Cal, I'm already in the family way."

An aristocratic eyebrow arched. "In Bismarck?"

"No, St. Louis."

"So that's why you came all this way."

Mattie lowered her gaze to the blue oilcloth. "I'm more than three months along."

"And your sickness on the *Big Muddy,* that was . . . ?"

She nodded, this time looking directly into the dark intensity of his eyes.

A broad grin spread over his face. "Well, I guess we *do* have a head start." And he let out a muffled whoop, startling diners who turned to see him lean across the table and kiss her soundly on the lips. "Why didn't you tell me?"

"I had to be sure of your feelings first. I had to know you're marrying me for the right reasons."

"And now you're sure?"

Again she nodded and he took her hand in his. "Mattie, I was sure from the first moment we met at the Nesbits' party. There's never been anyone but you since. And there never will be."

Mattie's eyes misted.

"But wait a minute." A humorous frown knit his smooth brow. "How do I know you're marrying *me* for the right reasons?"

They laughed together, their eyes seeing only each other.

"I do love you, Cal."

He grinned. "Then that settles it. We're getting married tomorrow. All three of us."

Gertie came to set steaming plates in front of them.

"I've asked Doc to be my best man," Cal said between bites of the savory stew. "He came riding in yesterday. That's how I knew you were coming."

"Dr. Austin?" Mattie had nearly forgotten the grizzled old man. She touched her napkin to her lips. "Cal, he's supposed to have killed somebody."

"He's been in some sort of a scrape all right. Said it might not be sensible for him to show up at the wedding, but I talked him into it. He saved my life, Mattie. I'd have been a goner if he hadn't pulled me out of the river."

"But Cal . . ."

"Don't worry. He's a wise old buzzard. I told him to clean up. Loaned him a vest." Cal grinned. "Now I see why he was so all-fired insistent about me meeting you. He knew about the baby."

Mattie nodded. "I guess we both owe him something."

"You bet we do."

That weird old man to be best man at their wedding? Mattie gazed out through the waffled window glass at the soft circle of light falling across the rough boots of the men lounging on the porch. "I never thought it would be like this," she murmured.

"What would be like this, darlin'?" Cal's face appeared even more finely sculpted in the pale orange glow of the lamp.

"My wedding day." Suddenly she felt she would cry. "It's all so strange."

"Now don't you fret. A night's sleep and you'll be good as new. Let's have some pie, and then we'll get you over to Steinbaum's. I'm sure those women will want to fuss over you some."

"I am a bit worn out."

"Course you are, and I'm being selfish not to let you rest." He stood to help her from her chair, and she took his arm as they left the dining room. In the lobby, he called to the woman at the desk. "See if you can get a game going tonight, Charlotte. I'm feeling mighty lucky."

Lionel Steinbaum opened the door at the top of the stairway and welcomed Mattie to the five-room flat he'd furnished for his family above the store. A new tufted horsehair sofa and chair stood at one side on the oriental carpet, flanked by several carved-mahogany chairs that matched the big table in the adjoining dining room. Abigail and Cindy, clad in nightdresses, came from one of the bedrooms.

"Oh, Mattie, it's nice here," Cindy blurted. "We took a bath in a real

French tub. And Abby has a double feather bed." She fluffed her hair, damp from its shampoo.

"It'll be yours tonight," Abigail said. "We want the bride to sleep well."

"But I couldn't take your bed."

"Fiddlesticks. How many times does a girl get married? Cindy and I will spread some comforters here on the parlor floor. Now let me get the teakettle of hot water. Your trunk is in there beside the bed and the tub is ready for you. We have everything all planned for tomorrow. Mama's stirring up a wedding cake."

"Make yourself at home, dear," Sophie called from the kitchen amid a clatter of tins.

Mattie sat on the edge of the feather bed and took off her shoes and stockings. Abigail, wielding the steaming teakettle, and Cindy, sloshing a bucket of cool water into the high-backed, enameled bathtub partially screened on the far side of the high bed, soon produced the water temperature they prescribed for her aching body. Abigail handed her a cake of perfumed soap. "Here's your first wedding gift. Papa has a little bit of everything downstairs." Abigail followed Cindy into the parlor. "When you're ready, I'll help you rinse your hair," she called.

Mattie stepped from her clothing and slipped into the water. "It's heavenly," she moaned. Smoothing the elegant soap over her body, she noticed for the first time the gentle swelling of her lower abdomen, but she was careful to shield herself when Abigail came in with more water to rinse her hair. Feeling deliciously clean for the first time in weeks, Mattie crawled between the sheets and fell asleep while Abigail and Cindy chatted happily about wedding cakes and hope chests.

She woke to the sound of rain on the window pane and the aroma of fresh coffee. Putting on her wrapper, she went into the parlor, tiptoed past Abigail and Cindy sound asleep on quilts on the floor, and found Sophie preparing breakfast in the kitchen.

"Up already?" The older woman clucked with pleasure at the sight of Mattie's sleep-flushed cheeks and renewed appearance. "There's lots to do, so we'd better wake those sleepyheads." She poured coffee and gave the cup to Mattie. "Lionel has gone down to the hotel to see if your Mr. Bodein has everything arranged. I made a list. We should have some music—Lionel will play his violin—and he knows a woman who has a real pretty flower garden. He's going to stop there to see if she has anything in bloom."

"You're very kind." Mattie sipped the coffee while gazing at the rain-drops trailing down the narrow window pane.

"Rain is a bride's good luck," Sophie said, sensing her thoughts. "On *my* wedding day, a cloudburst."

How good these people are, Mattie thought. Going out of their way to make things special for me—much as my own mother would have done.

"Bring your dress, dear, I'll press it for you. You need time to dress yourself exactly right today." She indicated two flat irons heating on the stove. "Why, Abigail takes hours just to get ready for a party."

As if on cue, Abigail appeared in the kitchen. "Today, Mama, I'm started already."

Sophie kissed her daughter's cheek as she hurried into the parlor to waken Cindy and fold her bedding. Abigail poured a cup of coffee and sat at the table with Mattie.

"Life is funny," she mused dreamily. "Somehow I thought you'd be marrying Captain Tanner."

"No, Abby. I love Cal. Now more than ever. And I can't imagine being happier than I am right at this moment." She placed her hand on Abigail's. "But the captain is a fine man . . . for someone else."

"I should be so lucky." Abigail stared out at the rain.

Fourteen

MATTIE ARRIVED at the International Hotel, along with the Steinbaums and Cindy, at exactly noon. Sophie insisted on this little propriety—the bride not seeing the groom before the ceremony. She chatted merrily about the good omen inherent in the continuing drizzle and held her umbrella to shield Mattie's apricot dress during their dash from the buggy to the hotel porch. "Hurry, Lionel," she urged her husband. "Get inside and start playing." Lionel, clutching a violin case under one arm, attempted to hold an umbrella over Abigail and Cindy, who looked regal in stylish hats provided by Abigail.

It all happened very fast, it seemed to Mattie. Lionel's violin began the familiar strain of Mendelssohn. The cluster of people waiting in the hotel parlor turned to peer toward the wedding party at the door, then stepped back to make way. She recognized Gertie and Charlotte Gaines, but most of those gathered were strangers to her.

The Reverend Parkington stood officiously before a table where two vases of asters and snapdragons flanked Sophie's silver coffee samovar and a small wedding cake. Cal, his dark hair and sideburns freshly barbered, stood next to the table, thumbs in the vest pockets of his white suit. His eyes swept from Mattie's high-piled hair to the hem of her dress and an approving smile spread across his face. Beside him Dr. Austin, wearing what Mattie recognized as Cal's brocade vest over a stiff new white shirt, nervously clutched a bouquet of orange day lilies.

Cal took the lilies from Doc and stepped forward to present them to Mattie. "For you, darlin'." He took her hands and, feeling her trembling, winked affectionately to remind her of all that was between them. Parkington acknowledged her with a nod and, clearing his throat, began in an exaggerated baritone, "Dearly beloved." Lionel finished the wedding march with a flourish and dutifully took his place near Mattie in order to respond when asked who gave the bride away. But the question was never asked.

Instead, a flurry of whispers rose above the sound of the rain, causing Reverend Parkington to lose his place. He glared with annoyance in the direction of the whispers and when he resumed the service he was already into the vows. He stumbled over the name Matilda Hamil, adding to Mattie's discomfort. When she heard the words ". . . pronounce you man and wife," she accepted Cal's embrace with pounding heart. However brief and unsatisfying the ceremony, she had survived the journey into the wilderness, she had found him, and now she was bound to him by love and law. He tilted her face to his and kissed her tenderly on the lips. But the exquisite moment was shattered by an authoritative voice.

"Grab that man!" A stocky gentleman in a cutaway coat stood pointing his finger at them.

Cal startled defensively in Mattie's arms, but it was Doc Austin who made a dash for the side door.

"That's him! That's Austin!" the man shouted, running after the fleeing doctor. Others followed, one brandishing a pistol. Some of those present muttered angrily.

"What's he up to now?"

"How does he dare show his face here?" They turned hostile faces toward Cal and Mattie.

"Look, we hardly know the man," Cal insisted. "What's he done?"

A scrawny-necked man, his spiny hair slicked back from a beak-like nose, shook his finger in Cal's face. "I knew there was somethin' shady about you, Bodein. Can't trust nobody these days."

"Now, Willard." Cal smiled engagingly at Willard Motts, the lawyer he knew as a mediocre poker player. "I told you we only just met the man. He seemed like a good sort."

"We met him on the boat," Mattie offered.

Motts' sharp nostrils flared. "That scoundrel came to this town as a respected physician, then he took to . . . well . . . *doctoring* the bawdy women down on Clore street."

"That's a crime?" Cal said.

"Well, it's an indelicate matter to discuss with ladies present. But his doctoring was of a shady nature. If you get my meaning." Motts' eyes narrowed to focus on Cal. "A woman died."

"A hurdy-gurdy woman?" Cal asked bluntly.

"No. One of our own. A beautiful young lady, daughter of our bank president Seth Thornton."

Mattie felt her face flush. If it had been one of the bawdy women—someone like Cindy—no one would have cared. But another kind of woman had obviously sought Dr. Austin's services and something had gone wrong. A lump rose in her throat when she remembered he had offered her the same kind of "doctoring" on the boat. But out of compassion. Certainly not greed. He hadn't asked for payment. Perhaps his outlaw status had resulted from a similar situation.

Cal raised his hands to calm the group. "Please, folks, it's our wedding day. I'm very sorry to learn about the trouble, but this is not the time or place to resolve it. Now I want you all to meet my Mattie and to join us in some refreshments." But his words provoked disdainful looks and mumbled apologies. Willard Motts led his wife toward the door. The Parkingtons and others followed. Soon the only remaining guests were the Steinbaums, Cindy, Charlotte Gaines, and the youthful P.J. Calahan.

"Golly, Mr. Bodein," P.J. blurted, "is he an outlaw?"

Cal rumpled the boy's hair, which resembled orange jackstraws. "Things aren't always what they seem, P.J. This could all be just a misunderstanding."

"No misunderstanding," Charlotte muttered. "Lucy Thornton's dead all right."

"Such talk for a happy day." Sophie Steinbaum, clucking cheerfully, stepped toward the table. "Come have some cake, young man. Everybody. It's my special recipe. Lionel, play something peppy." She began serving wedges of cake while Lionel played a lively tune and Abigail and Cindy danced.

"Don't fret, darlin'. It has nothing to do with us." Cal took the two pieces of cake Sophie offered and gave one to Mattie. "Soon as this rain clears, I'm taking you for a buggy ride." His good humor was reassuring. "I want to show you around."

"I can't wait to see everything," she said. Anything to forget Dr. Austin and the unfriendly wedding guests. "And we've so much to talk about, plans to make." She nibbled a bite of cake, beginning to share some of Cal's enthusiasm. She admired his unflagging spirit and energy. And such startling good looks; tall and tanned, dashing in his well-tailored clothes. A truly remarkable man. And even more astonishing, he was now her husband.

"Oh, Cal, I'm so very happy," she murmured.

"Are you, darlin'? It must rub off."

"Are you happy, too, Cal?"

"Mattie, I'm the happiest man alive." Then to the others, "Now if Lionel can manage a waltz, I'm going to dance with my wife."

Next morning, Mattie woke to a clearing sky that showed patches of blue above the rain-washed town. After downing the private breakfast delivered by Gertie to their room, she stood at the window breathing in the sweet air and looking out at her new home. She would learn all about it, the people, the community, its customs and peculiarities, every brick, stone, and plank of its buildings.

Cal hurried her preparations for their mountain drive. "The world is waiting for us, darlin'," he said, toting the picnic basket of food he'd ordered from the accommodating Gertie's kitchen. "We'll tour the town, then I'll take you up Grizzly Gulch to the Fike claim. Mattie, I think they may have found something up there."

Mattie tucked her most serviceable shirtwaist into a skirt that now seemed a bit snug in the waist, donned straw hat and shawl, and followed him downstairs. Yesterday's rain had settled dust, and the town glistened in the sunlight. Driving the black horse past tidy storefronts where proprietors were just opening for the day, Cal pointed out a bakery, a barber shop, a Chinese laundry, and other services they would be using.

The early morning bustle of the streets soon gave way to a rutted wagon-track road that wound upward into the foothills. As the buggy wheels jolted over rocks and dipped into small washouts, Mattie delighted in the late summer landscape. Fragrant pine and plush spruce groves loomed on either side and, at certain turns in the road, allowed scenic views of the valley as the black's nimble gait carried them higher. She glimpsed a mule deer in the shelter of the forest and smaller creatures scurrying out of sight as they passed. Cal teased her about the possibility of encountering a grizzly bear. Twice he pointed out claims staked by men he knew, and Mattie noted among the rocky outcrops the tumbledown sluice troughs and windlasses of abandoned mines.

The hot sun was nearly overhead when Cal announced they were getting close. "We'll take the shortcut and walk up. We'd have to go the long way around to get the buggy up to the claim." He turned off the road, and Mattie gripped the seat as the horse skittered down a grassy slope, crossed a stream, and pulled up on the opposite side at the foot of a cliff. "Best let them know we're coming. Don't like to surprise anyone up in these hills." He called out a long halloo that echoed along the narrow valley. "It's our signal," he explained. "The first time I came out here, Boot Fike got nervous before he recognized me and put a hole through one of the traces."

"My word!"

"Just protecting his claim. There's quartz up here, I know that much. And where there's quartz, there may be silver."

Silver. Mattie knew nothing about mining.

Cal called another halloo as he looped the lines over a bush, then picked up the food basket, putting his free arm around Mattie's waist to lift her from the buggy. "You're mighty pretty today, Mrs. Bodein." He drew her to him and gave her a quick kiss. "Boot and Alfie should appreciate our visit."

He led the way along the stream bank, skirting the cliff, then followed the water course up a brush-filled gulch. The climb seemed an eternity to Mattie, who struggled after him, pausing only to free her shawl snagged on underbrush or to clutch her skirt up in front to keep from stepping on it. She was gasping for breath when the hulking, thick-featured Alfred Fike appeared from behind an outcropping, a rifle over his arm.

Cal grinned a greeting. "Morning, Alf."

Fike eyed Mattie with suspicion. "What'd you bring her for?"

"Mattie and I were married yesterday. Fine day for a honeymoon drive. Thought we'd pay you a little social call."

"Don't need no nosy visitors snooping around." He spit tobacco juice at a spot near Mattie's feet and wiped his thick lips.

"Aren't we partners in this thing?" Cal said.

Scowling, Alf turned and led the way among the boulders and scrub pines. "Come on then," he muttered. "Boot's workin' the hole."

After trudging another short distance, they came upon a bubbling spring with a lean-to and other signs of habitation scattered among mounds of rubble. Two gaunt mules stood hobbled near a high-boxed wagon containing a few barrels and crates of supplies. A wagon trail opposite led down the other side to connect with the road farther down the rocky gulch. Alf bellowed "Boot! Company!" toward a narrow crevice, enlarged and framed with timbers to make a low entrance. Boot emerged, grubby and sullen, dragging his stiff leg through the rough passageway.

"So it's you." Blinking in the bright sunlight, the slight man wiped his sleeve over his dust-blackened face and politely tipped his hat to Mattie. He limped toward the cold fire pit where a few grimy utensils lay in the ashes. "Alfie, cook up some coffee. Can't you see we're entertainin' a lady?"

Cal set the picnic basket on a flat rock. "Looks like you boys are working hard."

While Alf hurried to start the fire, Boot eased himself to the ground, stretching his braced leg out in front of him. "When's that equipment gonna get here?"

"We gotta have dynamite," the oafish Alf blurted. His fire blazed up and he sauntered to the spring with the coffeepot.

"The shipment should be here in a month or so." Cal settled onto a fallen log and waited for Boot, obviously the dominant brother, to continue. But Boot sat silently rubbing the muscles of his good leg and watching scornfully as Alf returned from the spring, slopping water from the coffeepot the entire distance, threw in a handful of coffee from a sack, and set the pot in the fire.

"We've brought a picnic," Mattie said to lighten the mood. She didn't like Alf's vacant eyes, but she disliked the brooding look of Boot Fike even more. There was something sinister about him. She opened the basket and handed a chicken sandwich to each of the men, took one for herself, and seated herself beside Cal on the log. The gaze of both Fikes followed her, Alf openly staring, Boot observing her furtively. "There are more in the basket," she said, as the brothers wolfed their sandwiches.

"Having any luck with your digging?" Cal ventured after a while.

"Wouldn't waste time on this hole if it didn't show signs." Boot remained sullen. "Too soon to say yes or no." Alf dug into the basket for another sandwich.

"Can I be of any help? I mean, I'd be glad to take ore samples to be analyzed," Cal offered.

"It ain't your call to do nothing but get us those supplies," Boot said, sudden anger flaring. "You've already got yourself a third of anything we haul out, so don't come pussyfootin' up here again. When we bring in the goods is when you'll know about it."

"Fair enough." Cal handed the sack of ginger cookies toward the brothers.

The coffee boiled over and Alf got up to pull it from the fire with a stick.

"Sorry, ma'am," Boot said, his surly attitude changing to one of polite shyness. "Ain't got but two cups." He indicated the filthy, dented tins beside the fire. Mattie hurriedly produced the four cups Cal had asked the hotel to pack.

"Well, this is a right fancy picnic." Boot erupted with an unexpected cackle as he traced the cup's swirled blue-and-white enamel pattern with a grimy finger. "Alfie and I ain't used to such eats."

Alf, his mouth full of sandwich, grinned as he poured coffee all around. "We'll get a bellyache for sure." He bent over to reach into the basket again.

Boot's good leg shot out and gave him a sharp kick on the backside that sent him sprawling. "Don't mind him, ma'am. He's got no manners."

"There's plenty," Cal said. "Go ahead, Alf, have another."

Alf sheepishly took still another sandwich and sat in the dirt beside the fire to noisily wash it down with coffee. They sat in silence, Mattie merely pretending to sip the unpalatable beverage.

After a few moments, Boot cast a menacing glance at Cal. "Some diggers get cheated out of what's due 'em." His voice rose pointedly. "That ain't goin' to happen this time." The man seemed to have only two moods, shy and demonic. "You play straight with Fike," he growled, "and Fike plays straight with you."

"You can count on it," Cal said casually, getting to his feet. "And you can reach me anytime at the hotel."

Boot, struggling to his feet, suddenly grabbed Cal's shirtfront and jerked him forward. "Look, fancy man. I mean what I say. No one pulls a fast shuffle on Boot Fike. If you prize this dainty lady of yours . . ."

Cal's surprise turned to anger. "Now just a minute . . ."

"Only looking out for what's mine." Boot released his grip on Cal's shirt, his eyes narrow with suspicion. "I know you'll look out for what's yours." His glance darted toward Mattie.

"What are you trying to say?" Cal demanded.

"If we strike pay dirt, Bodein," Boot continued, "—and I mean just *if* we hit something—the assaying will be handled by a disinterested party. Got that? Everything fair and square."

Cal looked the belligerent Boot straight in the eye. "Rest assured I never do business any other way." He picked up the basket and took Mattie's arm, nodding to the two prospectors. "Good afternoon, gentlemen."

Fifteen

DOC AUSTIN had vanished, but his participation in the wedding had created a barrier between the good citizens of Helena and the new Mrs. Bodein. Greeted curtly in the street, Mattie found her attempts to be neighborly were politely rebuffed. After the unpleasant excursion to the Fike claim, Cal refused to take her with him on his visits to other prospectors in the mountains, and in the weeks that followed she spent much of her time at the Steinbaums'. While Abigail worked for her father in the store, Mattie sewed baby garments on Sophie's sewing machine and encouraged Cindy to learn to crochet.

"I'm no good at this." Cindy handed over the puckered doily she'd been struggling with for several days.

Mattie smiled at the snarl of loose threads and dropped stitches and put aside her own embroidering of a tiny flannel kimono for the baby.

"Maybe we should concentrate on your lessons. Did you finish the arithmetic problems I gave you?"

Cindy pouted. "I'm no good at numbers either."

Touched by the girl's misery, Mattie put her arms around the frail shoulders, but Cindy pulled away and flung herself face down on the sofa.

"Can't crochet. Can't do 'rithmetic," she wailed.

"You're reading now. That's quite an accomplishment."

"But I want to amount to something. Like you and Abby."

"Cindy, you're very young. Seventeen is just the beginning."

"I can't stay with the Steinbaums forever. I want to earn my own way. And I won't go back to . . . to how things were in Bismarck."

Mattie searched for a comforting suggestion. "How would you like to work for me?"

Cindy sat up, blinking at the idea. "Doing what?"

"With the baby coming, I'll need someone to help."

Cindy jumped up and whirled around the room, her misery forgotten. "That's it! I can be a nursemaid. A nursemaid with a little white apron and cap like I saw in *The Police Gazette.*" Mattie withheld her reservation about the girl's aptitude for child care.

"Come on, you two." It was Abigail. She had abandoned her tasks downstairs. "It's no fun being cooped up in that hot store on a day like this," she declared. "Let's take the buggy and go for a drive."

"Oh, let's," Cindy echoed. "It's nice out, and now that I have a job . . ."

"A job?" Abigail went into the bedroom and began changing her prim dress for something cooler.

"I told Cindy she can work for me when the baby comes," Mattie said. "I think we're both feeling a bit confined these days. That buggy ride sounds like a fine idea." Now free of morning sickness, Mattie welcomed a change of scenery, the chance to be active. "Let's ride up in the mountains. It's beautiful up there."

"Mama, would you like to go for a drive?" Abigail called to Sophie, whose industry was accompanied by the familiar banging of pots and pans in the kitchen.

Sophie appeared in the doorway. "For a drive?"

"We're going up in the mountains where it's cooler."

"Dead I wouldn't be caught on a mountain."

"Why not, Sophie?" Mattie asked. "Do the miners worry you?"

"Miners I don't bother about. It's them grizzly bears."

The girls laughed. "Grizzly bears?"

"They don't call it Grizzly Gulch for nothing," Sophie muttered.

"Mama, I assure you we'll give a wide margin to any critter larger than a chipmunk. Now come with us. You've been fussing around that kitchen all day."

"Do come, Sophie," Cindy said, already tying her bonnet.

"I said no, and that's what I mean." Sophie had made up her mind. "But you girls go on if it's so brave you are."

The young women enjoyed their afternoon up the mountain, refreshed by the cooler temperature and relaxed by the beauty of the fragrant forests. They saw no bears but were enchanted by the plentiful deer, a wolverine, several raccoons, squirrels, rabbits, and a coyote pair that crossed the road directly in front of them.

"This is glorious," Mattie said. "Just what I needed to put things in perspective."

"What's perspective?" Cindy asked. "Is that like a perspective husband?"

"You mean *pro*spective husband," Mattie corrected.

"Thinking of getting married?" Abigail teased.

" 'Course not." Cindy sighed dreamily. "But maybe someday I'll be married like Mattie."

"Maybe someday we'll both be so lucky," Abigail said.

"But meanwhile," Mattie interjected, "let's get out like this more often. There's so much to see and learn about . . . while you're waiting for husbands, I mean . . . and I'm waiting around for Cal."

Cal had rented a vacant building on Water Street and hired a carpenter to make it weathertight. He supervised the installation of shelves and ordered a sign painted across the high, false front. Bodein Enterprises. Mattie often went to admire his efforts, but as her pregnancy became apparent, the stares and whispers of other women in the streets prompted her to curtail even that pleasant activity. She relied more and more on her outings with Abigail and Cindy to ward off "cabin fever" and her increasing loneliness.

Cal also spent considerable time in the saloons "making contacts." He assured her such contacts were essential to promote the outfitting business and, more important, to enhance his reputation as a card player. She treasured their pleasant hours together, but often at night after she retired, he went out to "sit in on a few hands" in games that lasted into the wee hours.

"I'm doubling the spring shipment," he told her one evening as they finished their usual supper in the hotel dining room. "With payments on new orders and my poker winnings, we've got a respectable bank account. Soon be able to start thinking about building. We're going to have the best hotel and casino in town. Three stories high. The finest brick." He patted her rounded belly affectionately as they climbed the stairs to their room. "We'll have us an apartment on the top floor. I've got it all planned. High ceilings, fine woodwork, the best of furnishings."

"But Cal, raising a child in a hotel . . ."

"We'll build us a house when the casino begins to pay off." He tossed his hat on the bureau and settled back on the bed, his arms folded behind his head. "There's a corner lot available right on Broadway. Choice location." Noticing her lack of enthusiasm, he held out his arms. "Come here, darlin', and let me cheer you up. Aren't you glad things are going well?" Mattie stretched out beside him, her head on his shoulder. He *was* gentle and caring, working hard for their future, and she hated to complain. But she decided to share an idea she'd been nurturing.

"I feel useless all day," she began. "I've read everything I can get my hands on, and I'm spending so much time at the Steinbaums' I'm surprised they don't bar the door."

"I know it's lonely for you, but it won't be forever. We'll have us a real home before you know it."

She hesitated a moment. "Cal, I've been thinking. Your shipments will be here in a few days and there's no one at the store . . . to take orders, I mean, and run the place while you're making contacts."

"Thought I might hire P.J."

"P.J.? Why, he's only a boy. Doesn't he go to school?"

"I don't know that he's ever been to school. He was about four, I think, when his mama died and his dad brought him to Last Chance. His dad since died, too."

"But how does he live?"

"Does odd jobs at the boardinghouse. He gets by. Everybody likes him."

"Even so, you need someone with some business sense to keep your accounts. Someone responsible. Like me."

"Maybe. But where would I find someone like you?"

Mattie propped herself on one elbow to see if he were joking. Men are such dunces, she thought. Such marvelous dunces.

She laughed. "Not someone *like* me. Me! I could run the store."

Cal looked at her in astonishment. "You? With a baby on the way? Why, I couldn't have my wife . . ."

"But you could. I'm good with figures and you could teach me what I need to know about the merchandise." Just the idea made her feel more alive than she had in weeks.

Cal seemed surprised by her enthusiasm. "It might be too much for you."

"No, it wouldn't. It would make us real partners, give us something to share . . . besides the baby, I mean."

A grin overtook his skepticism. "All right, my girl, if that's what you want, that's what we'll do." He snuggled close. "But I'll still get P.J. to keep an eye on you."

"Cal, I don't think you realize I'm serious about this," she said. "I'd expect to be a full partner. With all the responsibility you'd give any other partner."

"Mattie, you're a wonder." He chuckled. "Here I'm offering to take care of you like a grand lady, and you say you want to work like a man."

He's still just humoring me, she thought. But he'll learn . . . in time. "I'd like to hire Cindy, too," she added. "She's bright and energetic, and I'd enjoy having her around."

Cal sighed in mock acquiescence. "Okay. Cindy, too." He tipped her face toward his. "I swear, I sure got me one hell of a woman."

Mattie made her first proprietary visit to the remodeled storefront the next morning. While Cal procured a rolltop desk and chair for her, she checked his order list and made notes on available shelf space to accommodate the coming supplies and equipment. In the busy days that followed, she set up a bookkeeping system and made out bills of sale for those who had ordered. In October, when both shipments arrived by freight wagon from Fort Benton, she worked with Cindy and the wiry P.J. stocking the shelves with pans, tubs and buckets, rope, cable, lanterns, sledgehammers, axes, picks, shovels, tents and bulk canvas, washboards, nails, bolts, and dynamite. Cal, pleased by Mattie's efficiency, allowed her full rein, suggesting only that the dynamite be stored in the shed out back, instead of under the counter where Cindy and P.J. had stacked it. Then, while Cal made the rounds delivering to prospectors, she and Cindy polished the windows and waited for business.

The stocks moved out quickly. By the time heavy snow fell late in

November, little remained to be sold. But prospectors had come down from the mountains looking for odd jobs that would get them through the winter and stake them for the next season, and Mattie catalogued their orders to be shipped in the spring.

Cal noted that the Fikes were not among the idle prospectors. "I'm more certain than ever that those two have hit something up there," he commented to Mattie, "or they would have quit for the winter."

"I'm glad they aren't hanging around town. Boot seems to resent our having a share in their diggings."

"He's greedy all right. But he and that lummox brother of his agreed to our partnership when I staked them. They're just grumpy now that there may be something to divvy up."

"Just the same, I don't like him," Mattie said absently as she totaled an order that would increase their inventory to include carpentry and blacksmithing tools, carriage hardware, harnesses and saddles, fishing tackle, cooking utensils and coal-oil lamps. "These are things folks have inquired about," she reported. "I see no reason to limit our sales to prospectors and miners."

"Let's advertise that we'll take orders for anything," Cal said. "It's bigger items of machinery and equipment that bring in the real profit. And we should carry a line of firearms and ammunition."

"Anything except clothing, yard goods, and household," Mattie said. "I don't want to take trade away from Steinbaum's mercantile."

Cal grinned. "Whatever you say, darlin'."

"And I'm ordering some books on mineralogy and metallurgy," she said matter-of-factly. "For myself. I want to know more about this mining business."

One cold late afternoon, Mattie sat reading in one of the chairs arranged for customers who liked to visit around the potbellied stove at the back of the store. She closed the book and gazed out at the snow-flakes swirling in the winter twilight, obscuring the view of the mountains she had come to love. Cal would soon be coming to take her to supper.

It was a strange sort of life here on the frontier, but despite the isolation and uncertainty she was beginning to feel a growing content-ment. More and more Cal relied on her judgment, his good-natured patronizing of her ideas changing to amused admiration. In some re-spects, he was overly generous, she thought. He often bought her presents she thought frivolous. A yellow silk parasol and filigreed Ori-ental hair combs hardly suited her new life as a storekeeper, but she accepted them affectionately. She delighted in his gifts of a walnut cradle and a hand-carved rocking horse, touched by his tender thoughtfulness even though it would be a long time before their child would be big enough to ride the little horse. When she felt the sharp jab of a tiny elbow or knee protesting the confines of her womb, she marveled at what a miracle the whole process was. A miracle that had carried her across a wilderness and bound her irrevocably to a man she loved. A miracle that gave meaning and purpose to this new way of living. Her child would grow up in this frontier place, knowing no other. In time, the Bodeins would be respected members of the community.

In front of the store, the dark figure of a man in a battered hat, a heavy overcoat covering him ears to ankles, loomed out of the blowing snow. He peered at the Bodein sign, then pushed open the door and came in. Mattie raised her heavy body from the chair as he came forward, squinting at her in the dim light.

"Mrs. Bodein?" He pulled off his hat.

"Dr. Austin!"

If the old man's white shaggy beard and unkempt hair weren't enough identification, there was no mistaking Doc's milky left eye. He put his finger to his lips and, brushing at the snow on his shapeless overcoat, slipped into one of the chairs near the stove, holding out his hands to its warmth. "Wind's gettin' worse," he said.

"What are you doing here?" Mattie's tone was more of concern than accusation. She glanced toward the door wishing Cal would hurry.

"I've come to collect my debt." He winked at her, but his good eye showed no humor.

Sixteen

CAL'S RIG pulled up in front, and he whistled to himself as he looped the lines over the hitching post and entered the store. His whistling stopped abruptly when he caught sight of the visitor.

"Doc!" He hurried forward to shake the old man's hand. "We've been wondering about you."

"Found me a shack in the mountains. Some abandoned claim. But I ran out of feed for Blacky and Buttercup. Anyway, I figured by now you'd have laid some groundwork for our little game."

"Now, look, Doc. I'm a respected citizen in this town, a businessman. You can't ask me to jeopardize that."

"No reason to. I just want you to trounce those skunks who ran me out. Willard Motts, that shyster lawyer who came to the wedding, he's one of 'em. And old man Thornton. He's the real cause of his daughter's unfortunate death."

Cal and Mattie stared at Doc, his expression grim in the light flickering through the isinglass on the stove door. "What do you mean?"

"Lucy Thornton came to me for help." He glanced toward the darkened front windows before continuing. "Her pa had thrown her out. She was in the family way all right. Said it was her pa that had done it to her. Said if I didn't help her, she would kill herself."

Mattie gasped at the shocking story. Cal stared skeptically.

"Seth Thornton's lower'n a rat's belly," Doc continued, his words tinged with venom. "When she hemorrhaged I sent word to him, but he wouldn't come. Said he'd disowned her." Doc shook his head sadly. "I couldn't save her. When I took her to her home, her pa and Motts came after me. Said they'd ruin me. There was a tussle and Thornton gouged my eye with his cane. I had to make a run for it."

Cal and Mattie exchanged uncertain looks.

"I didn't expect those weasels would be at your wedding or I wouldn't have showed myself. Guess you're friendly with 'em."

Cal nodded. "I've played cards with them."

"Good. Now it's not just the satisfaction of seeing 'em squirm I'm after," Doc continued. "I got to have a stake to get out of these parts."

"How much?" Cal didn't like the idea of dipping into his bank account to help the old codger, but Doc *had* saved his life.

"A thousand dollars ought to get me back east and set me up decent."

"A thousand!" This was steeper than Cal had expected.

Doc unbuttoned his overcoat in the glowing heat from the stove. The borrowed brocade vest was now as tattered and grimy as the rest of his attire. He bent toward them. "Here's how you work it. Invite those polecats to a special game. Let 'em win some to keep 'em dangling, make the stakes high, and when you get the greedy buzzards to thinkin' they're taking you, you clean 'em out."

Cal seemed intrigued with the challenge. "But what if *they* wipe *me* out?"

"They won't," Doc said. "You'll see to that."

Cal raised a sculpted eyebrow. "You're asking me to cheat?"

"I'm asking you to do whatever the situation requires."

Mattie, alarmed at the implication, interrupted. "Cal, couldn't you just loan him the money?"

"I can't fork out that much. We have commitments." He grinned to reassure her. "Besides, I rather like the idea of getting it from the hypocrites who've been giving us the cold shoulder."

"But if you lose . . . ?"

Cal turned to the old man. "Doc, I need every penny I have to secure a piece of land and get a start on building a hotel. I'd be risking my future here."

"Dag-nabbit! I risked my hide coming back here." Doc narrowed his good eye at Cal. "But I knew you were a man of your word. If I recall, you agreed to this when you were drying out at my camp on that sandbar."

Cal pondered a moment. "All right, Doc. I'll see what I can do."

Mattie clutched her husband's arm. "But Cal . . ."

"You got a good man here, Mattie." Doc glanced around the store. "Now do you have a cellar or somewhere I can keep out of sight till the action's over?"

"There's a loft." Cal pointed to a narrow open stairway in a back corner. "It's warm where the stovepipe goes through, and you can make yourself comfortable on that stored canvas. We'll bring you some eats and water."

"I'd be much obliged if you'd grain Blacky and Buttercup for me, too," the old man said, moving at once toward the ladder. "They're out back in your shed."

Mattie watched with apprehension as Doc's ragged figure disappeared into the dark opening at the top of the steps. He closed the trapdoor behind him and they heard him shuffling across the plank floor above them.

"It's all right," Cal murmured. "He won't be here long." He took her arm. "I'll get him some supper from the hotel and feed his horses. Then I'll see what I can do about settling that debt."

———

The opportunity to set up the special game came later that very evening in the private back room at the Last Chance Saloon, an establishment that attracted a prosperous group of businessmen, including the targeted Motts and Thornton. The two sat at a table with the balding, heavy-jowled brewer Otto Crouse when Cal entered the room carrying a bottle of whiskey from the bar. Crouse invited Cal to sit in.

"Feeling lucky tonight, Bodein?"

"That's just it," Cal said, pouring himself a shot of whiskey. "I'm feeling mighty lucky. In fact, I'm feeling so lucky, I just might like to double our limit." He took a fat roll of bills from his pocket and tossed it on the table beside the poker chips he had purchased on the way in.

The others eyed the money and glanced hesitantly at each other. They knew Cal to be a shrewd poker player, but tonight he sounded cocky and he was drinking, something they hadn't seen before.

"Suits me," Motts muttered. "Ante up." He tossed a ten-dollar chip onto the table. Motts, with his sharp nose and slicked-back hair, actually looks like the weasel he is, Cal thought.

Crouse began their usual game of five-card stud. His jack was high and he checked his hole card. "This is going to cost you twenty," he said, adding two chips to the pot.

"I'm in." Thornton fingered the gold chain across his portly middle. Moderate betting followed the deal around the table.

Crouse won the first pot with a pair of jacks. Willard Motts, who took the second with a ten-high straight, gloated as he raked in the pile of chips. "Maybe you aren't so lucky tonight after all, Bodein."

"The evening is young, gentlemen." Cal won an occasional pot but, as the game stretched toward midnight, had lost several hundred dollars before he began to feign panic and nervously poured more whiskey around the table.

"What's this about playing for high stakes tonight, Bodein?" Thornton snorted. "You aren't getting cold feet, are you, just because you lose a few rounds?" He downed his whiskey. "Let's up the ante, no limit."

Cal agreed to the higher stakes. From that point on, when his cards cooperated, he bet larger amounts on each hand, employing his considerable skill at bluffing, but always able to produce a winning hand when his bet was called. Soon chips and cash were stacked high on his side of the table.

Motts began to fidget and his betting became more reckless. Crouse grew increasingly agitated and Thornton continually checked his pocket watch, but the game continued until Cal held bank drafts from the three men totaling nearly three thousand dollars. "Well, gentle-men," Cal said, draining the glass he'd been nursing all evening. "It's been a long day. Time for me to hit the hay."

"Now just a damn minute." Motts rose from his chair. "You're not walking out of here with eighteen hundred of my money."

"Give us a chance to even this up," Thornton demanded. "Let's go one more hand."

"Never let it be said that I'm not a sporting man," Cal said. "All right, one more hand. Hundred-dollar ante."

Crouse shuffled carefully, tapping the deck to even the edges and ruffling it in his big hands before starting the deal. Motts had a queen of clubs showing, Thornton a club five spot, and Crouse the deuce of spades. Cal showed the king of diamonds. Each man checked his hole card.

"The bet is one hundred dollars," Cal said.

"Now wait a minute," Motts glared. "What are you trying to pull?"

"One hundred dollars says my hand beats yours."

"Come on, boys," Crouse grumbled. "We got to see this thing through." The three made out drafts to cover, and Crouse dealt an-other round face up. This time Motts had the queen of hearts added to his queen of clubs.

"Pair of queens," Crouse called out.

Thornton drew the seven of hearts, and Crouse another spade, the ace. Cal showed a second diamond, the ten.

"My queens have you," Motts said gleefully. "Calls for another hun-dred." He marked his draft.

"And raise you one," Cal said confidently.

"I'm out," Thornton muttered. "Christ Almighty, who got me into this?" He scooted back his chair, poured another whiskey, and downed it in one swig, grimacing more at the sight of his losses in the middle of the table than the taste of the liquor.

"A pair of queens can't beat the power in my ace of spades," Crouse said, covering the bet. Motts scowled as the ten of clubs fell beside his two queens, but he bet another hundred. Cal's card was the nine of diamonds.

"Three diamonds showing," Crouse announced. "Possible flush."

Motts sneered and raised. "Another hundred."

Cal covered. "And here's one extra says you don't have another of those pretty ladies hidden away."

"Ach! I'm out," Crouse grumbled.

Cal's hole card was the ten of hearts, giving him only a pair of tens. He needed another king to beat Motts' two queens, but Motts' nervousness revealed a lack of confidence, and Cal felt certain he didn't hold a third queen.

Crouse dealt the last round face down. Cal checked his card. The king of clubs.

Beats of sweat stood on Motts' ashen forehead. "It'll cost you a hundred to see my hand."

"And another to see mine." Cal pushed his chips ceremoniously into the pot. Then he leaned back in his chair, thumbs in his vest pockets, enjoying the weasely man's flustered scribbling of a draft to cover the raise.

Motts slapped it onto the table, his face livid. "All right, Bodein. Let's see that diamond flush."

Cal showed his cards. "Two pair. Kings and tens."

"Why, you bluffing bastard!"

Crouse turned over Motts' cards to reveal only the pair of queens. "Now, Willard. Bodein won fair and square."

"Okay. Okay." Motts sputtered. "But I want a show-down hand. Double or nothing."

"Sorry, gentlemen. It's past my bedtime." Cal began gathering the drafts into a neat pile.

"I'm warning you, Bodein." Motts puffed up in rage. "You owe me a chance to get even."

Cal, ignoring him, sorted the cash and drafts. "Would one of you mind telling them out front that I'm ready to cash in these chips?"

"You sonofabitch!" Motts made a move toward Cal but Crouse stopped him. Thornton pulled himself up to his full, portly height, his ruddy face mottled with rage. "Bodein, what Motts means is that if you don't give us a chance to even things up, we'll see that you're through in this town."

"I welcome a rematch, gentlemen, but some other time," Cal said. "Now I must say goodnight." He nodded to the three defeated gamblers and strolled from the room with practiced nonchalance.

Seventeen

MATTIE SLEPT POORLY that night, rising several times to peer out at the blowing snow, hoping to hear the sound of Cal's buggy in the empty street or catch a glimpse of him coming from the livery stable. Wind whipped at the windows, rattling the glass, and whistled around the International Hotel sign on the porch roof below. She put a stick of wood in the stove, then pulled a quilt from the bed and, wrapping herself against the chill, settled into a chair in front of the frosty window.

Cal had taken food to Doc and planned to check the action at the saloons, perhaps get up a game with the men Doc had mentioned. Until now, she had not worried much about Cal's gambling. He was so lighthearted about it, and he had built a sizable account at the new Bank of the Territories with his winnings. But surely his talent at cards would not always triumph. Could anyone be that skilled a player? Didn't luck play a part? What if the pressure of Doc's unusual request caused him to lose?

But she mustn't worry. She had accepted the fact that her husband made a good part of their living at the poker tables. Before long, the store would support them. And perhaps later, there would be a hotel and casino.

A horse and wagon crunched through the drifts in the street. Muffled by the falling snow, the harness jingled briefly as the wagon crossed the white swirl of light from the hotel lobby, then faded into the night, leaving a lonely silence. It wasn't Cal. She clutched the quilt tighter about her. After the baby came, she would not feel so alone when Cal was out. Three more weeks, Dr. Ward said.

She startled when Cal opened the door and danced exuberantly across the room. "Hallelujah, darlin', we're in the chips." He tossed his snowy coat and hat on a chair and knelt beside her, hugging her bulky body inside the quilt. "Mattie, I played Doc's game tonight."

"And you won?"

"Better than that. I cleaned out their cash and had them writing bank drafts to cover their losses. What do you think of that? But why are you sitting here in the dark? You'll take a chill." He lit the lamp, added wood to the embers in the stove, and helped her into bed. "Mattie, it was like taking candy from a baby. Look here. More than four thousand dollars!" He spread his winnings before her. "More than enough cash to pay Doc, and the rest, my girl, fattens our bank account."

Mattie would never understand the casual transfer of so much money, first across the gaming table, then to Doc, a man they hardly knew.

"Aren't you happy, Mattie? Aren't you proud of me? I didn't think it would be that easy."

"You know I'm proud of you, Cal." She caressed his cheek with her hand, his happy face alone a reward for her. And with the money there would be no delay in getting Doc away from the store. "Will Doc be able to travel in this weather?" she asked. "What if those men find out he's in our loft?"

"I'll settle with him in the morning and he'll be on his way as soon as the snow stops." He undressed and climbed into bed beside her. "Don't you worry about a thing," he murmured sleepily against her neck. Mattie lay listening to his soft breathing and the sighing wind till nearly dawn when sleep finally came.

When she woke to a gray day, snow still rustled against the windows, she felt leaden and her head ached. Cal, already groomed and dressed, stood at the chiffonier, recounting the money.

"Go back to sleep," he said. "I'm going to settle up with Doc and deposit this in the bank. Then I'll bring you a hot breakfast." He slipped the money packet inside his coat and sat down on the bed beside her. "You should stay in today, darlin'. No reason you need to get out in this storm."

The idea was inviting. "There won't be much business at the store," she murmured. "Cindy can handle things. And you and I can spend the day together."

Cal shook his head. "With Doc hanging around, I better mind the store myself," he said. "I'll send Cindy over here to keep you company."

He was right. It was better that Cindy not know about Doc hiding in the loft. But the reminder chased away all desire to go back to sleep, and by the time Cal returned with coffee and hotcakes, she was dressed and waiting in the chair by the window. He made her comfortable with her breakfast tray and, as he left for the store, kissed her affectionately, promising, "Tonight we'll sit around the stove together like a couple of old folks—and make plans."

Dawdling over the breakfast, Mattie watched the pelting snow drift around the buildings and form odd patterns across the deserted street. The hotel seemed unusually quiet. This would be a good chance to help Cindy with her studies. She had learned to read quite adequately during their spare time at the store and was now practicing penmanship. Mattie had grown fond of the girl, whose keen perception and energy never faltered. Cindy talked about wanting to enroll at the new high school, just opened in September with a freshman class of four young women, but Mattie hadn't the heart to tell her she would need many months of intensive tutoring in a variety of subjects before she could hope to qualify. And Cindy flitted from one thing to another like a butterfly.

A soft knock sounded at the door.

"Come in, Cindy," Mattie called, rising to greet her friend. But when she opened the door, Boot Fike stood before her, a long, heavy coat dusted with snow dwarfing his slight frame.

She gasped in surprise.

Fike's whiskered face was splotched red from the cold. He politely removed his hat. "Come to see your mister."

"Why, he's . . . he's not here." Her eyes darted toward the window, then, fearing to let them know she was alone, she added, "But he should be back any minute."

"We'll wait." Fike stepped into the room, favoring his braced leg. "Come on in, Alfie." His brother stepped into view from the hallway. Alf, his vacant expression pinched by a greasy sheepskin cap, wore a gunnysack that smelled of wet feed tied over the shoulders of his coat. He grinned at Mattie as he entered and closed the door behind him.

"If you gentlemen will just wait down in the lobby . . ." Mattie tried to leave but Alf pressed his broad back against the door, blocking her way.

"We'll wait right here." Boot limped to the window and peered out. "We got news for Bodein."

Mattie glared at Alf. "I'm afraid I must insist that you wait downstairs." If she could get them out the door, she would slip the bolt.

Alf reached out a pudgy hand and grasped her sleeve. Mattie pulled away in alarm.

"Let her alone," Boot barked, taking a leftover hotcake from the tray on the chiffonier and stuffing it into his mouth. Then he turned to Mattie. "Usually expect better manners from a lady. Came all this way in the cold. You could at least give us a friendlier welcome." He flashed a sidelong glance at her belly. "I see you've been making good use of these long winter nights."

"Hey, give me one of those flapjacks," Alf whined.

Mattie straightened her sleeve. "I'll get you some breakfast . . . downstairs." Again she moved toward the door, but this time Boot grabbed her arm.

" 'Scuse me, ma'am." He shoved her into the chair. "You're not going anywhere till we've had a chance to . . . talk." His eyes narrowed. Was it lust she saw there? Hatred?

"All right." She steadied her breathing. "Sit down. We'll talk."

Boot dragged the other chair up close and sat glowering at her. Alf shuffled toward them, his eyes focused on Mattie. But Boot lashed out, pounding his brother sharply on the knee with the edge of his hand.

Alf squealed, "Cut that out!" and shoved his brother's chair with all the force of his huge bulk. Boot fell onto the floor, the brace on his leg thudding against the pine boards.

Mattie dashed for the door. But as she reached for the knob, Alf, grinning from his momentary triumph over his brother, caught her around the waist and slammed her back against the wall. She tottered, stunned.

The door opened and Cindy burst in. "Mattie . . ."

Alf lunged at Cindy from behind the door, locking his arm around her neck. He tried to kick the door shut, but the girl's struggle threw him off balance.

Mattie ran from the room, her awkward belly slowing her as she hurried down the stairs. "Help! Someone, help!" The lobby was empty. Charlotte Gaines' usual post was deserted. She ran into the dining room. No one in sight. "Is anybody here?" she called frantically.

Gertie shuffled from the kitchen. "Just me today," she said. "Cook is snowed in."

"Two men . . . ," Mattie gasped. "Upstairs. They're hurting Cindy. We've got to get help!"

Gertie seemed bewildered by Mattie's anguish. "But there's nobody here. What two men?"

"Those Fike brothers. Get someone from the stable," Mattie directed. "I'll go for the sheriff."

Gertie now grasped the urgency and scurried to the kitchen for her coat. Mattie swooped a tablecloth from a table, wrapping it around her head and shoulders as she ran out into the street. Sheriff Karns' office was just a few doors away. Mattie had a nodding acquaintance with the sheriff, a pleasant, grandfatherly type, whose reputation was built more on pacifying minor complaints than with enforcing the law.

Wind-driven snow bit into her face and whipped at her flimsy wrap as she stumbled through the knee-deep drifts. The sheriff's office door was locked, but she could see lamplight from a side room. She pounded on the glass. "Sheriff Karns! Come quick!" She rattled the knob. "Sheriff Karns!" She heard a chair scrape and the sheriff appeared from the side room. Surprised to see her standing there in the snow, he quickly unlocked the door. "What is it, Mrs. Bodein?"

"Hurry," she pleaded. "Two men broke into my room. They've got Cindy Dougherty."

Her distress shifted Sheriff Karns into action. He buckled on his gun belt. "Who are these men?"

"The Fike brothers. Prospectors. Hurry!"

"Are they armed?"

"I don't know." Why is he wasting time asking questions? Mattie had already started back toward the hotel.

Karns grabbed his hat and coat and followed her. From the other direction came Gertie, flushed and puffing, gripping an iron bar with both hands, followed by the stocky blacksmith, Pete, carrying his hammer.

"At the end of the hall!" Mattie led the way up the stairs, then stood aside as the sheriff tried the door. It was bolted.

"Open up in there! It's Sheriff Karns," he shouted. They could hear muffled sounds inside, a scurry of footsteps. "Come on out, fellas. Let's talk this over." The response was the scrape of a window sash being raised. "They're going out the window!" Karns muttered. "Stay here." He propelled the hammer-wielding Pete into guard position before the door and dashed back down the stairs.

"Cindy!" Mattie called. "Open the door!" There was no reply. "Can't you break it down?" she urged the blacksmith.

"Better see what the sheriff says about that."

Panicked, Mattie pounded on the door with both fists. "Cindy! Can you open the door?" After what seemed an eternity, the bolt was slipped from inside and the door swung open. Boot Fike stood before them. The blacksmith stared at him, realizing for the first time that there actually had been an unsavory character behind the locked door. Gertie shrank back with alarm, holding the iron bar at the ready.

"There's been an accident," Fike said. "The little lady . . ."

Mattie pushed past them. In the corner near the stove, Cindy lay crumpled on her side, her clothing tangled around her upper body. Blood trickled from her nose. Her lip and cheek were bruised and swollen.

"Oh, Cindy!" Mattie knelt beside her and straightened the disarrayed clothing. Then she took the girl in her arms, holding her close, rocking back and forth.

"Lord a mercy!" Gertie murmured.

It was then that Mattie felt a cramp in her lower abdomen and a gush of warm wetness flowed down the inside of her thighs.

Eighteen

SHERIFF KARNS rushed into the room, his pistol drawn. "Damn! He got away!" He swung the weapon toward Boot Fike's throat. "This the other one?" His eyes widened as he saw Mattie huddled on the floor with Cindy.

"Ain't done nothin'," Boot snapped. "That brother of mine . . . got a little playful with the girl here."

Playful? Mattie resisted the impulse to claw the sneer from his face.

"Is she hurt?" the sheriff asked.

Gertie's round cheeks flushed with anger. "Now what does it look like to you?" She strode to the open window and slammed it shut.

"I'm locking you up." Karns prodded Boot toward the door with the pistol barrel, nodding to Pete. "I'll need some help to go after that other one."

"But I ain't done nothin'," Boot protested.

"We'll see about that after we fetch Dr. Ward."

"Lordy," Gertie blurted. "Dr. Ward rode out to Unionville early this morning. It's the Kubecki woman's time and old man Kubecki came on horseback to fetch the doc 'cuz she had such a time with her first one."

Dr. Ward in Unionville? Mattie winced as another cramp surged through her. The warm wetness had spread through her petticoats. She knew birth was imminent after the bag of waters broke. Oh, why now? Just when Cindy needed her.

"Someone please go after Sophie Steinbaum." Mattie held her handkerchief to the girl's bleeding lip. "Cindy lives with the Steinbaums above their store."

"I'll get her," Gertie offered, following the men out the door.

"Check back with you as soon as I can," the sheriff called over his shoulder.

Mattie hugged the trembling girl closer. If Cindy hadn't happened in, she herself would have been attacked. Of that she was certain. She caught her breath as another sharp contraction racked her body.

Cindy opened her pale eyes. "Did they hurt you, too, Mattie?"

"No. Just feeling a little shaky. Here, let me help you." The two struggled to their feet.

Sophie and Lionel arrived out of breath and anxious. "You poor child," Sophie clucked, putting her arm around Cindy's frail shoulders. "Let's get you home." She adjusted the rumpled cloak around the still-dazed girl, then noticed Mattie seemed shaken, too. "You're white as a ghost. You better stay here and rest awhile. That snow is drifting terrible."

Mattie sat down on the bed. "Lionel, Cal's at the store. Will you go tell him what's happened?"

"Right away," Lionel promised. "Now don't you fret. We'll look after Cindy."

"And I'll bring you a nice hot pot of tea," Gertie said.

Then all were gone. Mattie eased back on the pillow. She should have told Sophie about her water breaking. But even if the baby was coming, it would be some time yet. First babies took a while. She could tell Sophie what to do if the doctor didn't get back. She closed her eyes trying to remember births she'd attended with her father. She hadn't wanted it to be like this. The baby coming early. In a snowstorm. In the wake of this ugliness. The Fikes' brutality. Having a baby was supposed to be a beautiful experience. In your own bed. In your own home. With a kindly doctor standing by. In the springtime. With your husband bringing flowers. Not like this. Tears flowed down her cheeks. Not like this.

Gertie brought the steaming tea, mumbling her own anger and out-rage. "That poor little girl. They ought to string up those fiends." Then, noticing Mattie's tears, "Now, you mustn't take on so. She'll be all right."

"Gertie, do you know anything about delivering a baby?"

Gertie's cheeks crinkled into a smile. "Lordy, no. Ain't never had one myself." She blushed. "Never married, you know." Then, as she grasped the implication in Mattie's question, her expression changed to concern. "Oh, Mrs. Bodein. You don't mean . . . ? It's not your time?"

Mattie folded back a layer of her petticoat to show the spreading stain.

"Lord a mercy!" Gertie stood riveted.

"Bring some towels. And hot water. I want to wash up." Mattie shuddered. "Those men . . ."

"Now you just stay still till I get back." Gertie moved her heavy body with unaccustomed speed, her voice trailing back from down the hall, "Here's Mr. Bodein comin' now."

Mattie heard Gertie mumble a hasty explanation, and Cal hurried into the room. "Darlin', what happened? Lionel said Cindy . . ." He stopped when he saw her on the bed, her face tensed with another contraction. "My God, Mattie."

"It's the baby." She arched her back to relieve the ebbing contrac-tion.

"The baby?"

"It's coming early. My water broke."

Cal's dark eyes widened. "What should we do? Have you sent for Dr. Ward?"

"He's in Unionville. Sophie will have to help me. I know what to do."

Cal sprang to his feet. "I'll go after Dr. Ward."

"No, Cal. He's delivering Mrs. Kubecki." She held out her hand to him. "And I want you here, not out in this storm somewhere, when our child is born." Another stabbing contraction. Perspiration beaded on her face and she gripped Cal's hand till the pain subsided. "You better go for Sophie," she murmured. "The pains are too close together. Maybe something's wrong."

"I'll get Doc Austin. We settled up but he's still in the loft." Cal started for the door. "By God, he owes me a favor now."

"But he'll be arrested if he's seen. The sheriff is out looking for Alf Fike." She braced for another contraction as Cal dashed from the room.

Gertie was back with an armful of linens and a hot teakettle. "Lordy, looks like you're in a bad way," she sputtered, pouring hot water into the basin. "Mr. Bodein said he's goin' for help. Now let's get you out of those clothes." Soon the big woman had Mattie washed up and wrapped in a warm flannel nightgown. Mattie concentrated only on getting through the next wave of pain.

"Doc!" Cal shouted as he entered the empty store. "Doc! You've got to come quick." Racing up the steps, two at a time, he flung open the trapdoor. "It's Mattie." He poked his head into the darkened loft. "She's having the baby!"

Doc lay sprawled on a pile of canvas near the stovepipe, light from the grill around the pipe reflecting on his whiskered face. He pulled himself to a sitting position. "So soon."

"She's had a shock. Some prospectors . . . I don't know the whole story . . . but she needs you." Cal climbed into the loft and tugged the old man to his feet.

"Cal, I can't go out there. They'll throw me in the hoosegow. You know that. Ain't Dr. Ward lookin' after her?"

"Ward's in Unionville."

"Well, there used to be a midwife over in Chinatown. Name's Nu Ling. See if you can get her."

"Doc, you're coming if I have to drag you. Mattie thinks something may have gone wrong." Cal slipped off his coat and hat and handed them to Doc. "Here. Put these on and you won't be recognized. I'll wear yours."

Doc grinned through his shaggy white beard as Cal donned the lumpy old overcoat and battered hat, and he pulled on Cal's well-tailored Prince Albert coat and felt homburg. "They say clothes make the man."

"For God's sake, hurry." Cal led the way down the ladder.

Blowing snow obscured nearly everything in the street as they hurried through the drifts to the hotel. They encountered no one in the lobby or on the stairs. Gertie met them at the door wringing her hands. "I don't know what to do for her, Mr. Bodein." Then, recognizing Doc, she stood back, her expression a mixture of astonishment and relief. Doc hurried to the bed where Mattie lay in a tangle of sweat-soaked bedclothes.

"Dr. Austin," she whispered.

"Well now, Mattie, I see you're anxious to have this baby." Doc scanned the room, saw the steaming teakettle and the stack of linens, and winked his good eye at Gertie in approval. "I'll just wash up and see what we can do about it." He glanced at Cal and tilted his head toward the door. "Won't be needing you for a while."

Cal stood, distraught and forlorn-looking in Doc's overcoat and hat.

"Come on, Mr. Bodein," Gertie said, tugging his sleeve. "This ain't no time for you to be hangin' 'round. You look like you could use some good strong coffee."

"Gertie, you stay," Doc said. "I might need you."

Gertie's rough cheeks flushed. "Lordy, Doc, I ain't no nurse. I can't stand seein' folks in pain."

Mattie moaned with a primal urgency that propelled Gertie toward the door.

"We'll be just downstairs, darlin'," Cal said in apprehensive farewell.

Doc, shirt sleeves rolled to his elbows and smelling of pine soap, quickly examined his patient. "Yup, you're sure in a hurry." He arranged folded towels against her back and knees to make her more comfortable and covered her with a sheet. He put more wood in the stove, then pulled up a chair beside the bed.

Another wave of pain obscured Mattie's awareness. She dwelt in a faraway place where ocean waves came rolling onto the shore from far out at sea—rolling, rolling, engulfing her with pain, intensifying, higher still, holding her in a crimson agony beyond endurance, then ebbing, ebbing, gradually ebbing into a momentary void. Each cycle seemed an eternity. She tensed, dreading the next wave as it formed and surged toward her, gathering cruel strength. No, no. Not another so soon. She moaned and braced her body for the onslaught, more terrible than the last, pressing relentlessly upon her. She heard a frightening noise—her own anguished cry. Then the pain again subsided. She gasped for breath.

"Now, Mattie, things're goin' fine," Doc murmured. "I want you to loosen up and let it happen. Don't fight it. Your body knows what to do."

Mattie wanted to plead, "I can't. I can't." But she could only prepare for the next contraction. As it surged upon her, she heard Doc's quiet voice. "Now, don't tighten up. Just ride right along with it." He rubbed her hands, unclenched her fists. "Let it happen. Keep your breath coming. Puff. That's it. Puff." The soothing drone of his voice and the touch of his hand eased her fright and, in the depth of her struggle, mustered her strength to allow her body to be the instrument of this terrible yet irrepressible life force.

All sense of time was lost in the twilight of her suffering. But finally the pain peaked and she responded to a desperate urge to push the child out. "It's coming," she screamed. "It's coming."

"Yup, it's comin'." Doc expertly eased the crowning of the head. "Good size, too."

A few more pushes delivered the baby. A smile spread across Doc's whiskers. "It's a girl." Mattie felt only relief as Doc held up the limp, bluish child that was her prize. "She's had a tough time of it," he said, patting the baby's back as he held her upside down to drain the air passages. "Fast delivery's sometimes hard on 'em." But the tiny lungs did not fill with life-giving air. Doc rapped the back sharply. No breath came.

In moments, Mattie's triumph turned to yet another agony. She watched in helpless exhaustion as Doc suddenly held the small gaping mouth to his own and breathed into it. He patted the back and massaged the chest. There was no response. Why didn't the baby breathe? Oh, please. Don't let her die. Deftly balancing the baby, Doc poured cold water from the pitcher into the basin and lowered her into it. Mattie heard a faint wheezing gasp, then a kitten-like mew from the bluish bundle. Tiny arms and legs twitched.

"She's coming around." Doc's voice remained steady as the baby's gasping turned to a rapid noisy wail and her color flushed a healthy pink. But his hands were shaking when he placed the child in Mattie's arms, and she knew that for those few excruciating moments her daughter's life had been tenuous. Now the rosy round face, surrounded with wisps of dark hair, seemed incredibly small. Mattie touched a soft cheek, and the tiny rosebud mouth turned toward her finger, making sucking motions. The baby was very much alive . . . and she was beautiful. She had dark lashes and long slender fingers. Like Cal. Mattie raised grateful eyes to Doc.

"Thank you," she whispered.

"No need." He busied himself completing his tasks with inveterate skill, while the exhausted Mattie savored the miracle that was her daughter, safe and healthy in her arms and crying lustily.

"I think she wants to eat," Mattie said.

"Then you better not keep her waiting." Doc rolled down his rumpled sleeves. "She had her own idea about when to be born. I've a feelin' she'll always be in a hurry for whatever she takes a fancy to."

Nineteen

"RIGHT NOW she wants her father," Mattie said. "And I know he's waiting to see her."

"I'll hustle him up here." Doc took Cal's coat as he went out the door. "Maybe Gertie'll dish me up some supper."

Mattie lay back against the pillows. She felt a profound peace. A floating. Her body—the stranger that with wanton disregard for all other considerations had delivered her of a child—once again seemed acquiescent, hers once more, and pleasantly numb in the absence of pain. Her mind supremely conscious, in charge once more, she wanted to luxuriate in every moment of this new state of being.

The dark, dreary day had deepened into evening. The wind continued and snow still sifted against the window, but no storm could worry her now. She turned to watch the quiet breathing of the sleeping baby beside her and snugged the flannel wrapper around the warm little body.

Cal burst into the room, his cravat flowing askew, his shirt rumpled. How unlike Cal. Mattie smiled, but her effort to reach out to him revealed her exhaustion.

"Mattie. Darlin'. You all right?" He hurried to the bed, took her hand, and pressed her fingers to his lips. He smoothed the hair tangled around her face.

"We're both fine."

His gaze shifted from Mattie to the bundle beside her. Amused by his astonished look, Mattie lifted the baby so he could admire the fringe of dark, silky hair. Then she opened the wrapper to reveal the baby's hands, knees, and feet.

"Well now, ain't she something." He touched a tiny fist. "By Jove, Mattie, she looks like my mother."

"Does she, Cal? I'm glad." Mattie lifted the baby toward him. "Would you like to hold her?"

"Well, I don't know." He was both eager and hesitant. "Is there a trick to it?"

"No, silly. Just lay her in the crook of your arm and support her with your other hand." Awkwardly Cal followed instructions, beaming with delight when the little mouth puckered in a sucking motion. "You know, she does have the same shape face and dark hair as my mother. Let's call her Saya. That was Mother's name. A fine old southern name." He looked at Mattie as if sensing for the first time the enormity of his responsibility to this wee bundle.

"Saya." Mattie savored the sound of it. "It's unusual but I like it. Then her middle name will be Elizabeth after *my* mother."

Cal chucked the baby under the chin. "Hello there, Saya Elizabeth Bodein." He began to dance the child around the room, singing in nursery-rhyme cadence. "Saya's pretty as a picture. Saya's smart as a whip. Saya's got a silly daddy, who's going to make her proud."

Everything Mattie had hoped for seemed culminated in that very moment. How lucky she was. How rich and rewarding life could be. She would cherish this image of her extraordinary husband, his dark eyes filled with delight in the little daughter who looked so much like him.

The baby began to emit small plaintive cries. "If you two are through dancing," Mattie said, "I think it's time for refreshments."

Cal waltzed the baby back to her. "A pretty girl has to dance at her own birthday party, doesn't she?" He eased onto the bed beside them, cradling Mattie against his arm, watching with admiration while she held the baby to her breast. Saya nursed vigorously for a few moments, then fell asleep. Mattie, too, closed her eyes.

"My girls are all tuckered out," Cal said. "You rest while I see that Doc gets back to the loft."

In their joy, she had forgotten to tell him how Doc had breathed life into Saya. There was so much to talk about. But there would be time for that. Now she must sleep. She barely felt his parting kiss.

Downstairs, Cal found Doc in the kitchen joshing with Gertie as he topped off his meal with a slab of raisin pie. Both looked up expectantly when Cal entered.

"I have a *beautiful* daughter," Cal said. "I'm much obliged to you, Doc." He clapped Doc on the shoulder, then grabbed Gertie and swung her around. "Gertie, I have to tell you the truth, you're not my best girl anymore. There's someone else now."

"Pshaw, Mr. Bodein." Her eyes crinkled in merriment. "Sure glad you got your baby and your missus is doin' good, too. Seems like this's a real special day even with the storm and hardly no customers. Guess in some ways it was a good thing." She glanced at Doc. "Like I told the doc here, just the sheriff and a couple of his men was in a couple times for hot soup and coffee. Still didn't ketch that other brother." She waved the coffeepot at Cal. "Can I get you somethin'?"

"Not just yet." Cal took Doc's overcoat and hat from the peg where he'd left them and pulled them on. "I'll see that Doc here gets . . . gets where he's going." Better not mention the loft, he thought. "And then, my dear Gertie, you can serve up a fine supper for Mattie and me. I'm sure she'll be hungry by the time I get back." He looked out toward the street, pitch black except for the white whirl of snow in the lamplight from the lobby.

Doc placed some coins on the counter. "I'm much obliged, Gertie. Kinda like the old days, eh?"

Gertie nodded soberly. "I never did feel you was done right, Doc."

Doc tipped Cal's homburg in a courtly gesture.

Seeing no one in either direction, Cal stepped out into the blowing snow. The icy particles stung his face and he turned up the frayed coat collar as he motioned Doc to follow. They hunched into the cold, wading the drifts that clogged the dark street.

Before they'd gone far, a man's voice echoed above the wind. "Hold it right there."

"Get out of sight!" Doc whispered as he ducked into the alley.

Cal hesitated. "You go on. I'll cover for you." He looked around but could see no one through the darkness and swirling snow. Where had the voice come from? Was it him they were addressing? Had they spotted Doc? He heard nothing but the wind. Better lead them off Doc's trail. He crossed the street toward Steinbaum's mercantile. I'll just mosey along unconcerned, he thought, then circle around and head back to the hotel. Check on Doc later.

"Halt, I say! And get your hands up."

Cal stopped short in the shaft of lamplight slanting down from the Steinbaums' upstairs apartment. As he raised his hands in the air, he saw a reflection in the pitch-black store window and was startled by his own image in Doc's battered old hat and overcoat. My God! I'm not recognizable in this getup. Some overanxious deputy could make a mistake.

"Don't shoot!" he shouted into the whining wind. He lowered his right arm and began hurriedly unbuttoning the coat. The distorted image in the waffled glass held his glance. Like a carnival mirror he'd seen once in St. Louis. How he'd changed since St. Louis. His reckless days were behind him now. He had Mattie. And little Saya. He grinned into the dark window as he struggled to remove the overcoat.

A luminous streak of red flashed behind his reflection. The crack of gunfire. Cal's confident brow arched slightly in a grimace of surprise. He did not feel the hot blow of the bullet nor the cool press of snow against his cheek when he fell in the dim wash of light from the upstairs window. He did not see the shocked expression of the man sporting a deputy's badge who ran to him, pistol drawn, nor hear the deputy's astonished gasp as he looked upon the patrician features of Calvin Bodein, a bullet hole now leaking blood through a silky sideburn.

Twenty

CINDY LAY on the horsehair sofa in the Steinbaum parlor, her eyes wide but unseeing. Abigail sat nearby picking at her embroidery, twisting the silken thread and jabbing the needle through the layer of linen. When she could no longer see the tracing in the darkening room, she lighted a lamp and resumed her work by its yellow glow. "That's better now, isn't it?" Her attention shifted between the fancy work and the distraught girl on the sofa.

Cindy had barely spoken since they brought her home that morning, salved her bruises, and tried to make her comfortable on the sofa. She had refused to cry, and Abigail murmured reassurance as best she could, while Sophie scurried about the kitchen making fresh noodle soup and strong tea. Since then Cindy lay staring at the ceiling, ignoring all words of comfort.

In desperation Abigail decided to share a bit of news she'd been keeping for several days. "Cindy, I got a letter from Captain Tanner."

Cindy turned dull eyes at Abigail's announcement.

"He's planning to come out here when the river thaws. Isn't that splendid?"

Cindy turned her swollen face to the wall.

Lionel, having closed up the store for the night, trudged up the stairs, cursing Montana winters for slowing his business. His mind was more on the abused girl than on tidying his displays of union suits and overshoes. He found Sophie in the kitchen. "Is she all right yet? I could help maybe?"

"Poor little *shiksa*. It's a terrible thing that's been done to her," Sophie whispered to him across their small table. "Something like this she didn't deserve."

"Brutes," Lionel muttered, sipping the hot soup she placed in front of him.

The sound of a gunshot echoed from the street. Lionel hurried into the parlor as Abigail sprang to the window and peered out at the snowflakes dancing across the narrow shaft of light from their lamp.

"Maybe they got that hooligan." He pushed aside the lace curtain.

"Look, he's lying in the snow," Abigail cried.

Cindy bounded from the sofa and ran to the window. When she saw the crumpled figure below, she turned to Abigail and Lionel, a wild look of triumph in her eyes. "I hope he's dead!"

Abigail hugged the rigid girl. "Everything's going to be all right, Cindy."

"He'll get what's coming to him," Lionel offered. Then, smiling at Cindy, "I'm glad you're better."

"I'm not better," Cindy snapped with renewed bitterness. "I'll never be better. He made me . . . dirty."

"But surely you've . . . you've known men . . . men like that . . . before." Lionel couldn't help himself. He had to say it.

"No!" Cindy screamed, her eyes flashing. "Never! Not like that. Never!" She lashed out at Lionel with both fists. "Never! Never! Never!"

Abigail restrained her. "We understand, Cindy."

Lionel, regretting his remark, edged toward the door. "I'll go see what's happened."

"Wear your muffler," Sophie called after him. She joined Abigail and Cindy at the window, watching as Lionel approached the two deputies standing over the lumpy form in the snow. Suddenly he dropped to his knees, opened the loosened coat and pressed his ear to the fallen man's chest. Frantically he grasped the man's wrist and began rubbing it with snow.

"That's odd," Sophie said.

"It ain't Fike!" Cindy cried. "Why, it looks like . . ." The two young women rushed for the door.

"Your mufflers," Sophie called after them. But Cindy and Abigail were already halfway down the stairs.

"Bring him in here." Lionel held a match to the wall lamp behind the counter, illuminating the front of the store.

"Jesus," muttered the deputy in the heavy mackinaw, shaking his head. "Why'd he go for his gun?"

"It's Cal!" Cindy gasped. "Is he bad hurt?"

Lionel brushed a stack of woolen hosiery from the polished counter. "Put him up here."

"Someone get a doctor," Abigail cried, noticing then the trickle of blood oozing from a small dark hole near the temple.

The second deputy, helping to lift the wounded man onto the counter, peered closely at the surprised look in Cal's wide eyes. "Bodein don't need no doctor. He's dead."

"Dead?" Cindy moved closer. "But he can't be. I . . . Mattie . . ."

"Why didn't he identify himself?" the deputy repeated. "When I ordered him to halt, he put up one hand but went for his gun with the other. Doggonnit, why'd he do that? I didn't want to shoot nobody."

Lionel patted Cal's pockets. "There's no gun. It's a terrible mistake you've made." The group stood stunned.

The deputy shed his gloves and gently closed the dead man's eyes. "Gertie told us this afternoon his missus was havin' a baby today, too."

"Mattie's having her baby?" Abigail confronted the deputy but didn't wait for his shrug. She dashed out into the snow toward the hotel, followed by Cindy.

"Tell my wife we've gone to Mrs. Bodein," Lionel instructed. And he was out the door before Sophie appeared in the warm circle of lamplight at the top of the stairs with his muffler.

As Abigail and Cindy, bareheaded and cloakless, struggled to open the hotel door against the shrill wind, Gertie ambled curiously from the dining room into the brightly lighted lobby. "What's all the hubbub?" Gertie asked.

"Cal . . ." Cindy choked back the first tears she'd shed since her own ordeal. "Someone's got to tell Mattie."

"Mr. Bodein ain't here now, and Missus is sleeping," Gertie said. "I'm fixin' a nice supper for 'em when Mr. Bodein gets back."

"He won't be back," Abigail said, her dark eyes welling up. "He's been shot."

"Shot?" Gertie clapped a rough hand to her ruddy cheek. "Dead?"
Abigail nodded.

"Lordy! And her just havin' her baby."

"Is Mattie all right?" Abigail started for the stairs, but Gertie stopped her.

"You can't just barge in with news like this. Lordy, how'd all this happen?" Without waiting for an answer, she herded them toward the dining room. "He was just here not ten minutes ago. So proud of his baby girl."

"A little girl?" Tears streamed down Abigail's cheeks.

Gertie frowned. "You sure about Mr. Bodein?"

"He's dead all right." Lionel, shivering, had followed them into the warm dining room. "We carried him into the store." He shook his head in sad disbelief. "It's all a bad mistake. Deputy thought he was that Fike fellow."

"Lordy. Lordy." The distraught Gertie moved toward the coffeepot.

Cindy flung herself into a chair and buried her face in her arms. "It's all my fault."

"Don't be foolish," Abigail said, stroking the girl's hair. "How could it be your fault?"

"I said I hoped he was dead," Cindy cried. "But I didn't know it was Cal. I didn't want Cal to die."

"Course you didn't." Lionel, too, tried to comfort her. "It's nobody's fault. Just a terrible accident."

"But if it hadn't been for me," Cindy sobbed, "they wouldn't have been looking for Fike."

Gertie placed a stack of cups on the table and circled with the steaming coffeepot. "A real pity . . . with Missus birthin' and all."

Abigail sat forlorn. "How are we going to tell Mattie?"

"Don't see how we can . . . at a time like this." Lionel's face was ashen behind the flowing beard.

"I will tell her." The strong words came from Sophie. Face flushed with the cold but snug in her warmest cloak, she crossed from the doorway to Lionel and draped his muffler around his neck. "Mattie needs a mother now," she told the anguished group. "Or the next best thing." She started toward the stairs.

"If there's anything I can help with . . . ," Gertie called after her. Tearful and uncertain, Abigail and Cindy settled back to wait with Gertie. Lionel indicated he would talk with the deputies on the handling of the body.

Sophie sat quietly in Mattie's room, watching the young mother and her baby sleeping peacefully in the big bed. She lowered the lamp, determined to keep vigil as long as Mattie slept. A new mother needed rest, and heaven knows, a new widow needed every ounce of reserve strength. Both coming at once like this . . . Poor child.

It was nearly midnight when the baby stretched and whimpered. Mattie awakened instantly, weary and unfocused before she remembered, then a soft smile lighted her face as she reached for the tiny, squirming child.

The snow seemed to have stopped. Only the wind whispered at the dark window. Mattie startled at seeing her friend in the room. "Sophie, what are you doing here?" The baby began to cry lustily. "How long have I slept?"

Sophie straightened her stiff knees, rose slowly, and crossed to the bed. "So it's a baby girl." And with Mattie's concurring nod, "Has she got a name yet?"

"It's Saya. After Cal's mother." Saya's cries of distress ceased instantly as Mattie put the baby to her breast. "Look, Sophie, how she works at it."

"She's strong, like her mother," Sophie said. "While you feed her, I'll have Gertie fix you a bite. I can see you're famished, too."

"Yes, I guess I am. But Cal's bringing supper for the two of us. I'll wait for him."

"You tend to little Saya," Sophie said. "I'll check on that supper and be right back."

Feeding her new daughter delighted Mattie. The tiny mouth seemed perfectly fitted to her nipple. Nature's design was truly marvelous. Man and woman. Now child. So this was what life was all about. Saya nursed briefly, then fell asleep again. Mattie changed the damp square of flannel and had wrapped her daughter snugly for another snooze when Sophie returned with a supper tray of beef noodle soup, bread and butter, a glass of milk, and a pot of hot tea.

"But where's Cal?" Mattie asked. "We're going to eat together."

"Cal's been delayed," Sophie said. "You go ahead. You need your strength."

Delayed? I hope something hasn't happened to Doc, Mattie thought.

"New mothers need nourishment," Sophie continued. Her words were more a command than a comment. "The food will build you up again. The milk and tea will bring in your own milk." She placed the baby in the cradle, propped pillows behind Mattie, and set the tray beside her. While Mattie ate, she bustled about putting the room in order, chatting about babies and new mothers, child care and postpartum responsibilities. A whirlwind of conversation, Sophie talked of the shared joys of mothers and daughters, of herself and Abigail, of how Mattie's mother would have loved little Saya.

"Sophie," Mattie interrupted at last. "You're very kind. Having you here now is like having my own mother with me. Helping me to be a good mother to Saya. How can I ever thank you?"

Sophie stopped short. She had done what she could to strengthen Mattie for what was to come. She pulled a chair next to the bed, swallowing hard to hold back the emotion lumped in her throat.

"Sophie, what is it?" Something *was* wrong. "Sophie, what's keeping my husband?"

"Mattie." Was there a kind way to say it? "Mattie, dear." Sophie touched her hand. "There's been . . . an accident." Sadness shadowed her kind eyes.

"An accident?" Mattie sprang upright, panic pounding in her breast. "Sophie, is Cal all right?"

"No, Mattie. He's been shot."

"Shot!" The word cut Mattie like the bullet itself. "How? Where?" She gripped Sophie's arm, attempting to pull herself up from the bed. "I must go to him."

"It's too late, my dear."

Mattie felt her own heart stop. "Too late?"

"A sheriff's deputy made a terrible mistake." Tears streamed down Sophie's pudgy face. "Mistook your Cal for that Fike brother."

"I've got to go to him," Mattie cried. "Where is he?" She struggled to push Sophie out of the way. Her bare feet touched the icy floor.

"It's no good, Mattie. You're too weak to be out in this weather. Lionel is looking after him."

"I'm going!" Mattie screamed.

Sophie restrained her. "Your baby needs you now. You must take care of yourself . . . for her."

Mattie sank back onto the pillows, her heart pounding. A terrifying pain threatened to split the top of her head. Her thoughts refused to come together. The wind at the window became a mournful cry. Sophie took Saya from the cradle and placed her beside Mattie, but Mattie could not bear to look at her. She had come halfway across a continent to give this child a father. Now had he been snatched away from them both? Surely it couldn't be true. Had she dreamed it? Maybe this day hadn't really happened. Her thoughts raced in blurred frenzy. Cindy. The Fikes. The terrible labor. The relief of birth and little Saya's first breath. Now Cal. It couldn't be real. Despairing, she turned to the baby. Saya was real all right, a tiny, breathing body with a small round face edged in wisps of dark, silky hair; a living, helpless being demanding her complete commitment.

With a cry of anguish, Mattie clasped the child in her arms. She wept bitterly, her sobs muffled in the warmth of her new daughter. She could not stop the tears that fell onto the tiny flannel wrapper. A woman is like a river, her mother had once said. In a few short hours, Mattie's body had produced the gush of waters, the bloodied bluish lump that became a glowing child, the surge of life-giving breast milk— and now the flow of tears that would not stop. A woman is like a river. Mattie understood it now.

After a while, when she could cry no more, she murmured to the compassionate Sophie, "Will you bring him to us?"

Twenty-one

A FEW MINUTES LATER, the body of Calvin Bodein was carried to his wife's room in the International Hotel. Sophie Steinbaum had cleansed the bullet wound and applied a small patch of gauze to cover it before complying with Mattie's request.

"They've brought your mister," Gertie announced quietly as she held open the door for Sheriff Karns and a deputy bearing the makeshift stretcher. She arranged the two chairs next to the bed to support it and its grim burden. Mattie, sitting upright, thanked them with a nod, and the group withdrew downstairs to give the young widow privacy in her grief.

The reality of death came slowly as she studied the still body of her husband, focusing on the small square of gauze at his temple, the only impediment, other than the unnatural pallor, to his fine profile—the smooth brow, the dark eyebrows, the chiseled nose with its delicate nostrils, the wide, well-shaped mouth. She reached out to touch his hair, damp near the bandage where the wound had been washed. Only a moment ago he had danced around the room cradling his new daughter in his arms. Now he lay before her—a lifeless caricature of himself. Had she ever really known Calvin Bodein? How would she explain him to Saya? How could she tell her all that he was . . . and could have been?

She touched his hand. It felt cool in her own icy fingers and she glanced with annoyance toward the stove. Had the fire gone out? The window rattled and bitter wind howled the onset of winter. She hadn't counted on winter in Montana territory without Cal. How could she survive here alone? Oh, Cal, don't leave me.

As she pressed her lips to his hand, it slipped from her grasp and dangled askew between the bed and the improvised stretcher. Leaning forward, she tried to embrace him, her head against his chest, as she had done countless times in this very bed. This time there was no comforting thump of his heart beating beneath his vest, no male warmth of his body, no return of her embrace. Instead, his other arm slid from its resting place at his waist and swung briefly in an unnatural position, one knuckle rapping the floor. Oh, Cal. Tasting the salty, streaming tears on her lips, she wept with the moaning wind.

Sometime later when the baby whimpered, Mattie dried her swollen eyes, opened her nightdress, and lifted the child to her breast. The nipple was sore now from earlier feedings, but the sharp, new pain cleared her head.

"Your daddy's here to say good-bye," she murmured, tears looming afresh. "He won't be with us anymore." She gazed at the face of her husband, then turned back to the suckling infant. "He loved us, Saya."

A soft rap at the door preceded Sophie's entry into the room. She looked hesitantly at Mattie nursing her baby, then at the corpse of Calvin Bodein, the arms dangling with an awkwardness he never had in life.

"Tell the men to come for him," Mattie said.

Two days later, Mattie carried Saya downstairs for the brief memorial service conducted by the Reverend Jonah Parkington. She found his solicitations, like the man himself, repugnant. He had not spoken to her since the marriage ceremony he performed there in the hotel parlor almost six months before. Abigail and Sophie murmured over the baby. Cindy, her face still swollen, observed dry-eyed, while Charlotte Gaines and Portia Parkington offered terse condolences. Young P.J. Calahan stared at the polished pine coffin from the far side of the room. Lionel, who had asked a few fellow merchants to help him bear the pall, darted about organizing carriages for the trek to the small cemetery on the hillside at the edge of town.

Sheriff Karns, too, came to pay his respects. "I wanted to let you know," he said quietly, "that Cindy Dougherty makes no charge against Boot Fike so I had to release him. She says it was the other brother's doing. That Alfred. We're looking but there's no sign of him. Snow's too deep right now for us to get up to that claim they're working."

"It's good of you to come, Sheriff."

"My deputy feels real bad about this, Mrs. Bodein. We all do."

She scarcely heard the pious, somewhat vengeful words Reverend Parkington pronounced over the coffin. His spew of bewildering philosophy seemed irrelevant to the reality of Cal's death. To her own predicament. And despite the objections of the others, she insisted on accompanying Cal's body to its final resting place in the cemetery. Gertie, dressed for the occasion in a ruffled black taffeta dress, took Saya in her arms, saying, "I'll keep this one snug as a bug while you're gone."

The blizzard had left sub-zero temperatures in its wake, and the small group of mourners bundled into heavy coats and hats with mufflers tied around their faces to brave the intense cold. Numb to all but the crunch of snow underfoot and the clouds of breath vapor on the frigid air, the newly widowed young mother accepted the support of Lionel and Abigail to the carriage that stood waiting with the few others behind the undertaker's wagon. As they moved through the snowy streets, unnaturally quiet in the aftermath of the storm, only the clink of harness and the creak of buggy wheels penetrated her curtained isolation. At the cemetery, when Lionel helped her from the carriage, a brisk wind swept her breath across the white hillside to a black gash in the thick mantle of new snow where diggers had hacked through the frost line to excavate the grave. Oh, Cal, I can't leave you here.

She stared at the long, narrow box of polished pine placed by the bearers next to the mound of frosty earth. You don't belong in this cold, miserable place. You don't deserve this rude ending. Cal, it's not your style. She wanted to reach out to him. To hold him just once more. If only you could have stayed with us . . . just a little longer. If only I could have kept you safe somehow. New milk surged into her leaden breasts. The physical pain drew her back to Reverend Parkington intoning scriptures, his gloved fingers following the fine print in his Bible, as the gravediggers wielded ropes to lower the coffin. It tipped and scraped noisily into place in the frozen hole.

Mattie drew a farewell breath. The precious entity that was her husband was gone. Blown away on the icy wind. So little time together, and now they were forever parted. A parting manipulated by others. An untimely mistake. She sagged with loneliness. The Bible snapped shut, and the diggers pulled their ropes free. Lionel touched her arm, a gentle reminder that they should start back, and she turned away from the gaping grave.

In the weeks that followed, the intense cold continued. Mattie stayed on at the hotel, gaining strength after her confinement, grateful for Gertie's friendly mealtime prattle as well as the reserved conversation of other diners. Even Charlotte Gaines began clucking over Saya, now filling out and glowing with health. Cindy handled the sparse business with the help of young P.J., who had appointed himself the man to look after Mattie and the baby and, more specifically, to supervise Cindy at the store. Mattie found P.J. as friendly and accommodating as a puppy dog, and he seemed to thrive on this substitute for the family he'd never known.

Mattie found some comfort in caring for Saya, but her despondency prompted Abigail to invite her to a New Year's Day dinner at the Steinbaums'.

"Oh, I couldn't," Mattie protested. "I'm not well yet. It's too soon."

"Life goes on," Abigail told her. "Yours will, too. And the sooner you get on with it, the better for both you and Saya." Her tone softened. "Please come, Mattie. We miss you."

"You're a wonderful friend," Mattie said. "I owe you so much."

"Don't be silly." Abigail handed her a narrow pink satin hair ribbon stitched to fit around a baby's head. "Here. This is for Saya to wear to the party."

Mattie tried to feel lighthearted as she dressed herself and Saya for the festivities, then carried the baby out to Lionel's waiting carriage. "This is the beginning of a brand-new year, 1876, my little one." She smiled at her daughter's tiny round face and the pink ribbon laced through the silky hair. "It's a new beginning for us, too." She tried to sound cheerful, even if she didn't feel it. The baby, peering from the folds of quilt, blinked in the bright winter sunlight. She was so like Cal. But Mattie put thoughts of regret out of her mind.

Sophie welcomed them at the door with a warm hug. "So it's you already. And Saya. Such a darling child." Abigail and Cindy gathered around with New Year's greetings. "I'm saying," Sophie repeated, "this is a darling child." She took Saya into the parlor, where the baby remained the center of attention until she fell asleep in a padded bureau drawer Sophie had prepared.

At the festive dinner table, talk turned to business—as it usually did in Lionel's presence—and prospects for the coming year. "Some merchants are saying they won't stay here if we don't get a railroad through soon," he said. "I'm telling the Board members we've got to do something." Recently he had been named a member of Helena's mercurial Board of Trade after, Abigail had confided to Mattie, he became a silent partner in the new Bank of the Territories.

Mattie, impatient for spring shipments that would plunge her into a busy work schedule, agreed. "A railroad would put an end to this frustrating seasonal river shipping."

Abigail turned to her father. "If it's eastern backing they need, can't something be done?"

"The territory legislature is working on it," Lionel said. "They know that growth here—the town's very survival—depends on a rail line."

"Hundreds of people have left since the gold played out," Mattie said.

"Yes, but those were mostly disgruntled fortune seekers who moved on to more promising diggings," Abigail offered.

"Good riddance, I say." Cindy got up to refill Lionel's wine glass with port, then passed the decanter around the table. "We don't need that kind here." She helped herself to more of Sophie's baked chicken and giblet stuffing. Her bruises had healed, and the holiday atmosphere seemed to restore her appetite, if not her exuberant spirits.

"We still have more than three thousand people here. Lots of good solid citizens. That's an impressive number to build on." Abigail, in thought and deed, resembled Lionel. Beneath her dark-eyed beauty and feminine demeanor lay a keen mind that Mattie had come to rely on both for friendly companionship and for business advice.

"But not enough families," Sophie said. "More men than ladies. And some of those ladies . . . *oy.*"

"Naturally we need more decent women here," Abigail said. "But we have to be patient. Signs of permanence and respectability are everywhere. Don't we see buildings going up now in stone? Stone. Not flimsy frame structures that burn down every few years."

"But I worry about Saya growing up in such an isolated place surrounded by rough men." Mattie glanced toward the corner of the room to check on the sleeping baby.

Sophie nodded. "And a saloon on every corner."

Lionel gave his wife an exasperated look. "And fly-by-night barbers selling haircuts and hot baths. And washerwomen competing with the Chinamen at the other end of the gulch. More new businesses every day. And any house strong enough to keep out a stray hog serving as a boardinghouse . . ." He paused to savor the aroma of his port. "With such commercial demand, I say we're in the right place." They all laughed.

"And I say," Sophie interjected, "why let your pudding get cold when you can eat it hot?"

"And I say," Abigail added, holding her glass aloft, "a very fine new year to everybody."

"Happy New Year!" they chorused. Whether from the port, the company of kind friends, or even the pink hair ribbon, slightly askew now, around her daughter's curls, Mattie felt somewhat heartened. Abigail was right. Life did go on. No matter what.

After the new year, the Montana winter settled in, relentless as Mattie's troubling indecision. Could she raise Saya alone in such an isolated place? Could she make their living with her present modest business? Should she even try? Each day, she took Saya with her to the store, where the child slept in the bureau drawer, now a permanent fixture near the big rolltop desk.

"Going back to St. Louis doesn't make sense," she thought as she sorted through Cal's papers. "The trip with Saya would be too difficult even to contemplate. And I have no one in St. Louis." She smiled at the industrious Cindy, rearranging unsold sheepskin caps in the front window. In recent weeks, Cindy worked harder than ever, and Mattie was concerned about her nervous compulsion to be constantly useful. Her thin face looked pale and drawn.

"Yes, Cindy, I feel inclined to stay right here," Mattie announced. "This business should produce enough income, and Cal had some money put aside. I'm lucky. Unlike most of the states, the territory allows women to own businesses on their own. Without husbands, I mean. I see no reason we can't begin to make plans for—"

She turned just in time to see Cindy crumple to the floor. "Cindy! What is it?" She hurried to aid the stricken girl, who recovered almost at once and sat up, rubbing her forehead. Mattie helped the unsteady girl to a chair near the stove.

"I ain't feeling so good." Cindy made a sour face. "I think I fainted."

Mattie searched the girl's eyes. Surely the fates couldn't be so cruel. "Cindy, you're not . . . I mean, how long have you been feeling this way?"

"I don't know." Her pale eyes were those of an innocent child.

"Have you had any other symptoms? Are you regular, I mean, in your monthlies?" Mattie felt like an inquisitor.

"How should I know? I don't pay no mind to such stuff. I just got dizzy, that's all, when I jumped down from the window."

Perhaps the girl was right and there was nothing to worry about. "Cindy, you're working too hard," Mattie said. "Let's have a cup of tea. That window display can wait." She moved the cast-iron teakettle to the center of the stove and added a stick of wood to coals in the grate, easing the heavy stove lid back into place so as not to wake Saya. "We've been so cooped up," she said. "Spring will be good for us both."

Cindy's strength returned as they drank tea from the enameled cups.

"We'll do a good business here this year, I'm sure," Mattie confided. "Sometimes I think Cal would want me to go ahead with his hotel. The big profits would be in a casino, too, but without him to run it . . . well, I'm not sure I could make a go of it. Besides, without Cal my heart isn't in it."

"Maybe Captain Tanner can help when he gets here."

Captain Tanner? Hearing the name startled Mattie.

"Abby got a letter from him," Cindy continued. "He's coming upriver. He's not a captain anymore. He told Abby he wants to settle down. He's talkin' like he wants to marry her."

Tea spilled from Mattie's cup onto her lap. "Marry . . . ?"

"Funny how things work out, ain't it? I mean, *isn't* it?"

Mattie dabbed at the tea stain with her handkerchief.

Cindy spooned sugar into her cup. "I don't suppose he knows about Cal," she said absently.

By April, Cindy's frequently upset stomach and lack of appetite were accompanied by crying spells and angry outbursts over insignificant problems at the store, and Mattie grew more certain in her dreadful diagnosis.

"Cindy, you mustn't get so upset over nothing," Mattie advised one morning when the girl grumbled about little Saya's fretting. "Babies sometimes fuss before they fall asleep."

Sudden anger flashed in Cindy's eyes. "It ain't Saya. It's . . . it's that bastard Fike." She clutched at her apron, her face distorted. An animal-like sound rose from her throat.

"Cindy, you'll be all right." She tried to calm the suffering girl. "I understand."

Cindy pushed her away in a frenzied rage, screaming, "You don't understand nothin'!" A lurid laugh contorted her mouth. "Can't you see? I got a hot one in the oven. I'm knocked up."

The two women stood facing each other, the younger defiant and frightened, the other dismayed. Of course Mattie understood. Hadn't she been in a similar situation just a year ago? Hadn't she experienced the same devastation? Had to face the same trauma of an unfortunate pregnancy?

But no. It wasn't the same. Mattie's indiscretion was romantic and tender; Cal, decent and loving. Alf Fike's brutalizing of Cindy was too horrible even to contemplate. And Mattie now realized that Cindy would never be free of him.

"You're right." Mattie took her trembling hand. "I *don't* understand what you're feeling. But I'd like to help."

Again Cindy brushed her away. "You can't help me."

"Perhaps Dr. Ward . . ." Mattie left the suggestion unfinished as Cindy flashed a contemptuous look that said Dr. Ward already had turned her away.

"There's no way out. I'm stuck with this . . . this monster in me. This freak!" She tore angrily at the apron that concealed the barely noticeable weight gain.

"No, Cindy." Mattie put her arm around the stricken girl. "Not a monster. All babies are sweet. Innocent. Your baby . . ."

"*My* baby!" Bitter rage transformed Cindy's face into a livid mask. "This is not *my* baby. It's *his!* It's ugly . . . and mean!"

"Oh, no, Cindy. You mustn't talk like that. You've suffered a terrible wrong, but it's not the baby's fault. Your situation isn't ideal, but you're safe here with me. And your baby will be lovely . . . a playmate for Saya."

"He'll be a bastard," Cindy said through clenched teeth, "with a whore for a mama."

Twenty-two

THE TOWN WARMED with the spring sunshine and green swept up the gulches. Mattie's first consignment, shipped from St. Louis in April, arrived at Fort Benton on the second day of June, and after another week by freight wagon over the remaining 150 miles, was unloaded haphazardly in back of Bodein Enterprises. Mattie directed P.J. in the opening of barrels and crates, stocking shelves, and storing surplus in the loft. Cindy, her growing thickness concealed beneath a loose pinafore, was assigned the lighter tasks of arranging goods, dusting up, and tending Saya.

It was long after dark when Mattie, inventory list in hand, sank into a chair. Her helpers had gone home, and Abigail, who'd brought sandwiches for their evening meal, sat with her in the light of a single lamp.

"Well, that's that," Mattie sighed, "till tomorrow."

"When word gets around that the supplies are in, those miners will swarm in here like vultures." Abigail soberly surveyed the newly stocked shelves without her usual good humor. In the past weeks, she had eagerly anticipated the long-awaited shipments of new goods for the Steinbaum mercantile as well as Bodein Enterprises, but now she seemed worried.

"Mattie, there's something I must tell you," she began hesitantly. "I've had word from Captain Tanner. From Gar. He . . . he mentioned the possibility of our keeping company." Her announcement rang like crystal in the stillness of the darkened store.

"Why, that's . . . very nice, Abby." Mattie had almost forgotten the feeling that surged through her at the mention of Garnet Tanner. Weary with work and uncertainty, she'd kept him out of her thoughts. She had many more urgent concerns—like running an outfitting business, caring for her daughter, and worrying about Cal's slippery partnerships. She smiled warmly. "So why the long face?"

"I know he cared for you, Mattie. But when you married Cal . . . well, I accept that he's not in love with me."

"Of course he is, if he's courting you."

"He said in his letter he admires me and that perhaps we can build a future together. Oh, Mattie. I've thought of no one but him from the first day I saw him on the *Big Muddy*. Please, Mattie. I must have this chance with him."

"I have no hold on Captain Tanner."

"But when he sees you again, Mattie . . ."

"Abby, you're my dearest friend. The captain is a good man. I'm sure you couldn't find a better husband."

"You mean you don't have any special feelings for him?"

"Things are difficult enough, now that Cal's gone, trying to put together the pieces of my life with Saya." She smiled again to ease Abigail's discomfort. "It's too soon to think of anything else. I'm too busy." Then, sadly, "Too hurt."

"Forgive me, Mattie. I know how hard it's been for you." She bit her lower lip. "But there is another problem." Tears welled in her eyes.

"What is it, Abby?"

"Mama and Papa don't approve."

"I thought they liked Captain Tanner."

"Yes, as a captain. Not as my intended."

"I don't understand."

"Mama and Papa consider themselves Yankees now, so I don't see why it should make a difference to them. But Gar is . . . well, they don't approve of my marrying a gentile."

"Oh." The distinction had not occurred to Mattie.

Abigail straightened. "But I don't care. It's my life. And if you say I won't be hurting you . . ."

Mattie tried to sort out her own feelings. The captain seemed an uncommonly fine man. And he had told Mattie he cared for her. But when she married Cal, his desire to get off the river and settle down apparently had turned his affection to Abigail. Eligible women were few on the frontier. She gazed at her friend's lovely, animated face, her graceful, angular figure, eyes that, except for this moment, shone with good humor and good sense. How could he help but love Abigail? And if he did, surely Sophie and Lionel would not stand in the way.

Still, Mattie could not ignore her own uncertain future. The captain had lost his wife and child. He hoped for a new family. She could provide that. And Saya needed a father. Was her feeling for him simply her need for a strong supporting hand? Was she being selfish? Abigail, too, deserved a chance for happiness.

"You needn't worry about my having any claim on the captain," Mattie said.

Abigail clasped her friend's hands. "Thank you, Mattie. I had to know for sure."

Next morning, Mattie found several prospectors waiting at the store. For this busy season, she was leaving Saya in the care of Sophie, who brought the baby to the store for her feedings. Cindy and P.J. were already bustling about filling orders while the gathered miners palavered noisily among themselves. As she hurried in, conversation hushed and the men politely stepped aside to let her pass.

"Good morning, gentlemen." Mattie took off her rose-trimmed hat, one that always brightened her spirits, smoothed her high-piled hair, and stowed the hat under the front counter.

"Mornin', ma'am," they chorused, their faces reflecting a reverent awe of women like Mattie, a respect born of long isolation and social inexperience. As she turned expectantly toward them, a slight, dark-complexioned man limped toward her, encumbered by a brace on his right leg.

Boot Fike tipped his derby. Unlike most of the other men, he wore a clean shirt under his rumpled coat. "I figured my goods was in."

"I have no goods for you." She felt her face flush with anger. She looked out the window to determine whether his brother Alf might be somewhere near. Cindy, unaware of Fike's presence, continued weighing nails for a customer at the back of the store.

"Now hold on, lady. You accepted my order last fall." A mocking expression accompanied his syrupy voice. "If I don't get my supplies, I can't work our mine, can I? You remember we're partners, don't you? Since Alfie's gone, and your man . . . well, I was real sorry to hear about that, ma'am . . . I figure it's just you and me from now on."

"I'm no partner of yours."

"I see it different." Fike leaned on the counter. "We've agreed you owe me supplies for your share of the lode." He spoke softly. "I didn't hole up there all winter keepin' out claim jumpers for nothin'." He bent toward her, shielding his words from all but her with his hand. "We got silver."

"I don't want any part of your mine."

"Not just the mine." His eyes narrowed. "This store's part of the bargain."

"What are you talking about?"

"The deal includes your business." He looked around proprietarily. "You get a share of the claim, I get a share of the store."

"What!"

"Bodein didn't mention that little detail?" He grinned. "You and me are partners here, too."

"You're mistaken. Cal would never . . ."

"Ah, but he did. Signed the contract all nice and legal."

"I don't believe you. Where is this contract?"

"Safe with my lawyer, the honorable Willard Motts. Yes, ma'am. You and me will soon be on easy street. Now if you'll give me my supplies . . ."

Others were beginning to stare. She would have to think this through. Settle it another time. "I want to see that contract."

"Come with me to Motts' office."

"I'm busy." She indicated other prospectors waiting for supplies.

Fike caught hold of her arm. "Be at Motts' office at noon. And get my goods ready for me." He jerked his thumb toward his chest. "I got no time to mosey." Then he tipped his hat, nodded in a courtly manner, and limped out of the store into the June sunlight.

Mattie waited on the next customer, then the next, her thoughts tumbling. Boot Fike *can't* have a claim on the store. Cal would have told me. He said only that we were to stake the Fikes in return for a share in any strike they made. Cal wouldn't have bargained with those two hoodlums for any part of our business. She moved mechanically through the long morning, finally making up her mind to go to Motts' office to see the contract for herself, if there was one.

Sophie arrived just before noon in a state of agitation, Saya wailing in her arms. *"Oy, oy, oy,* what did I do to deserve such torment? My own flesh and blood . . ." She handed over the noisy child to Mattie.

"What's wrong, Sophie?" With Mattie leading the way, both women climbed the narrow stairs to the loft. Saya's cries ceased abruptly at the nipple and she gulped contentedly.

"It's Abby . . . and the captain . . . they're out in the buggy."

"Captain Tanner?" Mattie felt even more crestfallen.

"Came upriver on the *Dakota* along with our shipments." The distraught Sophie pressed her pudgy cheeks in her hands. "Rode in this morning and right away came to find my Abigail. I ask you, why my Abby?"

"I wouldn't worry. Captain Tanner is an honorable man."

"Honorable he may be. But he's not the one for my Abby. Lionel introduced her to a nice Jewish boy, but will Abby keep company with him? No."

"Don't fret." Mattie managed a feeble smile. "I'm sure things will work out." She wondered if the captain had asked about her, if he'd seen Saya at the Steinbaums'. But she shook off the memory of his gray eyes. The captain is the least of my worries, she thought.

"I have to go over to Motts' law office in a few minutes," she said, placing the wide-eyed Saya over her shoulder and patting her back. "I'll come to pick her up as soon as I can get away this afternoon." She nuzzled her daughter's rosy, round cheek and received a toothless smile in return.

"This one's no trouble," Sophie said, taking the baby and starting down the steps. "It's that strong-headed Abigail that's making me old before my time."

Downstairs at her desk, Mattie searched through a stack of invoices, found one marked "Fike Brothers," and handed it to P.J. "Please get this order ready right away," she instructed the freckled youth. "I don't want Fike to have to wait."

"Fike?" P.J.'s eyes widened and his gaze swept to Cindy, now assembling packs on the front counter.

Mattie nodded knowingly. "It's Boot. Alone. We'll give him his supplies and be rid of him. Tell Cindy there's nothing to worry about."

Arriving at Motts' office, Mattie saw that Fike was already there waiting for her.

"Mrs. Bodein," Willard Motts crooned. "What a pleasure." He self-consciously ran his hand over his slicked-back hair, then held a chair for her before taking his place across the desk. "You're acquainted with Mr. Fike, I believe."

"We're old friends," Fike offered before she could reply.

"Good. Good," Motts said. "Then I'm sure this little matter can be settled quickly. I understand there's a question as to the validity of this contractual agreement your husband made with this gentleman." Mattie sat silently while the attorney unfolded an official-looking paper.

"It's all here in black and white." He adjusted spectacles over his sharp nose and began to read. "Let it be known that this day, September 21, 1875, a partnership has been drawn up between the parties of the first part, Booker Fike and Alfred Fike, and the party of the second part, Calvin Bodein, to establish joint ownership of the mining claim in Grizzly Gulch known as the Fike Claim, with any and all of its assets, and of the business known as Bodein Enterprises, with any and all of its assets." He glanced over his lenses at Mattie.

"That's all?" Surely one brief sentence could not command her whole future.

"That's it. Signed by both of the Fikes and by your husband." He pushed the paper toward her.

Mattie looked at the signatures beneath the brief handwritten document. Calvin Bodein, in a strong familiar hand. Boot Fike, in a slanted scrawl. An "X" for Alfred Fike, whose name was written out below it in the same handwriting as the document.

"Everything appears to be in order," Motts said officiously.

"Why is my name not mentioned," Mattie asked, "since I'm a partner in Bodein Enterprises?"

Motts switched to a condescending tone. "Because, my dear, since this contract concerns that entire business, naturally, your interests are included."

"But this can't be." Mattie felt her judgment clouded by her loathing for these men. "I know Cal wouldn't sign something like this."

"The signature's notarized." Motts pointed to the notation in the lower left corner. "Witnessed by Seth Thornton, President, Commercial Bank."

Mattie rose angrily. "I can't accept this. Something's peculiar here. Why is there no copy of this among Cal's papers?"

Fike, too, jumped up, stumbling momentarily as he dragged his leg brace into position, then touched her elbow gingerly. "No need to take on like that, ma'am. We're rich, you and me." He glanced gleefully at Motts. "Tell her, Willard, ol' boy."

"That's a fact, Mrs. Bodein. Boot here brought in some mighty rich quartz samples. He's got silver, all right. And according to this contract, it's yours, too. You'll be a rich woman, Mrs. Bodein. Now why would you want to quibble about throwing in that grubby supply business of yours?"

Rich? One more complexity crowded into Mattie's throbbing head. Can this be true? Is he really offering me a portion of whatever he's found out there in that gulch? If so, maybe Motts is right. Why should I hang on to my little enterprise if I can trade a portion of it for greater gain? Would it be worth dealing with Boot Fike? And what does he want from me?

She turned to him. "Tell me why you're doing this."

"I'm only honoring our contract. When word gets out about my strike, you'd be comin' around for your share anyway. Never let it be said that Boot Fike ain't a fair man."

"If you're going to be so rich, you can buy me out of the store."

"I ain't a storekeeper and don't care to be. I don't intend to interfere with your running it." His eyes narrowed and his voice tightened. "Can't you get it through your head? This silver is only the beginning. There'll be more. Lots more. Together we can build something. Be important. I don't plan to stay a nobody all my life." Then, in a pleading tone, "I admire a strong woman like you. And you need a man."

"You're detestable," Mattie hissed, starting for the door. "I'd die in hell before I'd hook up with you."

"Take your time," Fike called after her. "I can wait." And as the screen slammed behind her, she heard him say to Motts, "She likes me. Did you see her eyes?"

Twenty-three

RUSHING from the suffocating law office, Mattie took a deep breath to calm herself. Cal would never have agreed to any such contract. Motts had to be a crook, too. And to make matters worse, Fike fancied her. She would have to dissuade him. But how? Maybe Lionel would know what to do. Yes, Lionel could help her. Starting toward the Steinbaum mercantile, she stepped into the street directly into the path of a horse and carriage.

"Whoa!" The bay horse threw back its head, snorting against the sudden tug on the lines. "Mattie." Abigail jumped down from the passenger seat. "We almost ran you down."

Mattie tried to compose herself. "I'm sorry. I . . . I must see your father right away." Only then did she notice Abigail's driver, who had climbed from the carriage and now stood beside them.

Garnet Tanner's sturdy frame, his sandy hair and mustache, were as she remembered, but the familiar captain's cap had been replaced by a jaunty straw skimmer. The gray eyes held the same warmth as he extended his hand. "Mattie, it's good to see you."

"Hello, Captain."

"It's just plain Gar, now." He took her hand. "I left the captain on the river."

"Gar." She withdrew her hand abruptly. His touch unnerved her even more than his easy manner.

"Abigail's been showing me around town." He smiled at Abigail. "I'm impressed."

"I want him to see he's come to the right place," Abigail said gaily. "But, Mattie, is anything wrong? What do you want with Papa?"

Mattie's turmoil could not be explained in a few words. "It's a business matter, that's all."

Abigail touched the captain's arm, obviously eager to continue their tour. "Well then, we must all get together soon."

"Yes, of course," Mattie said. "Welcome to Helena, Gar."

"Thanks." His glance lingered on her. "And give my regards to Cal."

Mattie stiffened. He didn't know. Why hadn't Abigail told him? "Cal . . . is dead," she murmured.

"What!" Tanner's smile faded.

Abigail looked stricken. "Oh, Mattie, forgive me." She turned to the captain. "Gar, in all the excitement I didn't have a chance to tell you."

The captain searched Mattie's face. "What happened?"

"A terrible accident."

"But when? How?"

"That's all behind me now." She smiled to ease Abigail's apprehension. "I'm doing fine, really I am."

"But we must talk." He gripped her arm. "I'll come to see you."

Mattie knew she could not postpone the inevitable. She would have to tell him face to face that there was nothing between them. "If you wish," she said.

"Mattie, why don't you come for supper with us tonight," Abigail said. "Mama's cooking. And Gar can see Saya."

"Abby, please understand. I must see Mattie alone." Gar's voice was considerate but firm.

"Oh." Abigail forced a smile. "All right, you take the buggy. I'll go on over to the mercantile, Mattie, and tell Papa you want to see him. Perhaps at supper."

"I won't be having supper with you tonight." Mattie groped for a plausible excuse. "Saya . . . isn't feeling well. She's getting another tooth and should be tucked in early. I'll talk with your father another time." She climbed into the buggy. "Gar, you may drive me back to my store if you like. We're at our busiest now with the shipment in." She turned to reassure Abigail. "Don't worry. Everything's fine."

Fine? The word sounded hollow. Boot Fike scheming to take her livelihood and Garnet Tanner ready to marry her best friend. She had never felt further from fine in her entire life.

As they drove along the street, Gar looked at her with both affection and accusation in his eyes. "Why didn't you let me know?"

"I'm sorry, Gar, but so much has happened. So much has changed."

"I tried to put you out of my mind, but seeing you again . . . Well, you know how I feel about you." He took her hand in his. "Mattie, tell me what happened to Cal."

"Shot. Mistaken in a snowstorm for an outlaw."

"My God."

Mattie nodded.

"But before that," he probed, "things had been going well? For the two of you, I mean?"

"Yes, everything was nearly perfect. Our baby . . ." She choked up with the painful memory. "Cal was killed the night Saya was born."

"I should have come sooner." He put his arm around her, but she pulled away.

"No, Gar." She resolved to make quick work of it. "Abby . . ."

"Mattie, if I'd known I wouldn't have considered anyone but you."

"But you do care for Abby, don't you?"

"Well, yes, I do, but . . ."

"Gar, I'm not the same person you knew on the boat. I run an outfitting business now." She turned to him earnestly. "I'm raising a child."

"But surely you don't intend to go it alone."

"Yes, that's exactly what I intend to do."

"Mattie, that's ridiculous. A beautiful woman like you, all by herself, trying to be an outfitter."

"What's ridiculous about it?"

"Well, it just isn't appropriate, for one thing."

There it was again, that insidious notion of appropriateness. Clearly, she and the captain did not see eye to eye.

"Gar, I'll say it as plainly as I can." She took a barely perceptible breath. "I could never marry you because . . . because I don't love you."

"Mattie."

She continued. "I feel affection for you as a dear and trusted friend, and I hope that's what you will remain."

He slumped back in his seat. After a moment he murmured, "All right. If that's the way it has to be."

Mattie felt leaden in mind and body as they pulled up in front of Bodein Enterprises among the wagons congregated there and she climbed from the carriage. Gar held her in his gaze momentarily, then, touching the brim of his jaunty skimmer, he flicked the lines and the bay stepped off down the street.

Cindy came running out, her hands fluttering nervously. "P.J. says Boot Fike is on his way here. If he comes in here, I'll . . ."

"Now, now. Calm yourself." Mattie saw two or three customers waiting to be served. "We'll give him his goods and be rid of him. Don't worry, he can't hurt you."

P.J. stepped from behind the counter and put his arm around Cindy, announcing quietly, "I'll look after her."

"Good." Mattie patted his shoulder. "Now let's take care of these other folks or we'll be here all night." And she plunged into a flurry of activity to ease her own apprehension.

Fike drove his two mules to the front of the store and backed the swaybacked wagon up to the porch. Mattie saw through the window that it was already laden with bags of flour and cornmeal, a barrel of salt pork, and other provisions. She immediately set P.J. to loading Fike's order: dynamite, digging equipment, construction tools, and cartridges.

Fike came inside, his thin lips curling into a grin as he signed the bill of sale she thrust toward him. He seemed in no hurry to leave, but leaned casually against the counter, his eyes tracing her body.

"Is there something else?" she asked, curtly.

"Well now, I was thinkin', Mattie . . ."

She bristled. "I'm *Mrs.* Bodein."

"That right? Seems I recall your hubby's dead and buried. That makes you Mattie again, don't it?"

"Not to you, it doesn't."

"Whatever you say—*Mrs.* Bodein. Just wanted you to know I've hired a crew to help me work the claim. Me and you'll be countin' that silver in no time." His farewell gaze swept over her again as he limped out the door. She watched him exchange a few words with P.J., then climb into the wagon, shifting the braced leg with his hands, and whip the mules into motion. As he pulled away he turned and shouted to her, "Be seein' you. Partner."

She slumped, dread gnawing in the pit of her stomach.

"That Fike must be crazy," P.J. muttered as he came back into the store. "He talks like he owns the place."

A few minutes later, Mattie, hatless and out of breath, revealed her apprehension to Lionel in his small office at the rear of Steinbaum's mercantile.

"You say Cal signed a contract with the Fikes giving them a share in Bodein Enterprises?" Lionel thoughtfully stroked his graying beard.

"His signature was there. But I know Cal wouldn't share our business. Not with those evil men."

"But he *was* a partner in their mining venture?"

"He staked them in return for a share in whatever they found. He had the same agreement with a few other prospectors."

"I don't know, Mattie. Unless you can prove something's fishy, you may be stuck."

Mattie stood abruptly. "Seth Thornton supposedly witnessed the signatures. I'm going to see what he has to say."

"I should come with you." Lionel reached for his hat. "Seth is a tough customer." As they walked down the street toward the solid, two-story brick Commercial Bank, he confided, "There's talk about Thornton's shady dealings. That's one of the reasons I put my support behind the new Bank of the Territories."

"I know he was the cause of his daughter's misfortune—and Dr. Austin's trouble," Mattie said.

Lionel nodded.

If Thornton was surprised to see the unlikely pair, he concealed it beneath manners as polished as his heavy gold watch chain. "Lionel. It's always good to see you." He rose and offered a handshake with a mirthless chuckle. "Have you decided to reopen your account? And my dear Mrs. Bodein. Come in." He indicated chairs. "How is your business coming along?"

Mattie dispensed with formalities. "You notarized a contract," she said, "signed by my husband and the two Fike brothers. I need to know more about it."

"Well, let me see." He glanced first at Mattie, then at Lionel. "I do recall a contract of some sort. Had to do with the Fike Claim, I believe."

"Did you actually witness my husband signing that contract?"

"Yes. Yes, I did. Last fall sometime, wasn't it? I remember Mr. Bodein and the two Fikes in Willard Motts' office. They asked me to come over as a witness."

"Seth, was there anything unusual about that transaction?" Lionel interrupted. "Mrs. Bodein feels her husband would never have agreed to the terms of that contract."

"Oh, he agreed to the partnership all right. No question there." Thornton pursed his heavy lips. "And, my dear, you got the best of the bargain. I'm told the Fike Claim is a rich one."

"A rich one?" Lionel looked quizzically at Mattie.

She shrugged. "Fike says it is."

Lionel's shaggy eyebrows raised along with his spirits. "So all right already. Mattie, you should think on this. Such a windfall don't come along every day."

Mattie sighed. Are there no principles among men? Even Lionel looks only at the money to be made, she thought. How can I do business with a man like Boot Fike? And what about Alf? Has everyone forgotten what he did to Cindy?

Lionel continued to reassure her. "With Fike you can deal . . . if you must."

"I couldn't agree more," Thornton said. "An opportunity like this is rare." Then, studying his fingernails, he added, "But, my dear, if you feel you want no part of the operation, I personally would be willing to buy you out."

Of all the contemptible, conniving thieves, Mattie thought. She rose to her feet, barely concealing the anger pulsing through her. "No, Mr. Thornton, I think not. I seem to own part of a silver mine and, as you gentlemen advise, I'm beginning to get used to the idea."

"How sensible, Mrs. Bodein. Now if you'd care to establish an account here at the bank, I'm sure we can provide you with sound financial advice."

Twenty-four

WHEN MATTIE accompanied Lionel to the Steinbaum flat to pick up Saya, she found her daughter in the arms of Garnet Tanner.

Abigail teased, "Isn't he a fine-looking father?" Sophie and Lionel exchanged glances.

Gar remained absorbed in watching the infant grasp his finger. "She's a beautiful baby, Mattie."

"And getting out of sorts, I imagine," Mattie said. "Cutting teeth can bring on a fever. I should take her home."

"She doesn't seem the least bit sick," Abigail pleaded. "Can't you stay for supper?"

Sophie quickly busied herself setting another place at the table. "You have to eat. Besides, I've roasted a fat hen. With dumplings. It's ready when Cindy gets here."

"The baby seems fit as a fiddle." Relinquishing Saya, Tanner looked into Mattie's eyes as if to say, "Looks as if we're going to be seeing a lot of each other whether you want it that way or not."

Mattie's resolve weakened. "Well, all right. Sophie's chicken and dumplings does sound tempting." Saya responded to her mother's voice with body-wiggling coos of delight.

Lionel did not exhibit his usual pleasure in the expanded family around the big dining table. The presence of Garnet Tanner produced an uneasiness in everyone; Sophie and Lionel seeing his qualities differently now as a potential son-in-law, Mattie distracted by her own uncertain feelings, and Abigail trying to act as if everything were normal.

Lionel tried, too. "Mattie, if that silver mine comes in you're going to need someone to oversee the mining operation. Why not hire the captain here?"

Gar shook his head. "I'm afraid I don't know much about mining."

"Why, that's a wonderful idea," Abigail joined in. "Gar, you could

learn the ropes in no time. Mattie's studying those geology and metallurgy books and dealing with prospectors. She knows more about those
things than they do."

Mattie seized on Gar's reluctance. "This whole mining thing is uncertain right now." She studied his rugged, lined face, the gray eyes
revealing his integrity . . . and longing. How could she go into a business arrangement that would bring the two of them together day after
day? That wouldn't be fair to anyone. "I've already written to St. Louis
inquiring about hiring a mining engineer," she said. "If I am in this
thing with Boot Fike, I have to have someone experienced to advise
me." Then, in a less tenacious tone, "But, Gar, this town needs better
freight service. If a well-run operation got under way, there are all
kinds of businesses here that would get behind it."

Gar nodded thoughtfully. "Setting up some overland lines might be a
possibility. I have lots of contacts in river shipping."

"You could certainly handle all our goods," Abigail said.

"And the Bodein shipments," Mattie added.

Gar smiled at them both. "Then consider yourselves my first clients."

Halfway through Sophie's delectable dinner, rapid steps sounded on
the stair, the door swung open, and Cindy and P.J. burst in.

"Surprise!" Cindy wore Mattie's rose-trimmed hat with her pinafore
and clasped a handful of daisies over her rounded belly. P.J.'s cowlick
stood up in tufts protesting the recent combing it had undergone. He
wore a stiff-collared shirt with sleeve garters.

"Yeah," he echoed. "Surprise."

"What on earth . . . ?" But there was no mistaking the meaning of
the dramatic entrance. The group at the table stood as one.

Cindy looked defiantly at each astonished face. "I'm a married lady
now."

P.J. glanced shyly at her. "We just got hitched."

"Don't have a real wedding ring yet," the bride announced. "But
Reverend Parkington said it'd be best not to wait for one." Cindy held
out her left hand to show a braided circle of wire on the fourth finger.
"Ain't this a caution?"

"I made it for her," P.J. said proudly.

"But why?" Mattie rushed forward to embrace them. "I mean, why
didn't you tell us? We should have been with you."

"We just decided," P.J. explained, "after you left the store this afternoon."

Abigail gasped. "This *is* quite a surprise."

"I say *mazeltov!*" Lionel clapped his hands. "And I'm kissing the bride." He stepped forward to give Cindy an affectionate peck on the cheek and shake P.J.'s hand. "Congratulations, my boy."

"Imagine, married." Sophie hurried to hug each of the newlyweds. "How nice. Come join us at the table. We'll call it a wedding supper."

"I'm happy for you, Cindy," Gar said.

"Well, Captain Tanner, I do declare." Cindy mimicked a coy southern belle. "We got more bridegrooms around here than we can shake a stick at."

"Did you say supper?" P.J. rubbed his palms together. "Golly, I ain't ate nothin' since mornin'."

"*Haven't* ate nothin'." Cindy rolled her eyes disdainfully.

"You neither?" P.J. glanced at his bride, but she turned away, muttering under her breath.

"Stupid."

After supper, Cindy and P.J. were dispatched to the International Hotel, where they would begin their life together with the wedding gift of twenty dollars hurriedly collected from the assembled well-wishers, Lionel contributing the major portion. Lionel lit up his usual after-supper cigar as those remaining gathered in the parlor.

"It appears a lot has happened I don't know about," Gar commented.

"Yes, Cindy had a very unfortunate experience," Lionel said.

"Unspeakable." Abigail seated herself next to Gar on the sofa. "It left her . . . well, you see how it left her. Poor thing. She had been doing so well, living with us, working for Mattie. Now she's like a lost child, whimpering one minute, belligerent the next. Hurt and angry underneath."

"P.J. just turned sixteen." Mattie felt a sadness, despite this unexpected solution to Cindy's dilemma. "He's a good boy and he's attentive to her, but you can see she's not in love with him."

"At least her baby will have a father," Sophie muttered.

"It's a pity," Mattie said. "I feel responsible."

"You?" Abigail frowned. "Why would you feel responsible?"

"If she hadn't come to my room that morning . . ."

"And it would have been you instead," Abigail said sympathetically. "It's not your fault. It's those despicable Fikes."

"So that's who it was." Gar's brow furrowed. "If we're placing blame, I guess it's my fault, too. I'm the one who took her to Bismarck and left her there. I couldn't help her much . . . till Mattie came along."

Then, earnestly to Mattie, "When she met you, life seemed to have new meaning."

His veiled remark unsettled Mattie. It was clear she would have to avoid seeing him altogether. "It's getting late," she said, rising to leave. "Now I really must get Saya home."

Gar stood to help her with the baby's things. "Cindy and P.J. may surprise us." He looked pointedly at Mattie. "Time has a way of setting things right."

Contrary to that prediction, the passing of time only brought Mattie more worry. Cindy and P.J. moved into a tiny cottage on miners' row. Lionel bought them a baby crib and Sophie contributed a layette from the mercantile, but as Cindy's confinement neared, her emotional outbursts and contemptuous verbal attacks on P.J. increased in frequency, and Mattie's hours at the store were often spent in arbitration between the two. Avoiding Garnet Tanner also required painstaking care. And Boot Fike had not reappeared.

Each day, Mattie carried Saya to the Steinbaum flat and left her with Sophie. Each day, she waited in vain for further word from Boot, hoping to resolve the question of her business entanglement with him. Even though she had found no confirmation of the contract among Cal's papers, perhaps Cal *had* agreed to share Bodein Enterprises with them. If he had, what could she do about it now? Boot said he didn't want any part of running the store. Would her share of the silver strike —if there actually was silver—compensate for splitting the store profits? The mining claim was legally registered, and any strike would be honest money, no matter how detestable her partner.

Still she felt uneasy. Cal had been clever in maneuvering the partnership. He had done it for her. For their future. But he hadn't known what kind of men the Fikes were. Just the sight of Boot turned her stomach, though his crippled leg and slight stature limited any physical threat, she thought. The burly Alf was the one she feared. Where *was* he? Had he left the territory as Boot implied?

Mattie shuddered. This apprehension and distrust was intolerable. Maybe if she talked frankly with Boot. Appealed to his finer instincts— he must have some down deep—to void the contract. She didn't want silver or anything else from him. She only wanted her store, and he admitted not being interested in it. The whole thing was crazy. She must get it settled. But how long would it be before he came down from the mountain? Perhaps she should go up to the claim to see firsthand what the mine was producing. He has a crew up there working with him. I have nothing to lose by confronting him.

That's what I'll do, she thought. I'll go see for myself, talk to him, get some answers that will clear up this whole messy business.

That morning, after leaving Saya in Sophie's care, she stopped downstairs in the mercantile to see Abigail and found her dusting shelves. The pleasant sound of Lionel's violin came from the back office, and Abigail smiled indulgently, tilting her head toward the music. Abigail had blossomed since the captain's arrival, her usual vitality enhanced by a glowing happiness.

"Mattie, I'm so excited." She waved her feather duster as Mattie approached. "Gar's taken a room at the boardinghouse till we're married. He's planning to set up that freighting business, and he's over at the bank now making some financial arrangements. Isn't that admirable?"

"Gar will do well, I'm sure." Mattie could not conceal her anxiety. "Abby, I have to get some things settled myself. I've got to talk to Boot Fike and I'm going up to the mine today. Will you come with me?"

Abigail looked at her sharply. "The mine? But, Mattie, should you be going up there? That Alf . . ."

"Boot says Alf has gone. Anyway there's a crew working up there now. Prospectors treat me as if I were made of porcelain. They're all so shy and respectful in the presence of a 'fine lady.'" Abigail laughed gaily, amused by Mattie's allusion to the upward shift in their social position in this new community. "Come on." Mattie coaxed, "If we get an early start, we can be back by mid-afternoon."

"All right. It's a lovely day for a drive. We can take our buggy." Abigail put on her bonnet, calling to Lionel in his back office. "Papa, will you keep an eye on the store? Mattie and I are going for a drive."

Lionel appeared in the doorway and waved. "It's hot out. Don't get a heat stroke."

"I'll ask Mama to fix us a picnic," she said, "while we harness up."

Abigail chatted gaily, holding the lines, driving the bay horse and buggy as they rode along the rocky wagon track winding up through the foothills. Mattie sat in silence, remembering her previous excursion up to the Fike Claim with Cal. Almost exactly a year ago. Now the summer landscape with its tranquil views of the valleys, the fragrant pine looming on either side, produced in her a renewed melancholy. Abigail's happy anticipation was as hers had been then.

"Mattie, I'm sure Mama and Papa will eventually accept Gar," Abigail confided. "How can they help it? A man like him. Can you imagine, Papa wanted me to start seeing some hosiery salesman who comes around the store? Says he's from a fine old Boston family but wants to settle here."

"A family is important, Abby." How Mattie longed for her own mother and father. Someone. Anyone. Saya was all she had now. But how could Abby, who had always been part of a loving family, be expected to understand? She took such things for granted.

"Of course families are important," Abigail said, "and I'll soon have my own."

Mattie scanned the rocky gulches for landmarks that would guide her. When she pointed out the grassy slope, the shortcut where Cal had turned off the narrow road, Abigail eased the bay down the incline and across the stream at the bottom, pulling up at the foot of the cliff, which soared above the tallest pines. "We must give a warning," Mattie instructed, remembering Cal's precaution. "Hello," she shouted. "Hello there." She climbed from the buggy. "We'll walk from here. It isn't far. Leave the basket. We'll picnic when we get this visit over with."

The women skirted the cliff and followed the creek up the rocky, brush-filled gulch. "Hello!" Mattie called again.

"My word!" Abigail gasped for breath. "Are you sure this is the way?"

"Quite sure." Mattie struggled on.

Then at the exact spot where Alf had appeared on her first visit, Boot, grimy and unshaven, stepped from behind an outcropping, his battered derby shielding his narrow eyes from the noon sun. His sweat-stained shirt, sleeves rolled up in the heat, revealed labor-toughened arms. A pistol bulged in the belt cinching his gaunt hips. Mattie gasped. She hated guns. Even before Cal.

"I was wonderin' when you'd come." Boot greeted them with a hint of humor in his voice, seeming pleased with himself.

"We need to talk," Mattie said.

He raised an eyebrow. "I knew you'd be here as soon as you come to your senses." His attention shifted to Abigail.

"We met on the *Big Muddy*," she said. "I'm Abigail Steinbaum."

Fike's grin widened. He touched his derby, bobbing his head in acknowledgment. "If I knew you fine ladies was comin' to call, I'd have slicked up some." He wiped his sweaty palms on his pants. "Steinbaum's daughter, eh? Mattie, you keep highfalutin' company."

Fike hobbled up the trail, leading the women into the camp Mattie remembered beside the bubbling spring. But now the scene had changed. The lean-to and dilapidated wagon were almost hidden by the increased mounds of rubble, crates of dynamite, and other equipment. A loaded ore wagon stood in the narrow wagon track winding down the opposite side toward the road. Several horses now grazed with the two mules along the creek. Two rough-looking men, strangers to Mattie, worked near the mine entrance.

Fike proudly indicated the loaded wagon. "You know, Mattie, it's no good hauling all this rock over to Unionville. Save a lot of time if we built our own stamp mill to crush it." He hurriedly arranged overturned chunks of log for seating near the cold fire pit, pulling his close to Mattie's. "It'd cost money, but a crusher's to our benefit. And Thornton's agreed to back us . . . for twenty percent. I think that's fair, don't you?"

He seemed to take their partnership—and her acquiescence—for granted. She shrank back.

"I know you're concerned about Alfie." He spoke earnestly. "And I want to put your mind at ease. Alfie's dead. Froze to death in the snow trying to get up here the night the sheriff was after him. I found him when the thaw came and buried him over yonder." He gestured toward a pile of rocks near the creek. "He ain't gonna interfere."

His cold, matter-of-fact disclosure shook Mattie. Abigail, too, stared with astonishment.

"Mr. Fike." Mattie couldn't bring herself to call him Boot. "About the store. Bodein Enterprises. Cal had no copy of the contract, and I . . ."

"I told you, my dear, you'll keep the store." He leaned closer. "I believe in a wife having her own money."

"Wife?" Mattie sputtered. "Surely you're not so presumptuous as to believe . . ."

"Presumptuous." Fike chuckled. "Now there's a ten-dollar word."

Anger surged through her. "I'll give you a few more," she blurted. "Conniver! Scoundrel! Liar!"

"Now wait a minute." He grabbed her roughly by the arm. "You ain't callin' me a liar."

"Don't you touch me!" Mattie commanded.

His leering, stubbled face loomed close to hers. "When we're married, you won't talk to me like that."

Mattie swung her free arm, chopping him in his Adam's apple. He clutched his neck with both hands. "Let's get out of here," Mattie murmured. Abigail, already on her feet, started running toward the trail.

"Stay right where you are, ladies!" Fike drew his pistol and pointed it at Abigail. Abigail froze, her face contorted with alarm.

"Abby, run!" Mattie sprang at Fike to knock the pistol aside, but he dodged, grabbed her by her coiled hair, and shoved the steely barrel against her ribs.

"Now you get this straight," he growled. "I expect to be treated with respect."

Mattie squirmed off balance, held fast by his grip on her hair. She saw that the two miners now were nowhere in sight. And Abigail had vanished down the trail.

"She can go." Fike shrugged. "Got no use for nervous women." He relaxed his grip, easing Mattie into a seated position on the log. "Now, my dear, we'll have some privacy to get to know each other."

Mattie, swallowing her increasing fear, began hesitantly. "Boot . . ." Yes, she would call him Boot. Disarm him. Charm him. Anything to get away.

"Booker," he corrected. "My name is Booker."

"Booker. I . . . I came to talk business." She straightened her back and fixed her eyes on his. She would have to humor him till Abigail brought help. That might take hours. She forced an apprehensive smile. "I think your plan for a stamp mill is . . . is very good. But it will take a year or more to get a steam boiler and weights shipped up the river from St. Louis."

"I knew you'd like the idea." He quickly replaced the pistol in his belt and sat next to her. "And Thornton's twenty percent? Had to grind him down from twenty-five."

"That was shrewd of you." The man was irrational. Volatile. Completely lacking in any concept of decent human interaction. She didn't dare take her eyes from his odious face lest he think she was looking around for a means of escape. It wouldn't be wise to set him off again. The two men must have gone into the mine, she thought. If I stall till they come out . . . "You've hired those men to help you?"

"Two good diggers. Down on their luck so I don't pay 'em much but beans and whiskey." He waited expectantly for her approval of his employment procedure.

"When will they be hauling out the first load?"

"This afternoon. The big fella, he'll take it over to the Unionville mill and the assay office."

"Can he be trusted by himself . . . with the accounts, I mean?" Mustn't appear too anxious.

"He's too numskulled to be interested in accounts." Boot chuckled. "No danger there."

"But shouldn't we go along to oversee things?"

Fike sobered and his eyes narrowed. "Now, don't think I'm that easy to fool. I can see right through you women." He clenched her upper arm in an iron grip and pulled her to her feet. "No, my sweet, you and me are going *up* the mountain today, not down. We need some courtin' time." He laughed coarsely. "My pa always told us, 'Don't marry no woman without tryin' her first.' "

Twenty-five

"NO, PLEASE." Mattie pulled back. She couldn't allow Fike to lead her up the mountain. Why had she assumed she could reason with him? She tried to reseat herself but he bent her arm behind her and roughly pushed her ahead of him toward the creek trail.

"Don't be upset," he snarled, wrenching her arm. "You're not the kind to get upset over nothing."

"Let go of me!" She twisted, kicking her heel into his shin. Frantically, she scanned the mine entrance for the two miners.

"Just come along pleasant like. You know I want everything nice for you." His voice softened to a whine, but his expression terrified her.

"Help!" she screamed. Maybe the miners would hear. "Help me!"

Fike's fist smashed against her temple. She staggered and fell, but managed to scramble on hands and knees out of his reach.

"You're not acting like a lady," he muttered, gimping after her.

Reeling from the blow, she fought to clear her head. His pistol worried her. If she could talk him out of it, she could make a run for it. "How can I act like a lady, when you . . . when you're wearing *that?*"

"You mean this?" Leering, he whipped the weapon from his belt. "If you don't behave yourself, I might have to use it." Enjoying the power it gave him over her, he brandished the pistol and mockingly took aim.

A shot rang out. Mattie flinched. But the expected jolt didn't come. Instead Fike took two awkward steps and fell backward into the dust. From her crouched position, Mattie whirled and saw Abigail standing a few paces away, a revolver in her hand. Her face and arms were scratched, her dress in disarray from her dash through the brush.

"Abby!" Mattie cried.

But Abigail's attention locked incredulously on the fallen man, his eyes glazing under the hot sky, a small stain spreading across his shirt pocket. "My God!" she gasped. "Have I killed him!"

"Abby, the gun . . . Where . . . ?"

"Mama put it in the picnic basket."

Mattie crawled to Fike's side, felt his neck for a pulse and, detecting none, rose to her feet, stunned and trembling. The two miners, having heard the gunshot, hurried from the mine entrance. "What's goin' on?" They stopped short when they saw Fike sprawled on the rubble-strewn ground. Mattie and Abigail stood bewildered, Abigail still holding the revolver. The men eyed the women more with curiosity than suspicion. One bent over the body.

"Deader'n a doornail," he said.

The other stooped to pick up Fike's gun. "Mean-tempered cuss. He try to hurt you ladies?"

Mattie nodded.

"Why you up here anyhow?" His eyes narrowed on her.

Mattie froze with renewed terror. "We . . . our buggy is down by the creek."

But the miner seemed to have as little interest in the women as he did in the turn of events that had left Boot Fike dead. "I'm 'sposed to take this wagon down," he said. "Might's well load him up, too."

The two men carried Fike's body to the wagon near the mine entrance and hoisted it atop the rocky load, leaving it staring at the noon sun. "Tell 'em we're bringin' him down," he called out.

"Let's go, Abby, hurry," Mattie gasped. The women plunged headlong down the trail, Abigail still clutching the revolver. Hair flying wildly, dresses snagged, they bounded into the buggy. Abigail dropped the revolver back into the basket and whipped the bay into a fast scramble up the grassy slope. Mattie's heart hammered fearfully as she looked behind to see if they were followed.

"Mama told me she put the gun in the basket because there might be grizzly bears up here. I didn't mean to shoot him, Mattie." Abigail's face contorted with anguish. "He would have killed you."

"You did right," Mattie murmured. "I owe you my life." Her own burning eyes refused to tear. Her breasts were full and aching. She had to get back to Saya. Keep her safe. Oh, why had she been so foolish as to think this visit would solve anything? And now what had she done to Abigail? Her dear friend. Surely Abby couldn't be blamed. No, Abby would be all right . . . with Gar to look after her.

Anguish tightened Mattie's throat. How she needed him herself. She needed him desperately . . . to help her through this trouble. But that could never be. Oh, please don't let Gar be there when we get back, she thought.

But Gar was there, with Lionel, standing out in front when the distraught Abigail stopped the lathered bay in front of the mercantile. Lionel caught the reins and looped them over the hitching post. Abigail fell into Gar's arms.

"Abby, what's happened? I was about to come looking for you. Sophie said you'd gone up to the Fike diggings."

"Why would you do a fool thing like that?" Lionel asked as Mattie climbed unsteadily from the buggy.

"We . . . I . . . ," Abigail sobbed. "He was dragging Mattie . . ."

Gar's attention shifted to Mattie, who held her hands to her throbbing temples as if to shut out the full realization of what had taken place.

Lionel grabbed Abigail by the shoulders. "Who? Fike?"

"He had a gun, Papa. I shot him."

Lionel gasped. "Dead?"

Abigail's terrified eyes answered his question, and Gar clasped her in his arms. "Good God, Abby." He looked from one to the other. "But what happened?"

"She saved my life," Mattie said, starting for the stairs to the Steinbaum flat. She had to hold Saya. "I'll get Saya. Then we'll go talk to the sheriff."

Bewildered, Lionel hurried to help her. "You're both safe. That's what matters."

———

"Those Fike brothers were bad apples," Sheriff Karns said after hearing out the somber group gathered in his office. Mattie, bedraggled, scratched, and bruised, clutched the wide-eyed Saya, while Abigail sat as if in a trance, her hair and bonnet drooping, Gar's comforting arm supporting her. Lionel anxiously fingered his beard.

"That clears up the question of Alfred Fike's whereabouts," the sheriff continued. "We'll check out that grave you mentioned, and it appears Boot won't be giving anyone further trouble."

"Abby had a right to defend her friend, didn't she?" Lionel asked.

"She did, and I can't see any reason to pursue the matter." Karns folded the signed statements he'd taken from Mattie and Abigail. "I'm here to see justice done, not to prosecute decent folks."

Gar sighed audibly.

Karns turned to Mattie. "Now about Fike conniving to get a part of Bodein Enterprises. The way I see it, it don't matter now whether that contract is valid or not, Mattie. As the sole survivor you legally own the whole shebang. Your business—plus the Fike mine."

Mattie caught her breath. The shock of Boot's death had blotted out the realization that, of the four persons involved, she alone remained.

"But there's still another matter," Sheriff Karns continued. "The part Seth Thornton played in all this. He did notarize that contract, damn him." Karns frowned as if he dreaded having to take action against the treacherous Thornton. "If, as you claim, your husband didn't actually sign it, there appears to be some skullduggery there."

"And Willard Motts," Mattie said. "He had to be in with Thornton on the forging of Cal's signature."

"Why do you suppose those two would do something like that?" Karns mused.

"Cal did win a considerable amount of money from them in a poker game."

"Poor sportsmanship, I'd say," Karns glanced questioningly at Mattie, ". . . *if* your husband won the money fair and square."

"Of course he won it fair and square. Surely you don't question Cal's integrity, Sheriff."

"He seemed like a straight shooter," Karns replied. "Never had any complaints. Guess I'll have a talk with Thornton and Motts."

"Otto Crouse was in that game, too," Mattie said. "You might question him."

"I'll do that." The sheriff reached for his hat. "I'll get back to you if I need anything more."

"But what about the mine? Does this mean I must oversee operations?"

"You're the owner," Karns said. "I guess it does. I'll get word to the two men up there when I check on that grave," Karns said.

"Much obliged, Sheriff." Gar shook Karns' hand, and Mattie managed an anxious smile as the sheriff chucked Saya under the chin.

Lionel took the silent Abigail's arm and led her to the carriage.

Back in the Steinbaums' parlor, Sophie shrieked her relief when told of the sheriff's reaction to Abigail's use of the weapon stowed in the picnic basket. After hugging Abigail and Mattie, she hurried to the kitchen to reheat the borscht, muttering, "Grizzlies is grizzlies!"

Mattie sat uneasily holding Saya, while Abigail, looking pale and shaken, sat with Gar on the sofa and leaned against his shoulder. Gar shifted uncomfortably.

Lionel slumped in his chair. "It won't be easy to put this behind us. Can't be helped, but a man is dead." Mattie knew he could not readily forgive her foolish decision to go up to the mine, a decision that now weighed so heavily on all of them.

A sudden stomp of footsteps up the stairs interrupted, and P.J. burst into the room. "Mattie, come quick, Cindy's had the baby."

Sophie bustled from the kitchen. *"Oy gevalt!* What next?"

Mattie jumped to her feet. "Why, she's early. Where?"

"At the house. By herself. Before I got home. She don't want me to get the doctor." He wrung his hands in anguish. "Hurry, Mattie. There's blood all over."

"Sophie, I may need your help." Mattie placed Saya in Abigail's arms and started after the youth. "Gar, please get Dr. Ward."

"Take my rig. It's out in front," Lionel called after them.

P.J. whipped Lionel's bay through the streets to miners' row and led Mattie and Sophie into the ramshackle one-room cottage. In the light from two small windows, they saw a table cluttered with dirty dishes, a small iron stove, and a few other sparse furnishings.

At the far side of a disheveled bed, Cindy lay curled against the wall in her rumpled and soiled pinafore, shock and hostility in her pale eyes. A newborn child, emitting a steady plaintive cry, lay in the bloody wastes of childbirth.

Mattie ran to the bedside. "Gar's fetching Dr. Ward," she said reassuringly, feeling the girl's clammy forehead and noting the intact after-birth on the stained bedding. "You're going to be fine."

"Don't want no doctor," Cindy muttered between clenched teeth. "Don't want you. Don't want anybody."

Mattie rolled up her sleeves. "We need warm water to wash this baby. And something to cut the cord." P.J. scurried to her command, gaping over his shoulder while she turned the red, wrinkled, and wail-ing child on its side and gently rubbed its back. The baby was thin but well formed, with dark hair and long, thrashing legs.

"It's a boy," Mattie said, once again marveling at the miracle of birth. "Cindy, you have a baby boy."

"Don't want him."

"Of course you do. He's beautiful. Wait till we get him bathed."

"*I don't want him.*" Cindy spat her words bitterly. "Just get out of here and let me die." Her face reddened with rage. "Get out! All of you!"

"We're going to take care of you," Sophie said softly. Having recov-ered from her momentary shock, she seated herself on the bed and stroked Cindy's tangled hair. "You just lie back and rest till the doctor gets here."

Mattie tied the newborn's cord with a bit of string and severed it with P.J.'s knife. "Where are the baby clothes we gave you?" She scanned the room. Cindy's and P.J.'s few garments hung on wall pegs near an upended wooden crate crammed with smaller items. "And the little crib Lionel made for the baby?"

Cindy glared defiantly, dark circles of exhaustion under her eyes. "I threw 'em out."

P.J.'s freckled face, which had taken on a more sober look of matu-rity since his marriage, sagged in anguish. "Must have been while I was at work. The crib full of things was here this morning."

"You keep your stinking nose out of it," Cindy screamed at her young husband.

Tears glinted in P.J.'s eyes. "Mattie, what's wrong? What's the matter with her?"

"She's been through so much, P.J." Mattie cleared a space on the table, poured warm water into a basin, and began to sponge the baby.

Gar and Dr. Ward pulled up in front of the cottage in the doctor's rig. Dr. Ward, a short man with muttonchop sideburns, hurried to Cindy's side and lifted her wrist to take her pulse. She jerked her hand away.

"I'm only taking your pulse, my dear," the doctor said in a loud, impersonal voice. "Your vital signs."

"No!" Cindy sat up suddenly, her face twisted. "Let me die! I just want to die!"

"You're not dying," Dr. Ward assured her, quickly administering his usual procedures. "No, you're very much alive, and I'm here to see that you stay that way."

Cindy curled away from him at the far side of the bed.

"Her color is better already," Mattie reported.

The doctor nodded. "These young girls snap back in no time." He walked to the table, thumped the baby's chest and back, and checked Mattie's handiwork at the navel.

"Does the girl have a husband?" The doctor seemed to address his question to Gar, who had remained standing uneasily near the door. "I like to keep a record." He took a pencil and a small notebook from his bag.

P.J. stepped forward. "I'm her husband," he said firmly. "P. J. Calahan."

The doctor, making hurried notes, showed no surprise. "Your wife's name?"

"She used to be Cindy . . . Cynthia Dougherty. She's Calahan now."

"And the baby's?"

"Don't know yet. We haven't talked about it." P.J. cast uneasy glances at the new mother huddled against the wall.

Dr. Ward tucked the notebook back into the bag, then turned to Mattie. "You ladies can get the little mother washed up. Keep her in bed for about ten days if you can. I don't see any reason to worry. We sometimes get this kind of reaction, especially in such a young girl."

When the doctor had gone, P.J. carried the basin out the open back door and tossed the baby's bathwater into the yard, narrowly missing a small overturned crib and scattered tiny garments. "Oh, no," he moaned, "she's dumped everything out here in back." He lugged the crib with its cargo of baby clothes back inside, scolding. "Christ's sake, Cindy! Shame on you." Cindy did not reply.

Gar put his hand on P.J.'s shoulder. "Come on, son. Let's go tell Lionel you have a baby boy." With an anxious backward glance, P.J. followed him.

Sophie poured another basin of warm water and began sponging Cindy's face and arms. "There, there," she murmured. "Everything's going to be just fine." Cindy, lying with her eyes closed, allowed Sophie's soothing touch.

Meanwhile, Mattie had dressed the wailing infant and stood rocking him in her arms. "He's hungry," she announced cheerfully when Cindy lay comfortable in a nightdress on the freshly changed bed. "He wants his mama to feed him. Look how his little chin quivers."

"I can't stand the sight of him!"

"Cindy, dear," Mattie murmured. "He's a lovely little boy. You must put him to your breast to bring your milk in. He needs you."

"No! No! No!" Cindy beat her fists on the bed, pounding close to the baby, forcing Mattie to quickly remove him from harm. As she lifted the crying child, she felt the familiar surge of milk in her breasts. Astonished to realize that any baby, not just her own, could stimulate the involuntary response in a lactating woman, Mattie held him at arm's length for a moment. She looked anxiously at Cindy, who turned toward the wall. The red-faced, thrashing bundle in her arms seemed to leave her little choice. Mattie seated herself, unbuttoned her shirt-waist, and put the baby to her breast.

"You can't take this on yourself, Mattie." Sophie shook her head sadly. "Already you're overdoing. I'm taking Cindy and the little one home with me. We'll get nursing bottles." She began gathering up the baby clothes.

"And Cindy," Sophie added, cheerfully, "as soon as we get you home, we'll think of a fine name for him. Something that sounds nice with Calahan."

Cindy snorted contemptuously. "He may be named Calahan, but he looks like a Fike."

Twenty-six

"HE HAS nice long fingers." Lionel watched with grandfatherly interest as Cindy administered a nursing bottle to her son, but since the incident at the Fike Claim he spoke with a weariness in his voice. "A violinist, maybe."

"I should live so long." Sophie rolled her eyes. "The boy will be at least a lawyer. Look, only three weeks old and he gets his way already."

"Jack won't be none of them," Cindy snapped. She had named the baby Jack after her father. "He'll be no 'count," she said.

"Well, you ain't helpin' him." P.J.'s face tensed with frustration and anger. "You ain't actin' like his mama."

"I'm givin' him this bottle, ain't I?"

Sudden hot tears rimmed his eyes. "You ain't lookin' like you want to."

"Who wants to take care of a no 'count kid all day?"

Mattie, who had dropped by on her way to work to leave Saya in Sophie's care for the day, bent over the new mother, adjusting the slant of the bottle to tip milk into the nipple. "Jack will be what you make of him. But he needs to know you care about him."

Cindy made a disagreeable face. "Care about somethin' that screams all the time and stinks?"

"Dammit, this ain't right!" P.J. jumped to his feet, wiping at his eyes with his sleeve. "I'm gettin' out of here." He stumbled toward the door. "She ain't my wife. Jack ain't my baby. Nobody wants me here. I'm goin' to . . . to San Francisco."

"Good riddance!" Cindy hurled the words venomously, and P.J. winced as if he'd been slapped across his freckled face. The door slammed behind him and his quick footsteps faded down the stairs and into the street.

"I'll talk to him at the store." Mattie exchanged looks with Sophie and Lionel as if to say, "What are we going to do with her?"

Sophie shrugged a silent "Don't ask."

But P.J. didn't show up at the store. Mattie was occupied all day with customers and bookwork, then swept the floor herself, digging into corners P.J. often missed.

"Excuse me." A tall man wearing a black suit and homburg, having entered unnoticed, peered at Mattie through wire-rimmed glasses. "I'm looking for Mrs. Bodein." He spoke with an eastern accent. "I have this letter."

"I'm Mattie Bodein."

"Benjamin Perch. You wrote inquiring about a mining engineer?"

"Well, I didn't expect anyone so soon." Mattie extended her hand. "I'm glad to meet you." He appeared to be in his late twenties, clean-shaven with large brown eyes behind the thick lenses and a strong, square chin that balanced his quick, discerning glance. She liked the look of him. Honest and direct.

"I have a certificate from the Missouri School of Mines and three years' mining experience in the Ozarks." He began rifling through the satchel he carried. "I was in St. Louis when Mr. Nesbit got your letter. I know his daughter Clarissa. She said you'd be a good outfit to work for, so I came ahead on the stage while the weather was good. Figured I could get here as quick as a letter."

"Clarissa Nesbit." The name held fond memories for Mattie. Clarissa had introduced her to Cal. "How is Clarissa? And her father?"

"Fine as fiddles." Perch pulled a handful of papers from his case. "I'm sure you'd like to see my references."

They huddled across the counter, discussing his qualifications, the mine's production and potential, available men and machinery, and financial resources. It was clear not only that Benjamin Perch knew his business but that he pursued it with vision and energy. Within half an hour he had joined Bodein Enterprises as chief engineer.

"I've already taken rooms," he said. "So I'll be going up to look at the mine first thing in the morning." He pumped her hand. "Clarissa was right," he said, nudging his glasses up on his nose. "I'm going to like working for you." And he was out the door.

"P.J. didn't show up at all today," Mattie told Cindy and the Steinbaums late that afternoon when she came for Saya. "Did he come back here?" Saya, who sat playing with a large wooden spoon in the middle of the parlor floor, jabbered happily as she held out the spoon to her mother.

Cindy looked up from her indolent sprawl on the sofa but said nothing.

Sophie came from the kitchen with baby Jack in her arms. "You don't think he meant it about going to San Francisco?"

"Had he ever talked about going west?" Mattie directed her question to Cindy.

"He wouldn't go way out there," Cindy said absently.

"Are you sure? He was quite upset this morning."

"Who cares?"

"Cindy, if you're to make a home together you must try to be kinder to him. You're not being fair."

"Fair!" Cindy jumped to her feet, her eyes flashing. "He's at the store every day. With you. While I'm stuck here with babies." Her voice trailed off into a whine. "Mattie, please let me come back to work."

"But what about Jack?"

"Why can't I leave him here with Sophie like you leave Saya?"

"Two babies would be too much for Sophie alone."

"A young girl I'm not." Sophie cooed at Jack's narrow, sober face to coax a smile.

"I haven't been able to find someone to stay with Saya at the hotel," Mattie said. "But I'm looking for another place to live. When I find something, I'll hire a housekeeper to take care of her there. Then perhaps Sophie can look after Jack."

Cindy pouted. "But I want to come back to work now. I know you need me now that P.J.'s gone."

"Surely he'll come back by tomorrow." Mattie lifted Saya from the floor. At eight months, she was getting to be an armful. "If he doesn't, I will need help at the store." She offered an encouraging smile to Cindy.

Two days later Benjamin Perch came down from the mine, his city grooming gone awry and his clothing smudged and rumpled, but his brown eyes keen and eager as ever. When Mattie finished with her last customer and closed the store for the evening, Benjamin proudly spread a stack of charts and figures on the counter.

"The main lode is silver-lead," he announced.

"How much is there?"

"Can't tell yet. Could be considerable. Then again, maybe not. It's slow going with just the two diggers. But we're lucky we don't have to haul the crushed ore to the railroad at Corinne, Utah, as they did a few years back. The silver can be leached out with mercury right here at the Unionville works."

"And we freight only the processed ingots to Corinne?"

"Yes. I understand ore once had to be shipped clear to San Francisco from here, sometimes even across the ocean to Wales." Benjamin's frown indicated his distaste for such expensive procedures. "If they bring a railroad through, we can save even more time and money. Let's see now . . ." His stubby pencil never stopped. "If we find copper traces, we'll have to send that ore to a smelter somewhere. Maybe Colorado."

"Helena's new government assay building is completed now so we'll soon have more processes available. When will you know what metals might be in the mine?"

"Still have to trace a couple more of the leads. Those two miners up there may not be heavy on brains," he continued, "but they can dig like crazy. And they're loyal. Even seemed surprised to be offered a fair wage. But, Mattie, if you agree, I'll hire a bigger crew. A few more men can bring out considerable ore before winter sets in."

Mattie approved of his initiative, and both were intent over his figures when Abigail appeared at the door.

"Abby, come in," Mattie called. "You haven't met our engineer, Benjamin Perch."

After peering at the dark-eyed young woman in the ruffled pink gingham dress, Benjamin pushed his glasses up on his nose to get a sharper view, then leaped to attention to acknowledge the introduction.

But Abigail turned to Mattie. "Mattie, I hate to worry you, but . . . well, Cindy was particularly sullen this morning, and when Mama was busy in the kitchen, Cindy rushed off with the baby."

"Rushed off?"

"She mumbled something about going up Grizzly Gulch, but you know how she is. Mama didn't think anything of the remark till she discovered they were gone. We thought she'd just gone for a walk because she's been up there several times with us and knows the road, but she hasn't come back and we're getting worried."

Mattie frowned. "She took baby Jack up Grizzly Gulch?"

"No, not Jack. She took Saya."

"Saya!" Mattie reeled at the words. Her hand trembled as she reached for her hat.

"Gar went to look for her. I knew you'd want to come, too. I've brought our rig." Abigail was already holding the door open.

"I'll come along," Benjamin said. Though the names Cindy, Jack, and Saya meant nothing to him, he seemed to want to keep Abigail in sight. "Perhaps I can help."

"Cindy lives with us and Jack is her baby," Abigail explained to him as they climbed into the buggy, Mattie tense between them. "Saya is Mattie's little girl."

"Abby, you swore you'd never go up the mountain again," Mattie murmured, ". . . after the incident at the mine. If you'd rather not come along, Benjamin will come with me."

"Don't talk crazy." Abigail urged the horse into a fast pace. "Saya and Cindy are my family, too."

"I may have seen this Cindy," Benjamin said, "this afternoon, on my way down from the mine. I thought it odd at the time."

Mattie clutched his arm. "Did she have Saya?"

"About halfway down the mountain, as I came around a bend, I saw a young woman in a yellow dress run into the trees. At the time, I thought I had frightened her. She *was* carrying a baby, I think."

"What on earth is she thinking of," Mattie murmured, "taking Saya up to the woods so late in the day? Hurry, Abby! We've got to find them quickly."

Abigail whipped the bay into a gallop but by the time they reached the spruce groves, it was nearly twilight.

"I know she wouldn't hurt Saya," Mattie reassured herself. Then the realization, "But Cindy hasn't been herself for some time."

They rounded a turn among the shadowy trees, and there in the road ahead stood Cindy, her pinched little face distorted with panic at being discovered. When she saw them, she darted into the forest.

"Cindy, wait!" Mattie cried.

Before Abigail could stop the bay, Benjamin was out of the buggy, his long running stride carrying him down the overgrown trail behind the furtive figure in the yellow dress. Mattie jumped down after him and followed. In a small clearing a short distance into the woods, Benjamin caught up with Cindy and grabbed her by the arm.

"Let me go!" She struggled but Benjamin held her firmly.

"I won't hurt you," he murmured, poking his dislodged glasses higher on his nose. "I'm Benjamin Perch."

Cindy knew the name and that he worked for Mattie. "Then leave me be," she said. "I ain't none of your business."

Mattie rushed into the clearing. "What have you done with Saya?"

"Too many babies around here." Cindy's dull response panicked Mattie.

"What do you mean? Where is she?"

Cindy gazed about the clearing, avoiding their eyes. "In the woods."

"In the woods?" Mattie gripped the girl by the shoulders. "But why? Why, Cindy?"

"If Saya ain't around, Sophie will take care of Jack."

"Oh, no!" Mattie caught her breath, forcing herself to speak slowly and deliberately. The girl was more deranged than anyone realized. Mustn't frighten her. Must stay calm. "Where did you leave her? Show us, Cindy."

Cindy gestured vaguely toward the road and on up the mountain.

"Come. You must take me to her." Frantic with fear, Mattie tugged the girl back toward the buggy. "Abby, she's left Saya in the woods."

"Somewhere up ahead," Benjamin added, helping them scramble onto the rear seat as Abigail started the horse at a fast clip.

Cindy seemed dazed. "I don't suppose you'll want to teach me my lessons now," she mumbled.

Mattie, her heart beating wildly, put her arm around the confused girl. "First we must find Saya."

"Everybody's mad at me."

"Cindy, you must understand. No one's mad at you. We all care about you. You've had a hard time of it. But your trouble has nothing to do with Saya. She's a tiny girl who cares about you, too."

The buggy wheels clattered as Abigail whipped the horse up the rough wagon road over rocks and across washouts.

"Show us where you left her," Mattie pleaded. "We have to find her before dark."

"By the creek."

"Where by the creek?" With horror, Mattie imagined her baby crawling toward the swift current.

"Where the bears drink."

Mattie gripped the buggy seat to steady herself.

"How far?" Benjamin demanded.

"By a big tree."

"There are thousands of big trees up here," Mattie agonized.

"It's burnt black," Cindy said. "The creek is down below." Almost at once she pointed into the shadows ahead. "There it is." A tall jack pine grew beside the road, one side blackened by a lightning strike.

Mattie's heart leaped into her throat. Maybe there was still a chance. "Hurry! Show me." She climbed from the buggy, her legs turning to jelly beneath her as she scanned the darkening woods.

At that moment, a man on horseback emerged from the trees a few yards ahead. He carried a child in his arms. It was Gar. With Saya.

A cry escaped Mattie's lips. She felt her life blood surge through her once more.

"Mattie!" Gar dismounted, cradling the round-eyed Saya as best he could, and started toward her.

Mattie found herself running, too. Tears streamed down her face as she took the baby in her arms. "Oh, Saya." Sobbing her relief, she clung to her child, pressing her lips against the silky baby curls. Gar was kissing Saya, too, enfolding them both in his arms. Then he was kissing Mattie's tears. "Oh, my dearest," he murmured. "Everything's all right now. Saya's safe."

"But how . . . ? Where . . . ?"

"A deer skittering down the slope caught my attention. Then I heard the baby crying. I found her propped among some rocks next to the creek." His eyes reflected love and joy and anxiety all mixed together. He touched his lips to her damp forehead.

"Oh, Gar." Mattie, cuddling Saya, stood for a long moment in his embrace. This was the way it was meant to be. She knew it now. There was so much to be grateful for. So much lost time to make up. So much love to give . . . to receive.

Then she remembered Abigail.

"What are we doing?" Her anguish came in a whisper as she slipped from Gar's arms.

But Gar again drew her to him. "No more pretending, my love," he murmured. "I could never marry Abby feeling the way I do about you."

Her resolve faded. He was right. There could be no more pretending. They would face whatever came. Together. She raised her lips to his.

After a moment they turned back to the buggy, Mattie carrying Saya, Gar's supporting arm around them both. Abigail and Benjamin stepped down as they approached. Abigail's dark eyes flashed with shocked comprehension.

"Abby, we didn't want this to happen." Mattie reached out to her, but Abigail pulled back.

"I'm sorry, Abby," Gar said. "We didn't mean to hurt you."

"Didn't mean to hurt me?" She glared at them, angry tears welling. "You said there was nothing between the two of you. Oh, how could I have believed you?"

"I hope we can make it up to you," Gar said.

Cindy sprang from the buggy screaming, "Everybody's crazy!" Animal-like she sprang at Gar and struck out with her fists, pounding him on the face and chest.

"No, Cindy." He clasped her tightly in his arms. "It'll be all right."

"No. No, it won't!" Her pale eyes were wide with rage. "Everybody's hurting everybody."

"Just calm down now. The baby is safe."

She responded with a renewed barrage of blows.

"Stop it, Cindy." He gripped her flailing fists. "Everything's fine. You're going to be all right. We'll help you."

"You can't. You can't."

"Why, Cindy? Why can't we help you?"

Her hysteria ceased and her frail body went limp. "I don't know!" The words came in a long, mournful wail. "I'm empty!"

He embraced her tenderly then, stroking her hair, and she clung to him crying softly.

"Cindy, dear," Mattie said, "we'll find a way."

Cindy sobbed. "I just want to die."

Abigail went to her. "No, Cindy, nobody's going to die."

Cindy looked at her, bewildered.

Abigail's voice was brittle. "No one dies from heartache."

"Oh, Abby." Cindy turned to Abigail and the two stood holding each other.

With Gar's comforting arms around her, Mattie wept, too. Saya was safe. Gar loved her. But Abby . . . And Cindy . . .

Benjamin climbed into the buggy and picked up the lines. "It'll be dark soon," he said.

Twenty-seven

GARNET TANNER paced the hotel lobby waiting for Dr. Ward to come from Mattie's room upstairs. He had insisted on fetching the doctor to check Saya after her ordeal on the mountain. Actually it was Mattie he was most worried about. He hoped the doctor would make sure that she, too, was all right.

Charlotte Gaines, behind the lobby desk, noted the sandy-haired captain's strong shoulders, the sensitive mouth, and intelligent eyes. Unusual. She had heard this interesting newcomer was in town but as yet hadn't had the chance to meet him. And wasn't he engaged to Abigail Steinbaum? What was he doing here fretting over Mattie Bodein?

Charlotte had to admit that at first she didn't like Mattie much. A tenderfoot easterner, a little too refined, too soft-looking. She felt Cal Bodein needed someone more suited to his way of life. Someone who'd been around a little. Someone more like Charlotte herself. But in the months since Cal's death, she had changed her mind about Mattie. She showed real gumption, going it alone, running her own business. They'd had several conversations and she had actually listened to Charlotte's advice.

Now, here was a man of obvious decency concerned over Mattie's welfare. Heaven knows, she needs someone to look out for her, with Thornton and his cronies trying to pull a fast one. Charlotte knew what they were up to. But it wasn't her place to stick her nose in. She hadn't gotten where she was today—secure in a good hotel job—by sticking her nose in.

"The baby has another tooth coming through," Dr. Ward announced as he came down the stairs. "But the trip up the mountain didn't hurt her any." He accepted Gar's payment and tipped his hat to Charlotte. "Mattie's still a little shaken but they're both fine."

"Thanks, Doctor," Gar called after him.

"Someone have an accident?" Charlotte ventured.

"No, nothing like that." Starting toward the stairs, he turned and, for the first time, smiled at her. "Saya's cutting a tooth."

Charlotte raised a practiced eyebrow as he hurried up the stairs.

Gar knocked softly and Mattie came to open the door, holding her finger to her lips to tell him Saya was asleep in the cradle. She had dressed in the same apricot-colored dress he remembered her wearing on the *Big Muddy.* It emphasized her complexion, her honey-toned hair coiled at the nape of her neck, and the blue eyes that he had never stopped thinking about. He closed the door for their first moment alone. She melted into his arms and they kissed, tenderly, passionately, then stood in the darkened room, holding each other.

"This will never do," Gar murmured, scanning the room. "There's not even a place to sit and spark . . . to court you properly."

"I have chairs. We can sit." She stepped away but he drew her back.

"I don't want you out of my arms for a moment. Marry me, Mattie."

The moment was sweet indeed. She had waited so long—she suddenly realized just how long—for those words from him. She wanted to put every qualm, all grief and regret, behind her. But an uneasiness remained. He seemed to want her just as she was, despite all that had gone before. The circumstance of Saya's conception would, for some, forever brand her a "loose" woman.

"Gar," she ventured. "Have you no doubts? I mean, about my . . .

my past?" She knew some men jumped at the chance to get close to an "experienced" woman. And widows were fair game.

"Your past?" He looked at her, amused. "You mean there's something you haven't told me?"

"No. It's just that at my age . . . I mean, a woman with a child . . ."

"Mattie," he murmured, pulling her to him, "Saya is part of my love for you. You don't know how much I've wanted a child. But I never imagined I'd find a woman like you in the bargain."

"I only wish . . ."

"Now, no regrets. Ever. Life is what we make of it. Starting today."

"I've never met a finer man than you, Gar. I knew that from the first. But my duty was to Cal . . . and our baby."

"Mattie, your loyalty to him made me care for you all the more. I admit for a minute or two on the boat, when Bodein showed up, I wondered if I'd misjudged you. But then the brave way you proceeded, the decency you showed . . ."

"I did love Cal, you know. And he loved me."

"When I thought I'd lost you to him," he murmured, "I convinced myself that Abby could take your place. I know now that no one could ever take your place." He touched his lips to hers, and she sensed with exquisite joy the depth of his caring. But his mood remained serious.

"As for Abby," he said, "I regret that."

"I've hurt her, too, getting her into the Fike predicament."

"Maybe in time she'll forgive us. After we're married we'll make it up to her somehow." He scanned her face lovingly. "You will marry me, won't you, Mattie?"

"Of course I will." She hesitated. "But I want Abby to be happy for us. If we wait . . . just a little while . . . maybe she'll understand, and we can start our marriage the way it should be."

"We've waited this long. I guess a while longer won't matter—as long as I can see you every day, be near you."

She touched his face with her fingertips. A wonderful face, with a remarkable man behind it.

"That will give us time to find a place to live, too," he continued. "Mattie, I've a little money put by. Enough to provide a decent home for the two of you." He indicated the sleeping child in the cradle wedged into the space beyond the bed. "It just so happens that Otto Crouse is building a new house, a mansion they say—apparently his brewery is doing pretty well—and Mrs. Crouse has ordered all new furniture from Europe, so they're selling their old house completely furnished."

Mattie felt her heart would burst with love for him. "Why, I know the Crouse place," she said. "A big stone house with ornamental iron-work on the upstairs porches."

"I haven't seen it. But I'm told it has a shady yard. Nice for Saya."

"Oh, Gar, you're dear beyond words."

"A woman needs a home, I know that." He nuzzled her nose. "Even if she is the smartest little businesswoman around."

"Gar." She seized the moment to bring up the idea. "Come into the business with me. Benjamin's doing a fine job with the mine. He has the men working on the vein of silver-lead and they've found traces of zinc and copper. We can't tell yet how much of each there may be. But if this thing grows, I want you to help manage things."

"Sure, if you need me. But don't be disappointed if it's all a flash in the pan. I've talked with lots of disappointed prospectors around town. Most of these claims play out fast."

"Yes, I know that's a possibility." Perhaps she *was* getting excited over nothing. The Fikes could have simply made a lucky but limited strike. It all happened too fast to keep things in perspective.

"In any case, the town needs better and cheaper shipping," Gar said, "and I'm going ahead with the freight line."

"That's wonderful, Gar. And we'll have to find a new location to expand the outfitting. The store's bursting at the seams with the new inventory."

"I'll make some inquiries." He took her hands as they sat facing each other in the two chairs. "Mattie, I'm getting acquainted with the business people here. I'm amazed at how many of them know me already and call out to me on the street."

Mattie gazed lovingly at his weathered face. "I'm calling out to you, too, Gar." She pressed her lips to his, then stood, drawing him to her.

"Oh, Mattie, my dearest."

"Hold me, Gar. Love me."

"I do love you, Mattie," he whispered. His lips sought her neck and a moan of pleasure mingled with his kisses. She wanted more. But instead of leading her to the beckoning bed, he gently released her.

"Not here, Mattie. It wouldn't be right." She understood his consideration of the sleeping child . . . and his awareness of the room she had shared with another.

He grinned then. "But I don't believe in long engagements, do you?"

It was after dark when Tanner emerged from Mattie's room to Charlotte Gaines' knowing nod.

Next morning, Charlotte's sagacity was confirmed when Gar came to have breakfast with Mattie and the baby. As they seated themselves in the dining room, Gertie appeared with the high chair for Saya and a dish towel to tie her in. "Mornin', Mattie. Mornin', Captain Tanner. And how's my little sweet patootie this mornin'?" Saya giggled as Gertie tickled her tummy. "How you feelin', Mattie? Heard you had a scare yesterday."

"Yes, we did." Did the whole town also know about the two of them?

Gertie answered the unspoken question with a special smile of approval. "Word travels fast around here."

They ordered the ham-and-egg special, with oatmeal for Saya, who grabbed into the bowl with both fists as soon as it was placed in front of her. While Mattie attempted to spoon cereal into her tiny mouth, Saya gave a happy sputter of recognition. Abigail was coming toward their table. She wore her rose velvet suit topped by a saucy plumed bonnet. Only the faint shadows beneath her eyes betrayed a sleepless night.

"I wanted to see you both," she said soberly. "I behaved badly."

"Abby." Mattie stood to embrace her. "We're the ones who should apologize."

"We wouldn't hurt you for the world." Gar jumped up and held a chair for her. "Please. Sit with us."

"I think I knew all along," Abigail said. "It's just that . . . well, coming the way it did."

"Your friendship means everything to us." Mattie pressed Abigail's hand.

"So," Abigail continued, "I've decided the best thing for me to do is to go back east."

"What?"

"I think we'd all be more comfortable."

"No, Abby," Mattie pleaded. "You can't leave. We want you here. We need you here."

"Don't make any hasty decisions," Gar said. "In time, you'll feel different."

"I doubt it," she said curtly. Then, without looking directly at either Gar or Mattie, she stood to leave. "I know you two have lots to talk about."

Mattie rose to her feet, her heart aching in empathy for her friend's misery. Gar stood, too, not knowing what more to say, and they watched her go.

Sheriff Karns, just coming into the lobby, held the door for Abigail's exit, then spotted Mattie and Gar in the dining room. "I was looking for you," he said, approaching. "Guess maybe you've heard my news. I've been appointed a territorial judge."

"I did hear something about that. Congratulations, Judge." Gar extended his hand. "Got time to sit?"

Karns tentatively took a seat. "Got to get back to the office. Tryin' to wind up my duties as sheriff." He tweaked Saya's nose, making a clucking sound to amuse her, before continuing. "Just wanted you to know I had an interesting visit from Charlotte Gaines last night."

"From Charlotte?" Mattie tensed for another disagreeable surprise.

Karns continued. "She told me that a couple of months ago she overheard Seth Thornton and Willard Motts talking about getting even with a certain gambler."

"Charlotte came and told you this?" Apparently Mattie had not misinterpreted Charlotte's increasing friendliness.

The sheriff nodded. "She said Otto Crouse was there, too. Crouse told them to forget it, that it would only hurt you, Mattie. But the money they'd lost to your husband in that poker game was a real sore point. They wanted to get it back and didn't seem too particular how they did it."

Gar scowled. "Those crooks."

"According to Charlotte, Thornton knew your husband had staked the Fike brothers in return for a share in any mining profits."

"Yes, I think everyone knew that."

"So Thornton talked Boot Fike into claiming your husband had chipped in a share of Bodein Enterprises, too."

Mattie tried to follow the logic. "But how would that benefit Thornton and Motts?"

"Apparently they thought you would give up your interest in an unproven mine to protect your store."

"Did they know there was silver in the mine?"

"Yup, Fike confided in Motts when he had the quartz assayed. Motts figured to get his hands on some of it, so he got Thornton to offer some financing in return for a percentage."

"But Fike couldn't do that without consulting me, his co-owner," Mattie protested.

"Not legally, but they counted on you being easily convinced."

"So they forged Cal's name to that phony contract," Gar summarized.

"There was another reason." The sheriff seemed reluctant, almost embarrassed to tell them. "Motts says Fike thought a legal hold on you would lead to a romantic one."

"The idiot!" Mattie murmured.

"What they didn't count on was your making a fuss when you didn't find a copy of the contract among your husband's papers."

"Can Thornton and Motts be prosecuted?" Gar asked pointedly.

The sheriff cleared his throat. "That's the touchy part. I talked to them both this morning. They claim there was no such contract."

"But they showed it to me."

"Probably destroyed it so it can't be used against them," Gar said.

"They deny everything." Karns shrugged. "I'm afraid, Mattie, since you have no copy of the contract and Fike is dead, and since Thornton and Motts are out of it on all counts, there is no point in pursuing the matter further."

"But they'll go on scheming and cheating." Gar's anger surfaced. "They'll do this again to someone else."

"They may. But if I know Charlotte Gaines, word will be all over town and folks won't be anxious to do business with them. Thornton's been on thin ice anyway since that episode involving his daughter."

"What about Motts? He's a scoundrel, too."

"Well, Motts is Motts. He'll keep on attracting a certain type of clientele, and there's not much we can do about it unless we can prove he violated the law." Karns stretched his long legs and got to his feet. "But neither Thornton or Motts has any legal claim or access to anything of yours, Mattie. You're free to operate any way you wish." He cast a sly glance at Gar. "And from what I hear about the size of the lode, you won't be wanting for much from now on."

"What do you mean?"

"You don't know yet? Ran into your man Ben Perch at the assay office just a few minutes ago. He's flying so high his feet are barely touching ground. The samples he brought in show the highest concentration of silver found around these parts in a long time."

Gar's sandy brows furrowed. "Are you sure about that?"

"Sure as I am about anything these days."

Mattie took a deep breath. "Sheriff—or I should call you Judge now —I appreciate all you've done."

"My job," he replied. "I'm wishing you well from here on in. And bring this little tyke around now and then." He patted Saya's curls. "Got no kids of my own, you know." Saya happily patty-caked her sticky hands.

"Thank you, Judge Karns, I will."

When Karns had gone, she leaned across the corner of the table to kiss Gar full on the lips. She didn't care who was watching. The old tyranny of appropriateness no longer held much meaning for her. "Isn't it wonderful?" she said ecstatically. "Oh, Gar, let's be married right away. I'm sure we can talk Abby out of going back east. Our getting married might even make it easier for her to stay. Resolve things, in a way."

Gar stiffened and pulled away. "Mattie, this changes everything."

"It certainly does. Now we'll be able to live comfortably. Expand the business. Oh, there's so much I want to do for Saya. And for you, Gar."

"No, Mattie, I can't marry you this way. It makes me look like some damn bounder, turning Abby down to marry you just when you come into some money."

"Don't be silly. It doesn't matter where our livelihood comes from."

"It does to me." He pushed his chair back from the table. "We'll have to wait till I get my own business on its feet."

"But, Gar . . ."

"That's the way it will have to be, Mattie. I won't have my wife keeping me."

Twenty-eight

MATTIE KNEW what she must do. The money from the mine, instead of bringing happiness, would be a wedge between her and Gar. Wealth wasn't important, anyway. Money for money's sake actually seemed immoral.

She lay awake most of the night formulating her plan. Seth Thornton already had given her the answer. His greed would work to her benefit. She would sell him the mine and put the money in trust for Saya. Yes, that was the perfect solution. Then Saya would never have to forgo suitable schooling. She could become a doctor, or whatever she might want to be.

At first light, Mattie rose, bathed, and arranged her hair. Should she play the helpless widow or the shrewd businesswoman for her visit to Seth Thornton? His reaction to her could make a considerable difference in her future. After considering her wardrobe and finding nothing appropriate for either image, she sighed in disgust. What does it matter? she thought. I am what I am. And I guess Seth Thornton knows it by now. Abigail put on her blue silk travel suit, which had begun to fit her again in the weeks since she'd stopped nursing Saya.

Seated before the bank president in his office, she began abruptly. "Mr. Thornton, I've decided to take you up on your offer to buy the mine."

Thornton smiled quizzically as he fingered the gold watch chain across his middle. "You've changed your mind?"

"Yes, I find I'm not interested in managing mine operations."

Thornton's delight erupted in a hoarse cough. "Well, this is unexpected. As I told you, I'm interested. But I'd have to have fresh appraisals, samples assayed, that sort of thing, before I could consider such a move."

"I would have thought you'd already have heard about the rich samples Benjamin Perch brought down yesterday."

"Well, I did hear a rumor, but . . ."

"I'd like you to meet with Mr. Perch and the assayer, visit the mine with any consultants you choose. Make me an offer. As soon as I hear from you, and we agree on a price, I'll arrange to have the papers drawn up."

"All right. All right." He drummed his fingers on the desk as if uncertain whether to stall or to hurry the transaction. "But why the hurry?"

"I think it best to proceed at once," she concluded, "before I change my mind again."

At that same hour, Gar strode into the Bank of the Territories with equally determined purpose. He was pleased by Mattie's good luck at having come into the silver—actually he had to credit Calvin Bodein's foresight—but for him to simply accept such a windfall seemed opportunistic. That kind of thing could make a man complaisant. Lazy. Eventually lose his self-respect. He'd waited years to get off the river and build something solid. But with his own hands and mind. Having it handed to him from the woman he loved was out of the question.

At the Bank of the Territories, he made arrangements to draw on his savings for the purchase of livestock and equipment. He planned to spend the next few days making the rounds to reliable area stockmen and wagoners, bargaining for the best prices. With a little luck he could get Tanner Freight Lines in operation immediately. Maybe show some return before snowfall.

But first he must see Abigail. Things had to be set right. Mattie's happiness depended on their continuing friendship with Abby. On Abby's staying in Helena. He found her at the mercantile, arranging a display of gentlemen's hats with Lionel.

"Abby, we have to talk."

"I have nothing to say."

"You always have something to say, Abby. That's one of the things I like about you." His lighthearted remark did little to dispel Abby's gloom.

"What good will talk do?"

"Talk is always good," Lionel interjected, dismissing them with a wave of his hand.

Abigail glared at both men, but allowed Gar to lead her outside. He helped her into his new surrey, where they sat while the handsome chestnut horse, another of Gar's recent acquisitions, lazily switched his tail in the morning heat.

"Abby, whatever you think of me, don't let it ruin your friendship with Mattie."

Abigail sat in silence.

"You're a fine person," Gar continued. "A lovely, capable, desirable woman. But in suggesting marriage I was deceiving myself as much as I deceived you. I was selfishly trying to forget my love for Mattie. All I can say in the way of apology, Abby, is that it was a mistake. Please try to forgive me."

"I'm not angry, Gar. I understand how it is with you and Mattie. But since the day I . . . I shot Boot Fike, everything seems to be all confused and uncertain."

"I know," Gar murmured.

"It's like everything is turned upside down."

"Abby, all of us are starry-eyed and shiny till life gives us our first painful kick in the teeth. That's when our mettle gets tested."

Abigail nodded.

"But when we bounce back, we have a whole new perspective. Less certain we have all the answers. But more determined than ever to do the best we can with whatever resources and prospects we have."

"My prospects are pretty dim."

"Abby, there's nothing dim about you whatsoever, including your prospects. You're smart. Principled. A dazzler in the looks department. You'll never have to settle for second best."

"Gar, how can I fall out of love with you when you flatter me like that?"

"I didn't come here to flatter you. Mattie and I both need your friendship. Your good sense. We have some problems of our own."

"You and Mattie?"

"Abby, I just found out Mattie's coming into big profits at the mine. How do you suppose that makes me feel? We're going to have to wait to be married till I can see some results from my freighting."

"Now who's acting like a horse's behind?" Abigail demanded. "I never heard of anything so crazy. I also never heard of having money being a problem. I always thought it was lack of it."

"A man should be able to take care of his wife."

"You will, Gar. Give yourself time. I don't see that that's any reason to postpone the wedding."

"Everyone has their own concept of integrity. I guess that's mine."

"You're a fool."

"Maybe so. But I could never marry Mattie, be a father to her child, with no sure prospects of my own. She doesn't deserve that."

"Then why don't you get going on whatever you feel you have to do to deserve her?"

"I'm working on it. But I had to clear the air with you, too." He grinned, sheepishly. "I guess we want your blessing."

She smiled then, placing her hand on his. "All right, you have my blessing." The pompous sound of it made them both laugh.

"And you won't go back east?" Gar said.

"Papa and Mama have already talked me out of that."

"Abby, if there's ever anything we can do for you . . ."

"There is. You can both come to supper tonight. Mama wants to see for herself that Saya is all right."

Within a few days, Gar rented a barn with pasture land just outside of town and purchased thirty head of mules and oxen. He bought and repaired three used freight wagons and ordered three new ones to be delivered by spring when he planned to increase the livestock. Then he began calling on prospective shippers.

"Mattie, I think this is going to work," he announced during one of their meals together at the hotel. "I telegraphed the river companies to let them know I'm in business here, and the responses look promising. Lionel put in a good word for me with several merchants around town, and I've got shipments to bring from Fort Benton and Salt Lake already."

"I'm glad, Gar."

"But the best part is that the assay office here and the Unionville stamp mill need ingots hauled to the railroad at Corinne right away. Mattie, I'm in business." She had never seen him more exuberant and eager to tell her all he had accomplished. "Just wish I had more than three wagons. By spring, Tanner Freight Lines will be a solid enterprise. Meanwhile, I've got a couple of teamsters ready to go to work."

"Have I told you how proud I am of you?" she said.

"Mattie, let's go see the Crouse place. If you like it, we can be married as soon as it's ready for us."

"Of course I'll like it. Oh, Gar, I want so much to have our own home, a place for Saya."

"You couldn't want it any more than I do, Mattie. Tomorrow, I'm making the first wagon run to Corinne with the drivers. Takes about a week round trip. Then, after a look at the Salt Lake run, we can meet the preacher."

She gazed lovingly at this man who would be her husband. His integrity showed in everything he did. People liked him, and wanted to do business with him. Because of him, Mattie was beginning to feel a part of the fledgling town. For the first time since she came west, she felt she belonged.

But she hadn't told him she had sold the mine. She had accepted Thornton's second offer, a compromise between Benjamin's projection of the mine's worth and the figure lawyer Motts advised Thornton to offer. It seemed more money than she could imagine, and she overruled Benjamin's reservation at accepting such a conservative amount.

She immediately had Lionel's attorney draw up a trust limiting disbursement of the money. Mattie would have access to a modest living expense each year, should she need it, and Saya would be able to draw on the trust for her education. It also stipulated that when Saya came of age, the entire trust would be dissolved and the money divided between Mattie, Saya, and—here she was hopeful—any future children Mattie might have.

Now she hesitated to tell Gar what she had done. What if he, like Benjamin, thought it a wrong decision? What if, despite his protests, he was counting on the silver income?

"Gar," she began, "I've made a rather momentous decision myself. I've sold the mine."

"You've what?"

"To Seth Thornton."

"You sold it?"

"And put the money in trust for Saya."

He took a minute to sift this startling information. "Why, that's a fine idea."

"I couldn't bear the unpleasant associations I have with that mine. The Fikes. Thornton and Motts."

"Mattie, you're a wonder. That protects you and Saya, and puts an end to all the uncertainty and expense of operating the mine."

"And if we should fall on hard times, I'll still be able to draw a small income each year."

"That makes sense. But I intend to see that you'll never need to. Now, I have a surprise for both of you." He lifted the child from her chair. "Come on, Saya, we're going to see your new house."

A cooling breeze from the mountains brushed their faces as the spirited chestnut, pulling the new surrey, stepped into a trot. "Say, I have something else for this young lady," Gar said, digging into his vest pocket. "I'd forgotten all about this." He held out a man's ring, a gold signet ring with a blue-and-orange crest and the inscription "Virginia Cavaliers."

"Why, that's Cal's!"

"Doc Austin asked me to give it to your baby."

"Doc Austin?"

"I ran into him in St. Louis just before I came upriver. Hardly recognized him as that strange old bird aboard the *Big Muddy* last summer. But he knew me. He's hung out his shingle there. Building a good practice, he says."

"Oh, Gar, that's good news. Dr. Austin delivered Saya. She would have died if it hadn't been for him." She touched her lips to Saya's soft cheek. "But how did he get the ring . . . ?"

"He told me he left Helena in a blizzard and would have frozen if he hadn't stumbled onto some Indians he and Cal had encountered when they came upriver. Cal had given the ring to the chief. After the blizzard, Doc stayed on with the Indians to nurse some kids who had come down with diphtheria, and the chief gave him the ring in gratitude."

Mattie took the ring that brought back so many memories. "How good of Doc. Saya will cherish this." Saya poked a chubby finger at the bright insignia.

Gar leaned over the child to kiss Mattie tenderly on the lips. "Damn, Mattie, but I love you."

"And I love you, Gar."

Saya stared up at the loving bond between the two people who would shape her future.

Twenty-nine

THIS SEPTEMBER Sunday afternoon in the new house would be special for friends and neighbors invited to the wedding of Matilda Hamil Bodein and Captain Garnet Tanner. Sophie bustled about the dining room showing Mattie's new housekeeper how to arrange the buffet table, while Abigail, elegant in a gown of powder-blue faille, placed a large bouquet of chrysanthemums on the mantel. Though Saya napped peacefully in the nursery upstairs, Mattie stood flustered, unable to concentrate on what might still need doing. Her hands shook as she tugged at the bustle on the satin gown she had made for the occasion, a rosy ivory, bride-like she thought, but dignified and appropriate for a widow. Abigail had helped her do her hair in ringlets, pinned high on her head, with two soft curls hanging at each side.

"This won't stay buttoned," Mattie complained, holding out her arm so that Abigail could fasten one of the pearl buttons at her wrist. Her free hand fluttered about aimlessly. "Is my hair mussed?"

"You're beautiful," Abigail said, amused. "A regular picture." She took Mattie's trembling hands in hers. "I'm happy for you, Mattie."

"Thank you, Abby. It's all so . . . so overwhelming."

"It couldn't happen to a nicer couple," Abigail said.

"Something wonderful will happen for you, too. I know it will."

"I've learned this much. In this town, anything can happen."

"Abby, this town couldn't do without you. And neither could I." They laughed together and Mattie kissed her affectionately. "Now," she scanned the room, "is the table ready?"

"Stop fussing. Everything's perfect." Abigail peered out the window. "I hope Cindy doesn't forget to bring Jack's bottles. She's been totally absorbed in making herself a new dress for your wedding."

Mattie continued to be distressed by Cindy's emotional struggle. "She seems to be doing better now that she's back at work."

"Well, she hasn't had any more crazy spells."

"It was good of Lionel to hire a nursemaid to help Sophie with Jack." Abigail nodded. "Papa and Mama are both fond of the baby."

"Is Cindy showing any more interest in taking care of him?"

"No. And it's been more than a month since P.J. left."

"She never mentions P.J. either," Mattie said.

"Let's not talk about unpleasant things on such a lovely day." Abigail smiled reassuringly. "I'll see if Mama needs my help."

Mattie walked through the entrance hall touching the polished walnut banister on the open staircase. She loved the Crouse house. Its imposing stone. The ornamental ironwork. The matching fence enclosing the elm-shaded yard. Everything as solid as Otto Crouse himself. The Crouses' old furnishings had responded well to Mattie's personal touches. In the nursery the little rocking horse Cal had given Saya stood vigil beside her new crib, shelves in the library held the few books Mattie and Gar had brought with them, and in the sunny, front bedroom upstairs new linens and a plump feather mattress on the high carved walnut bed awaited their first night together. By unspoken agreement they had postponed consummation of their love, though she and Gar had spent many fond evenings in the house, planning and arranging while Saya crawled about the spacious rooms exploring her new freedom. It was Gar's suggestion to have the wedding here. "I want this to be a special beginning," he said.

A very special beginning, Mattie thought as she stepped out onto the front porch. The lazy, warm day held the same fragrance of autumn she remembered from her girlhood in St. Louis, and she took a prayerful breath as two carriages pulled up to the hitching post. Gertie, resplendent in a Mother Hubbard of flowered cretonne, stepped from the first. "Lordy, Mattie, what a fine day." She joked heartily with Dr. Ward, alighting from the other carriage. "Doc Ward, what you doin' here? It's a preacher we need, not a sawbones."

Mattie ushered them laughing into the parlor and other guests began to arrive. Otto Crouse sank comfortably into his old leather chair, lamenting the fancy new furniture his wife had foisted on him in their new place, while Mrs. Crouse roamed the house clucking approval of Mattie's changes. Charlotte Gaines, lavish with good wishes, offered to dress Saya, who awakened from her nap. Judge Karns asked if he could put off donning his black robe till just before the ceremony.

Cindy came with Lionel, the cinnamon silk dress she had made for the wedding twisted and wrinkled from her awkward grip on the lustily protesting Jack.

"The bottles I remembered," Lionel said, setting aside his violin case and handing Abigail the parcel tucked under his arm.

"You can put Jack in Saya's cradle in the spare room," Abigail instructed Cindy. "I'll warm his bottle." With a sigh of resignation, Cindy trudged up the stairs, Jack wailing in the crook of her arm. Lionel made his way to a corner chair, took his violin from its case, and lovingly began to tune it.

"Is it time yet for the groom to show up?" Gar, wearing a new gray cutaway, stood at the door, his strength and pride evident in his stance, despite the exquisite, full-blown pink rose he held. His eager expression softened when he caught sight of Mattie in her ivory gown among the guests. She returned his tender gaze, and they moved toward each other as guests murmured approval. Lionel began a lively tune.

Gar held her at arm's length, admiringly. "I didn't realize exactly how very dear you are till this very moment."

"Thank you, my love." She pressed her cheek against his.

"Look who showed up at the hotel." He stepped aside, and behind him stood P. J. Calahan, twisting his hat in his hands.

"P.J.!" Mattie linked her arm through his. I'm so glad you're here. We've missed you."

"Sorry to bust in like this. On your weddin' and all."

"Don't be silly," Mattie said, leading him inside. "It wouldn't have been a celebration without you."

But P.J. held back. Stretching his boyish frame to full height and squaring his shoulders, he announced so all could hear, "I've come for my wife."

Everyone turned to look at the new arrival.

"P.J.!" Cindy's shrill voice echoed from the top of the staircase. She stood for a moment transfixed, then pounded down the steps toward him, her dress ballooning around her thin legs.

P.J. took the stairs two at a time and they met midway. "Cindy, don't be mad. I had to come back."

Cindy blinked back tears. "Thought you were gone for good."

"Too many people in San Francisco. Didn't know nobody. Got me to thinkin'. We said for better or worst."

Her faint smile faded. "But I'm bad for you."

"You couldn't help it." Shyly, he took her hand. "We'll try harder this time."

"But I'm not a good mama. I'm not going to be a good mama. Ever." Her jaw tightened. "And you can't make me. I hate it."

P.J.'s freckled face showed new determination. "I never had no mama at all," he said quietly. "But I do have a wife. And you need me, Cindy, you know you do. Jack needs a daddy. I figure this our best chance all around." He took a small velvet box from his pocket. "Look what I brought you. A real weddin' ring."

Cindy opened the box and took out the gold band inside. She squinted at it. "There's writin' on the inside."

"It says . . . ," he blushed, "P.J. loves Cindy."

"No foolin'? It says that?"

He slipped the ring on her finger.

A wistful smile lighted her pale, narrow face. She studied the ring on her finger, then, shyly, touched the cinnamon silk of her dress. "I made this myself."

"I like it," P.J. said, looking into her eyes.

"Hold on here," Gar interrupted, waving the rose. "Whose wedding is this?"

The guests, having stood in pleased silence witnessing the young couple's reunion, burst into applause and Lionel added a flourish to the music. P.J. and Cindy, embarrassed by the attention, came down the stairs hand in hand, and the guests broke into happy chatter.

"Where's Jack?" P.J. whispered. "I got somethin' for him, too."

Cindy's smile vanished and she glared at him. "Don't you dare wake him up . . . till after Mattie's married."

Sophie brushed at P.J.'s coat, more to reestablish an affectionate connection than to smooth the wrinkles. "You look like you need a regular meal," she scolded.

"Shall I start the wedding march?" Lionel asked Mattie.

Before she could answer, Benjamin Perch appeared at the door, scanning the room anxiously. Mattie, leading Gar by the hand, went forward to greet him. "Welcome to our home, Benjamin. I thought we'd have to start without you."

"Sorry to hold things up, but I must see you, Mattie . . . in private."

"What is it? Can't it wait till after the ceremony?"

"I think not." He hesitated, eyeing Gar.

"Come into the library, both of you." Taking Gar's hand, she led the way and closed the door behind them.

"Mattie, it seems impossible but . . ." Benjamin struggled to get the words out. "The mine's played out."

"Played out?"

"The vein of silver-lead. Cut off just like that." He made a chopping motion with his hand. "Only two weeks of stepped-up operations and we came to solid granite. We've probed along a few other trace leads but there's nothing."

"Nothing?"

"Kaput." The wire-rimmed glasses emphasized his woeful expression. "I was wrong, Mattie. I gave it my best, but . . . well, I was wrong. Now I feel like I've cheated old man Thornton. Gave him bad advice. Whatever he may be, I never intended that."

Gar whistled softly. "You mean Thornton's stuck with a worthless mine?"

"And I'm out of a job," Benjamin added apprehensively. "I was sure that hole would produce for years. There was every indication."

Mattie looked from one to the other, too astonished to speak.

"Thornton is fit to be tied," the young engineer went on. "Says we've ruined him. Says he's going back east. Says there are no decent folks left here."

"He's living proof that one sees others from one's own perspective," Gar said.

Benjamin continued his lament. "I don't know how I could have made such a mistake. I'm glad things turned out right for you, Mattie, but . . . well, doggonnit, it makes me doubt my own judgment."

"Don't be so hard on yourself," Gar said. "You made an educated guess. That's all anyone can do."

"There was every indication to proceed as you did." Mattie smiled to ease his distress. "And I can't thank you enough for all you've done for me. I'd rehire you in a minute if I were still in the mining business."

"You would?"

"Maybe there's a place for you in *my* operation," Gar said. "Do you have any interest in shipping?"

"Oh my, no." Benjamin shook his head vigorously. "My life is in those rocks. I plan to go over toward Butte and look into the copper situation."

"Then I wish you good luck, Ben." Gar offered his hand. "I'm glad you're staying in the territory. You'll still be close enough to come to see us."

"You're a good friend," Mattie said. "In fact," with a mischievous glance at Gar, "if I weren't already betrothed, I think I could fall in love with you."

Gar grinned as he took her arm. "Not only betrothed, my clever darling, but about to be wed. Now let's get this celebration under way."

Their laughter as they came from the library alerted the waiting guests, who stepped aside to reveal Judge Karns standing before the fireplace wearing his official robe. Abigail stood nearby holding Saya, who wore the pink satin hair ribbon around her dark curls and a pink ruffled dress and pearl-buttoned slippers Sophie had crocheted for her. Lionel struck up the wedding march.

With the moment at hand, Mattie and Gar smiled almost shyly at each other. Gar, realizing he still held the lavish rose, handed it to Mattie. "Didn't think I was going to find one fine enough," he said. "It may be the last of the season."

Mattie touched the rose to her cheek. "Yes, my love, but this is a season that will last."

The judge cleared his throat. "Are we ready to begin?"

ABOUT THE AUTHOR

Dee Marvine, born Deloise Hall on a Nebraska farm, spent fifteen years as a corporate writer and magazine editor in Chicago. She now writes full-time in Big Timber, Montana, where she lives with her husband, artist Don Marvine. *Last Chance* is her first novel.